Daughter of the Mystic Moon

Nicolle Morock

Nicolle Morock

Contents

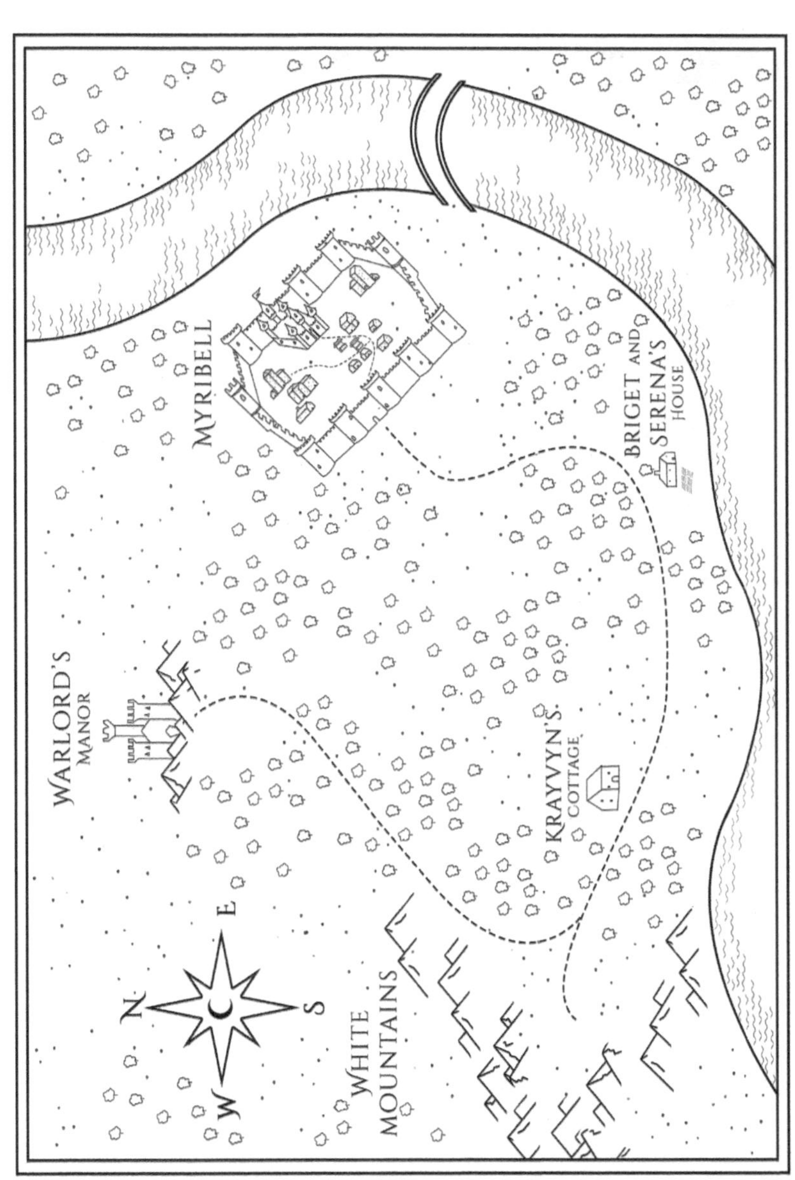

MYRIBELL
WARLORD'S MANOR
KRAYVYN'S COTTAGE
BRIGET and SERENA'S HOUSE
WHITE MOUNTAINS
N
E
S
W

Chapter 1
Myribell

Meetings

STANDING ON THE EDGE of the carriage road that traversed the forbidding forest beyond Myribell's walls, a swarthy man hid his face beneath the hood of his cloak. Only the whites of his eyes were visible in the darkness until he smiled, and his grin was unnerving. After baring his teeth like a predator for a moment, he spoke. "A princess should not be alone in the woods this late at night."

"Who says I'm alone?" Shaylea, the princess of Myribell, asked, shooting a quick glance up at the trees above her. She sat comfortably on a jeweled leather saddle atop a large deep bay horse.

Unconcerned, the man ignored her question. "Why did you call this meeting, Your Highness?" he hissed.

"I may have need of your services," she replied. "I want to know if your price remains the same?"

"After all these years? Of course not!" He scoffed. "It's higher!"

"How much?"

"Twenty percent, or more, depending on the need," he smiled slyly. His scarred hand rested on the hilt of his poniard.

"That much? I'm not sure you're worth it."

"Oh, I am. You know I am." The cockiness in his voice sickened her. At that moment, she had no choice but to agree with him.

He could see the contempt flash in her eyes. Princess Shay, atop her stallion, dressed in shades of royal purple, luxurious fabrics, black leather riding boots, and no doubt carrying at least one dagger under that sweeping cloak. She was the most dangerous sort of princess—selfish and spoiled, dishonest and disloyal, the only heir to the throne and well aware of the king's good health.

Her streaming blond hair and perfect, fair skin could not hide her selfish heart. Rumors swirled around her since childhood. The citizens whispered that young Princess Shay cavorted with the meanest boys and wanted nothing to do with proper courtiers. As a teen, she took any opportunity to escape her escort's gaze and find a way to cause trouble for whatever unfortunate soul crossed her path. Many innocent passersby ended up in prison for not immediately recognizing the princess and bowing formally with their eyes downcast. Guilty over the death of her mother, her father looked the other way. Ten years after the dark wizard last met her, there she sat, in her late twenties and deceptively beautiful, just glaring at him.

"Well, Princess, do you have a job for me or not? It's quite risky business to be here, even under cover of darkness."

"Risky for you only, but I am aware. I may have a task for you. For now," she smirked, "I just wanted assurance that you will still come when I beckon." She deftly maneuvered the braided reins, swung her horse back toward the town, and took off into the darkness.

The grim wizard admired how she sat on her steed, yet scoffed again. "Sadistic; but what a horsewoman." He adjusted his cloak so that his scarred hands were free of the fabric, and he clicked his tongue against the roof of his mouth twice. An obedient chestnut stallion stepped out from the shadows. He swung himself up and rode in the opposite direction of town toward the caverns of Mount Pilkin.

...

On a sunny morning in Myribell, a light breeze brought just a touch of the coming autumn into the air. Late summer was a beautiful time within the walls of town. The farmers' market teemed with people selling brightly colored vegetables, hand-woven fabrics, and cured meats and cheeses. Vendors sold fresh flowers on every corner. Under the protection of their fair-minded king, Liam, people freely exchanged money for goods, and they bartered for what they couldn't easily afford. Six days a week, this was the scene in the center of town.

A young woman with light brown hair and olive-toned skin stopped at a farm stand to sniff the fresh-picked apples. Serena was an average sort of beauty—her height, her build, and her dress could blend into any crowd—but her eyes sparkled, and she was always smiling.

"How are you doing, Harold?" she asked the attendant.

"Fine, lass! The day is better with you here."

Serena blushed a little. "These are wonderful!" She exclaimed as she placed a few apples for herself and her mother in her burlap cloth tote. She handed Harold some money, took an apple back out of the sack and sniffed it. "Just great!" Turning to find her mother, she instead came face-to-face with a tanned stranger. The man gave her a warm smile. "Oh, pardon me." She said and stepped back.

"No, I beg your pardon." He stepped to one side and gestured to let her know she could pass him. As she did, he said, "You made me really want one of those apples."

Serena paused and turned back to face him once more. This time, she really looked at him. His jet-black hair was tied back; his goatee neatly trimmed. Serena tried to read his eyes, but they were under a heavy brow. He was smiling at her with his mouth closed, and his skin told her he spent much of his day outside. His clothes were those of a hard worker—stained and rough at the seams.

"My name is Trevor," he said as he held out his hand.

"I am Serena," she smiled brightly and gave him her hand. He took it and kissed it gently. The action surprised her because she only expected a handshake from a common laborer. Although eyes were friendly, she fought the urge to wipe her hand on her skirt and wondered why his energy felt grimy.

"It's a pleasure to meet you, Serena." His voice was mellow and smooth, and she liked how he said her name.

"And you," she answered. A touch on her shoulder startled her, and she turned around to see her mother standing behind her. Briget looked like an older version of Serena—a little shorter and with a few tendrils of gray mixed into her sandy brown hair—but still very much a natural beauty.

"I was just looking for you," Serena said.

"I found you first," her mother answered. She looked beyond Serena at the tanned stranger behind her. "It's time to go." Briget's gaze was icy, not curious, and Trevor's smile faded briefly. It returned when Serena pivoted on her heel to toss one more smile in his direction.

"Enjoy those apples," he said.

"We will," Serena replied, and she and Briget left the market. As they walked to their little farmstead just beyond the town walls, Briget was thoughtful. She finally broke her silence and asked, "Who was that man you spoke with at the market?"

"I don't know. He said his name was Trevor. He was rather handsome and very polite. I nearly ran right over him!" Serena answered cheerfully.

"Trevor, hm?" Briget mused.

As they walked the rest of the way home in silence, Serena replayed the meeting in her mind and wondered why her mother suddenly seemed so guarded.

...

That night, in a small house on a corner near the eastern wall of town, an older man, husband and father of the house, awoke to the sensation of a presence in the room. Startled, he turned to wake his wife, but she was not in the bed beside him.

The presence was menacing. Like a creeping shadow, it overpowered what little light the moon gave through the open window. The air felt charged, as if before a thunderstorm. The man's breathing became labored, his heart straining to beat in his chest. His ears burned and rang. His mouth went dry; he could not call out. In less than a minute, it was over, and his body gave no clue to his cause of death.

Chapter 2

Day 1

"DID YOU HEAR ABOUT the blacksmith?" The morning air buzzed with questions and rumors spawned by the sudden death of the king's favorite craftsman.

"I heard he died in his sleep."

"I hope it's not the sweating sickness."

"Do you think it was too much cider?"

"His wife is beside herself with grief. She told my neighbor she got up to check on the children after hearing a noise in the hallway, and when she returned to the room, the door was shut tight, and her husband was dead beyond it."

"Maybe she did it."

"Why would she?"

The gossip was unstoppable. It had been years since an unusual death had occurred in the realm, years since the three wizards reigned terror in the night. In those days, the deaths were gruesome and never meant to be mysterious. The wizards left their mark by using magical means to physically destroy their targets. Those days were gone. The mighty trio was shattered, and two vanished without a trace. The youngest was now living a quiet life, peaceful to the onlooker and simple to those with means.

Serena returned to town that morning to buy fresh bread from the baker. It was a rare treat that she and her mother enjoyed when they had a little extra money. She heard the rumors flying, bombarding her as soon as she passed through the city gate.

She felt trapped by the walls, overwhelmed by her senses. It wasn't just what she heard. It was what she felt as she walked through the crowded streets.

Serena was a sensitive soul--a natural empath. Without trying, she could feel emotions and sensations that those around her were experiencing. When she was a child, she couldn't understand or explain it. Thankfully, her mother recognized her ability at a young age. Briget saw her three-year-old daughter limp as if her leg was broken after standing near a relative who truly had a broken leg, and she knew. When the relative left, Serena reverted to her usually playful self within minutes. Briget asked the child if she was mimicking the woman, and Serena was adamant that her leg really hurt when the woman was there.

It wasn't long before Briget began training her young daughter to protect herself from outside energies. Through grounding and meditation exercises, Serena learned to build an invisible wall of protection around herself when she needed it. Once she was a little older, and she felt in control of her gift, she learned to use it for her benefit and to help others. Intuitively, she could tune into a person's emotions and temper her own responses to their actions and words. She became a calming presence to those around her; friends and family would confide in her, never knowing why they felt an immediate rapport with the young woman.

Now, she was mastering channeling energy to ease the physical pain and suffering of those same people. Citizens in town who knew her father well said that she was following in his footsteps. She had to trust them because she only vaguely remembered Waylon, but she had heard the stories of his bravery. He had died defending the king.

To honor his sacrifice, the king took a special interest in the welfare of Serena and Briget. While never visiting in person, he always made sure they had what they needed and would not starve or thirst or go without when hard times, such as drought, fell upon the land. He would have given more, but Briget was a proud woman who did not want pity and never asked for anything beyond necessity...and only asked when all other options were exhausted.

Serena found a little green space near the center of town where there weren't so many people. She paused for a moment and closed her eyes, took a deep breath, and felt the sunshine on her face. A light breeze bristled her hair, and she could hear the cooing doves on the rooftops above. She focused on their soft sounds. After taking another deep breath, she pictured the sun's warm light wrapping her in a layer of positive energy from the top of her head to the ground beneath her feet. She took another slow, deep breath and opened her eyes. The world was brighter, and its stresses lost their grip on her. Smiling, she continued her walk to the bakery.

A wide assortment of bread and muffins filled the bakery window. The warm smell of fresh baked goods hit her as soon as she opened the door. She inhaled it and savored the aroma. The baker smiled at her and said, "Welcome, Serena!"

"Good morning!" She greeted him. "How are you today, George?"

"Well enough, my dear! I'm happy to be alive. Not all of us are so lucky today."

"Do you know what happened?"

"No more than the next man." George stood on tiptoe to reach the salt canister on the top shelf, then wiped his floury hands on his apron. The apron strained over his generous belly. His kind eyes looked around cautiously, and he lowered his voice to almost a whisper. "I tell you, I haven't heard this much chatter since those three wizards were out there. This kind of sudden, mysterious death..." He shook his head. "Do you remember those days?"

"Yes, I do. I was just a child, but I vaguely remember them."

"Ha! You are still a child!"

"I'm nearly twenty now." She grinned.

"Well, so you are! Still, you will always be a youngster to me. I remember the year you were born. It was an icy winter that year."

"So I've heard." Serena watched him pull bread from the open oven as they spoke. "How is your shoulder?"

"It is well, thanks to you, dear! What delicious creation can I serve you today?" he asked in a jolly voice.

Serena looked around the shop. "Mother wants barley bread for dinner, but I don't see any."

"That's because it is in the oven as we speak. If you come back in a little while, it will be warm and ready for you."

"In that case, I'll return in an hour!"

"Shall I wrap up two loaves?"

"Just one, please. That's all we can afford this week."

"Nonsense!" George said with a warm smile and patted his left shoulder with his right hand. "The second loaf is my gift in gratitude for your healing service."

Back out on the narrow street, Serena looked around for a diversion. She wasn't expecting to wait for the bread, but the thought of it fresh from the oven made spending the extra time worth it. She strolled back over to the little green where she had grounded herself just a short while before. It seemed a pleasant spot to spend an hour and much more peaceful than the busy market ripe with rumors regarding the death of the king's blacksmith.

When Serena arrived at the green, she saw a laborer assembling a heavy wooden bench near the center of the grass. She could only see his back, but she felt he was familiar. Although she'd spent her whole life in Myribell, there were still many people who lived within the city gates and the surrounding countryside whom she didn't know. At first, she hesitated but then approached him to satisfy her curiosity.

As Serena walked toward him, he stood up to stretch his back and admire his work. The fabric of his shirt stretched taught over his shoulders. Sensing her approach, he turned to see her coming, and Serena recognized his warm smile immediately. It was Trevor, the man from the market the day before.

"I bid you good morning," he greeted her.

"Good morning," she replied.

"What brings you here?" Trevor asked. He studied her face so intensely that she felt her cheeks blush.

"I came to town for fresh bread," she answered and pointed toward the bakery.

"Ah, but what brings you *here*?" He asked again and made a sweeping gesture with his hands as if showing her the green grass beneath their feet.

"Oh, here? I'm... um... just waiting for that bread." Even though she spoke the truth, she felt a little silly saying it. The way he looked at her made her uncomfortable. No one had ever looked at her that way before. "I just wanted a peaceful spot to wait, and this one seemed tranquil enough."

"Perfect timing, then!" He declared and took a rag from his trousers' pocket to wipe off the new bench seat. "You may be the first to try it."

"You made this?" she asked, impressed.

Shod horse's hooves clip-clopping up the cobblestone street interrupted the conversation. Serena and Trevor both turned when the horse stopped at the edge of the green. One of the king's guards sat atop the tall brown steed. He pointed at the bench and asked, "Where did that come from?"

"I just put it there," Trevor answered directly.

"By whose authority?" the guard demanded.

"By the authority of the owner of this little piece of land."

"That would be the king," the guard said.

"You are correct, sir."

"That must mean you are one of the king's carpenters."

"Again, correct."

"What's your name?" The guard's demeanor never softened.

"Trevor Ash," he answered and gave a quick bow.

The guard studied him closely. "Well, Trevor Ash, I will be checking up on you."

"I'm sure you'll know where to find me."

The guard dug his heels into the side of his horse, and it trotted away.

Hearing Trevor's full name strummed a chord with Serena, but she couldn't put her finger on why it was familiar. She absently watched the guard leave while trying to remember.

Trevor's voice interrupted her thoughts. "I wonder what he has against benches?"

"No telling," Serena said. She looked at the seat once more. It was crafted from solid, thick, dark wood, but the finish looked soft to the touch. "Did the king really order this?"

"Yes, he did." There was a hint of pride in his voice. "He's ordered several more like it, too."

Serena reached down and touched it. "Nice," she observed.

"Please, try it!"

"I think I will." She sat down gracefully, her long skirt smoothed out around her effortlessly. "It is comfortable for a hardwood bench."

"So, it meets your approval?" Trevor smiled.

"It does," she said, returning his smile.

The sound of horse hooves interrupted yet again, but this time there were two of the king's guards. The taller, heavier one bellowed, "Trevor Ash?"

Trevor turned to face him, gave another quick bow, and replied, "Yes."

The shorter, younger guard piped in, "The commander of the Royal Guard requests your presence. Please, comply immediately." He looked very proud of himself, and Serena guessed he was new to the job.

"Comply?" Trevor repeated. His face lost all expression.

The larger guard answered, "Yes. I see you have no horse here. We will give you time to walk." That was all he had to say. The two guards rode toward the castle's main tower.

Serena stood beside Trevor and touched his arm. The rough linen cloth of his shirt was wet with sweat from carrying the bench to the green. He regained his composure and smiled at her light touch.

"Well, my lady, I am required elsewhere. I only wish I knew why."

"I'm sure we'll meet again," Serena assured him. "Good luck at the castle."

"Thank you."

She watched him walk away and then sat back on the bench to mull over what she had just witnessed. When she touched his arm, she tuned into his emotions, which otherwise would have been hidden by his blank expression. She sensed something akin to fear, but not as strong, in response to the guards' request. The emotion was not one she had herself felt before, so she could not discern it as distinctly as she was used to, and it puzzled her.

...

The main tower stood at the back of the town. A wide main road ran from the Grand Gate at Myribell's entrance, straight back to the tower gates. The walled town was the capital of the kingdom, and most of the population lived within its walls.

A smaller entry for pedestrians like Trevor was beside the large tower gates. He took a deep breath as he approached the thick oaken door. This was the first time he'd been required to comply with a request for his presence in a long, long time. The only other time, he had not gone willingly.

The heavy door creaked open, and Trevor crossed the stable yard to another side entrance—this time to the main building. Just inside, a young, red-haired guard in a basic uniform made of light woolen cloth, a chain mail vest, and without a helmet met him.

"What's your business here?" the youth asked.

"I was requested. I'm Trevor Ash."

"Ah," the guard looked around. "You're shorter than I expected."

"You're more casual than I expected," Trevor replied.

The guard stood up straight and pointed down the dark hallway to his right. "The commander is waiting."

Trevor walked slowly through the hallway, which was shorter than it appeared, and opened another ponderous door. He entered a room with gray stone walls, bare of any decoration. A few tall windows provided light. The room was just large enough to house about twenty soldiers at a time, and Trevor was glad to see only one standing over a long table at the far end of the room. The thick-set man looked familiar, and his booming voice brought back terrible memories when he spoke.

"Trevor Ash," the commander bellowed.

Trevor's voice was weak in comparison. "Yes, sir?"

The commander's stance softened a little upon being addressed properly, and his voice lowered a bit. "Thank you for coming in promptly." He walked from behind the table and approached Trevor, who had stopped in the center of the room.

"I wasn't sure I had a choice," Trevor answered.

"Actually, you did, but not much of one." The commander sized him up carefully. "You look well."

"I am better than I have ever been, sir."

"Why is that?"

"I work for my living, and I enjoy what I do. I appreciate the fresh air and sunlight."

The commander laughed. "Years of darkness will either make a man love the light or hate it."

"I love it."

"And you would be wise not to do anything that would cast yourself back into the darkness."

"I never will, sir. You're looking at a changed man."

"Where were you last night?" The commander's tone changed, and he stiffened a bit.

"In my room at the boarding house."

"Alone?"

"Yes, sir." Trevor didn't like where the questions seemed to be going.

"Can anyone vouch for you?"

"I'm sure Dame Critchen can. We spoke before I retired, and she keeps an eye on everything in her house. May I ask why you summoned me here?"

The commander held Trevor in his gaze for a long moment. "Did you have anything to do with the death of the king's blacksmith?"

Trevor did not hesitate. "No, sir, I did not."

The man relaxed. "Very well, then, you're free to go."

"Can I ask wh..." Trevor started.

"You may go now." The commander interrupted him and waved him off as his voice echoed in the otherwise empty room.

Trevor choked back his question. "Thank you," he mumbled and turned to leave. He walked a few steps toward the door, paused, and turned back to the commander, who had not moved. "I just want you to know, sir, that I enjoy my freedom. I consider it a gift, and I treasure it. I would never do anything to jeopardize it."

The commander nodded his approval. "That is good to know." With that, Trevor strode home to his room in the boarding house.

...

The August sun was setting over the hills, and the western sky was a brilliant pink hue, slowly fading to peach and gold as the eastern sky turned deep blue, speckled with stars. Serena and her mother sat in their front yard on a couple of stools watching the sky and snapping beans. Their work was almost done for the day, and it would soon be time to dine on vegetables from the garden and the baker's delicious barley bread. A light breeze blew through the leaves of the surrounding trees, and the gentle sound made Serena sleepy.

The day began peacefully enough, but her trip into town changed that. After her brief interaction with Trevor, a silver-haired, hunched woman, who smelled of lavender and sage, stopped her on the way back to the bakery with a warning, "Stay away from that man—the king's carpenter. He is a man of mischief. A black cloud will follow him all the days of his life."

"Why are you telling me this?" a bewildered Serena asked her.

The old woman looked around cautiously and answered, "Your mother would want you to know."

"Who are you?" Serena demanded. She'd never seen that woman in her life.

"Never you mind. Heed my words!" The woman said and scurried away.

Hours later, the conversation still haunted Serena. Why would a stranger warn her to keep her distance from a man who worked for the king? It made little sense. Someone in the king's employ couldn't be that bad, right? The king was more careful than that would imply. Still, Trevor was called away to meet with the commander of the Royal Guard, which might mean trouble for him.

Serena wanted to ask her mother about the woman and the carpenter, but she feared the answer. There was something intriguing about him, and she wanted to see him again, preferably for more than just a few minutes at a time. Was it more than just a coincidence that they'd run into each other two days in a row?

"What's troubling you tonight?" Briget interrupted Serena's thoughts. "You're quieter than usual."

"My trip into town was stranger than usual."

"How do you mean?"

"Well," Serena started, "the whole town is buzzing with news and, of course, rumors about the blacksmith's death. A lot of the people seemed genuinely scared about it. Then, there's the carpenter..." Her voice trailed off. The thought escaped her lips before she could stop it.

"The carpenter?" Briget asked. "What about him?"

"Oh, um... I... I guess he was called to meet with the commander of the Royal Guard."

"How do you know that?"

Serena swallowed hard. "Because I was with him when he was summoned."

Briget's voice was calm, but her words seemed measured. "Where were you with him?"

"On the little green near the bakery," Serena answered quickly. "I was relaxing, waiting for the bread, and he had just placed a nice little bench there, commissioned by the king himself."

"What did you say his name is?" Briget asked.

"Trevor Ash." It came out almost as a whisper.

"Hm..."

"What, Mother?"

"Be cautious with him, Serena," her mother warned. "He has a history."

"We all have a history." Serena waved her hands nonchalantly.

"His is murkier than most."

"Murkier?" Serena stopped snapping her beans and paid full attention to Briget.

"My dear, most of the people you've encountered up to this point in your life have been genuinely good people. I've made sure of it. Some have made mistakes, but at their core, they are truly good souls. Not all people are like that. Some are born with a natural tendency toward evil. They thrive in the darkness when the rest of us walk in the light."

"So, you're saying that the king's carpenter is evil?"

"I'm saying he has a history of evil, and although he is unlikely to behave that way now, it is also unlikely that his soul has changed that much. He cannot do the things he used to, so now the king employs him as a laborer, hoping he'll continue to walk in the light and convert his soul."

"Do you think it will work?" Serena inquired earnestly.

"For his sake, I can only hope, but people don't change easily." Her mother looked her in the eyes. "I can see I need to teach you more about protecting yourself psychically because your interest in him won't fade with my warning."

Serena said nothing in response. She'd only met the man twice, but something about Trevor Ash intrigued her. His energy differed from anyone she'd ever met before, and although she'd led a sheltered life, she had encountered all sorts of people on her trips into the town. She couldn't help but wonder what made him so different, and Briget didn't seem ready to explain any more than she already had.

...

Night fell over Myribell, and very few slept peacefully. Some mourned the blacksmith, and some worried about the mystery surrounding his death. Others couldn't relax, sensing a growing shadow over their town, their homes, and their loved ones. Those who did sleep had nightmares, except for one.

Trevor Ash knew he was dreaming as he stood alone surrounded by a thick brown fog. A deep male voice called his name from somewhere, but he couldn't see the source through the mucky haze. "What do you want?" Trevor asked.

The voice answered, "To know your heart."

"You already know it. I'm here, aren't I?"

"You are," the voice whispered. "And what of the girl, Serena?"

"She's hardly a girl."

"Your interest in her?"

"Unchanged."

"Leave no room for doubt, Trevor." The voice gave a low, unsettling laugh. The brown fog faded, and Trevor found himself standing in the middle of his stark room next to his cot. He shook the dazed feeling from his head and laid back down. His mind was racing with possibilities and thoughts of Serena.

...

In their cottage outside the city gates, Serena and her mother were up late. Briget was brewing an herbal infusion while Serena sat comfortably in a chair, staring at the space between her two palms that were in front of her with just a few inches of space between them.

"You're right, Mother," she said. "I see it better when I stop trying so hard."

Briget nodded from across the open kitchen. "I knew you would. You've always been able to feel the energy. With practice, you'll be able to see it much more easily and probably in color. You'll have a visual to confirm your empathic reading."

"Why haven't you shown me this before?"

"I thought feeling it would be enough for you." Briget sighed softly and leaned on the kitchen counter. "Things are changing quickly, and I'm afraid you'll need more tools than you have to deal with what lies ahead. The blacksmith's death is a foreboding of dismal times to come."

Serena dropped her hands to the arms of the chair and looked at her mother. "How do you know?"

"Because I've seen it before." She lowered her gaze to the floor in front of her for a moment and then looked at Serena once more. "You have, too."

"But I don't recall much. I know it was just over a decade ago, but I was only a girl."

"Right, and I kept you sheltered from as much as I could. I didn't want your childhood to be as scarred as mine was." Her mother looked down again. "It was bad enough we lost your father. I couldn't let you see all the other losses around us, so we kept you shielded."

"We?"

"Family, friends, and neighbors. You've had a lot of love and support from people you may never meet. We really have been truly fortunate."

Serena stood, crossed the room, and hugged her mother. "I know," she said. "I may not know much, but this I know."

Briget returned her daughter's hug. "You know more than you realize, Daughter."

Chapter 3
The Adventure

Day 2

DAWN BROUGHT RELIEF TO the people of Myribell. Despite their nightmares and fears, no one died in the night. Still, many felt a shadow hanging over the town despite the bright morning sunlight.

The elders shared Briget's sentiment that the darker times were on the verge of returning. The younger ones just felt out of sorts but couldn't explain it. All compared stories of horrible dreams. Some were of catastrophe, others of dying loved ones, and a few even dreamed of their own deaths.

The king himself was not immune to the visions of that night. He awoke with the comprehension that someone was once again plotting against him and the peace that he held so dear.

Years before, he had a trusted advisor—two, in fact— whom he could ask for insights. One was brutally murdered while honorably defending his majesty. The other asked to be left alone for the safety of family and friends.

The king employed many whom he knew he could trust with his life. His soldiers had not only sworn allegiance to him, but they had proven themselves time and again. Those who worked within the castle walls were all known to him by name. He considered them extensions of his own family. They ate what he ate and enjoyed small luxuries most other kings would only offer their courtiers. For this reason alone, all agreed Liam was a great king.

Outside the castle proper, but within the city gates, he recognized a large percentage of the faces and knew family surnames. He enjoyed trips to the artisans' shops. Rarely did he have more than one armed escort because within the city walls during the era of peace, security wasn't needed. The people adored King Liam, and he adored them.

Like everyone else, he now sensed a change in the atmosphere of his realm. Someone was raising long forgotten energy. He feared it was someone within the city walls, and to learn more, he needed to ask for help from outside the walls.

King Liam eased himself out of bed, moving slowly as his stiff joints made themselves known. His beard was grayer, and his muscles were softer than the last time he'd spoken to his advisor. Despite his age, he still felt healthy enough to handle whatever he may face in the days to come.

He rang the bell next to his bed and waited patiently. When his chamber servant arrived, he asked the young man to find Captain Mikal Sage and bring him as soon as possible.

...

Serena stood on the bank of the river that ran behind their land and watched the morning fog finally lift. The sun was approaching noon, and the fog was thicker and lingering later than normal. The water's song reminded her of the chorus to a song she couldn't place—something from her childhood.

She appreciated the view as the grassy bank on the far side of the water slowly appeared through the dissipating haze. Patches of gray mist still clung to the water and fish left ripples where they broke the surface to capture hapless, unsuspecting bugs.

The world seemed peaceful, but her stomach told her otherwise. It felt tight, like she had swallowed a rock, although she'd hardly touched her breakfast of fresh eggs and fruit. Her mother had sensed this long before she did, and that made her anxiousness worse. Serena took a deep, slow breath of fresh, river-cleaned air and released it even more slowly. She did this three times until "the world felt a little lighter and the sun a little brighter" as her mother had taught her when she was five years old.

She focused her attention on the far bank and tried to visualize each blade of grass. Movement in the woods beyond distracted her from her meditation. She tilted her head. Was it a deer? They visited the bank often enough. She tried to focus harder but saw nothing more. Deer were well camouflaged. It was probably just a...

An unearthly shriek tore through the forest. Birds clamored to flight and filled the sky above the trees. She'd never run in fear, but she wouldn't risk being seen by a predator because of her movement, either. Like a rabbit, she stood perfectly still and waited for what came next.

But nothing came.

She stared across the river into the woods, but nothing moved.

Her mother called to her urgently from their cottage behind her. "Daughter? Serena? Are you alright?"

Serena shook herself free of the icy feeling the shriek had given her and answered, "Yes, Mother!" She turned and walked briskly toward the house, careful not to run. "I'm here. I'm coming!"

Briget was waiting for her at the back door, arms outstretched toward her. "Quickly! Come inside!"

Serena darted past her mother. "Did you hear that... that..."

"Scream?" Briget finished for her as she shut and bolted the door. "I did. Do you know where it came from?"

"The woods across the river."

"Did you see what made it?"

The young lady shook her head. "No, I mean, at least I don't think so."

Briget took her daughter's hands and looked her in the eyes. "What did you see?"

"Motion." Serena returned her mother's gaze and took a deep breath. "I was down there to clear my mind, and I noticed movement among the trees. I guessed it was a deer, but it didn't feel right. I was trying to see more when I heard the scream and froze."

Briget let go of Serena's hands, broke their connection, and started pacing the floor. She had seen what her daughter described as if she had been there, too, thanks to her own gifts.

"What was it, Mother?" Serena's voice was curious but unsteady. She could still hear the echoes of that horrible sound in her mind.

"Banshee." Briget stopped pacing and looked at her daughter.

"A banshee?" she asked, bewildered. "But whose?"

"I wish I knew."

"Not ours?"

"We have no stories of them in my family, but I'm unsure about your father's side. I doubt it was for us."

"Then whose? And why did I hear it? And why in the forest across from our riverbank?"

"I'm asking myself the same things," Briget said as she sank into a dining chair. "This can't be good."

An aggressive knock at the front door jolted both women. Briget stood and hastened to it.

"Wait, Mother! What if..."

Briget didn't let her daughter finish. "Banshees don't knock." She straightened her hair and opened the door a crack to peer out. The man standing rigidly on the step was about six feet tall with sandy blond hair in a short cut, holding a silver helmet to his chest and wearing a long sword at his hip. She opened the door wider and asked, "May I help you?"

"I seek Briget, widow of Waylon, the king's most talented advisor." The clean-shaven soldier never broke his stance.

Serena took her place at her mother's side and asked, "Who are you?"

"Captain Mikal Sage, madam, of the king's guard."

"I'm no madam," Serena boldly corrected.

"My apologies, miss." He gave a quick, stiff bow from the waist and glanced at her with a slight smile.

Briget answered in a pained voice, "I am Waylon's widow, and this is our daughter, Serena. To what do we owe the pleasure of your visit?"

"The king requests you attend His Majesty in the castle, if it's not an inconvenience." Mikal marveled at the wording King Liam told him to use. A king worried about inconveniencing a farmer? How strange!

Serena was puzzled at the phrasing, too, and even more puzzled when, without hesitation, Briget told her to ready the horses for a visit to the castle. She stood dumbfounded for a moment until Mikal broke the awkward pause.

"Madam and Miss," he addressed them, "If you prefer, I brought his carriage."

...

The ornate black carriage drawn by two majestic gray horses passed through the city gate. Serena had never been in such a beautiful coach. The seats were a golden colored velvet and softer than any chair she'd ever occupied. The cushions kept her from feeling all but the worst bumps in the road. She marveled at the gilt paint outlining the interior panels and the larger-than-usual windows that allowed sunlight to flood the cabin.

Her mother sat next to her, silent and staring straight ahead as if in a daze. Captain Mikal rode up front with the coachman. Serena stared out the windows at the city as they passed all the familiar places. She could smell the fresh rolls at the bakery and hear people haggling in the market. They were passing the green when she noticed Trevor placing a second bench there. She thought it was a pity to have the one unmarked green space in town broken up by man-made things. At least they were quality seats.

Trevor was finishing his work on the green, admiring the bench he had completed that morning when he looked up in time to see the king's carriage pass. Yet the king wasn't inside. Instead, he glimpsed a familiar young lady looking back at him. He quickly wiped his hands on his work vest and straightened his ponytail. Then he remembered his bidding and started walking toward the castle.

...

King Liam sat comfortably in his library, surrounded by leather-bound tomes and maps. A round table large enough to seat eight people was just to the left of the center of the room as a visitor entered, and to the right was a plush reading chair with a small table that held a lantern. Candelabras adorned the spaces where light from windows near the high ceiling couldn't reach.

The reception of guests typically occurred in the all-too-formal throne room, but Briget was no typical guest. She was a friend who disliked the ostentatious world of royalty. Liam understood her reasons and respected them because he respected her and her deceased husband, Waylon. They didn't care for titles—only good hearts and trustworthiness earned their friendship, and they were wonderful friends.

Captain Mikal Sage entered the room first and saw the king was ready for them. He opened the door wide and stood aside, announcing them by first name only. "Sire, your honored guests Briget and Serena have arrived."

The king stood as the ladies entered. Serena gave a formal bow, an act she thought would be expected. Briget, on the other hand, walked briskly to greet His Majesty with a warm embrace. He then backed up, took a long look at her, and kissed her hand gently.

"My dearest Briget!" He smiled. "It has been far too long!"

"I agree, Sire," she answered. "I am sorry I've been absent for nearly a decade, but I know you understand my reasons."

Serena and the captain stood and watched in silent amazement. Serena did not realize that the king and her mother had ever met, much less been on such familiar terms.

The king glanced beyond Briget at her daughter. "And this lovely young lady is Serena? The child I once held in my lap, all grown up?"

Serena gave a shy smile and nodded slowly. "I'm sorry, Sire," she finally said. "I don't recall ever having visited you before."

"You shouldn't, I think," said the king. "You were barely walking the last time your mother brought you here."

Serena relaxed a little but struggled to comprehend this surprise. She had been inside the castle? She had been held as a toddler by the king? Why did she not know this?

Her mother seemed to read her mind. "Serena, your father and I spent quite a bit of time inside these four walls." She motioned to the room where they stood. "This library was where we worked." She turned back to Liam and said, "I can only imagine you asked us here for a reason other than a walk down memory lane. Forgive me, but am I right?"

The king nodded. "You are correct."

Briget looked at the floor between them. "The darkness," she whispered.

"I hoped this day would never come," Liam answered solemnly.

"I know you did." She lifted her eyes to meet his and then looked back at her daughter and the captain. "If you don't mind, Sire, Serena has not heard the stories of these matters, and now is not the time for her."

The king nodded to Briget in comprehension. "Captain Mikal."

"Yes, Sire."

"Please, take our guest to the small dining room and ask the cook to make her my favorite meal. She should make enough for all four of us. Briget and I will join you in a short time."

"Yes, Sire." Mikal offered Serena his arm to escort her out. Serena silently wondered what the king's favorite meal was.

Serena accepted his arm and forced a smile. She glanced back at her mother as they left the room. Who was this woman she thought she'd known so well? Clearly there were secrets Briget had yet to tell.

While they walked silently through the maze of corridors, Serena decided that as a distraction from her questions regarding her mother's past, she would practice getting a sense of a person by his touch. It only seemed natural to choose Captain Mikal, since her arm was still formally intertwined with his. She cleared her mind the best she could and touched his upper arm with her free hand.

A flood of sensations came to her quickly, and she forced them to slow to a trickle as Briget had taught her. First, she focused on his heartbeat—strong, steady, and calm. Calm was good, especially for a soldier. His breathing matched his heart despite their quick pace through the castle halls.

Next, in her mind's eye, she saw three children of varying ages. Two were boys and one was a girl. All were dressed in simple clothing. She wondered if they were his children. Instantly, the same three were older, and the brothers surrounded their sister in her sickbed. She saw Mikal glance up at a mirror. He was the second brother, and she was suddenly seeing his sister's death from his perspective.

Before sadness overcame her, she saw a battlefield in a valley below him. Mikal was standing on a cliff looking down into the smoke, sweat, blood, and death. He looked to his right at the king, who was younger and more serious than when she met him that morning. Beyond the king, she saw more officers.

The years flipped by like pages in a book, showing more images of the king until she saw him through Mikal's eyes as he was today, possibly even that morning, asking for Briget, his trusted advisor from years past, to be invited to his grand home.

Serena felt a moment of shock and disbelief. Her mother was an advisor to King Liam? But that was her father's position, wasn't it?

Her little experiment only filled her with more questions, and she suddenly realized they were entering a small, private dining room. Despite its size, ornate decorations filled the room; even the chairs had crushed velvet cushions the color of a clear winter sky. Eight places at a mahogany table were set with fine porcelain and silver.

"Here we are," the captain announced. "Excuse me a moment while I find a cook." She released his arm and watched him hurry through a narrow door on the opposite side of the room.

Serena was lost in thought, staring blankly at the beautiful silver candlesticks on the table, when the sound of a man clearing his throat startled her. She whirled around, expecting to see Mikal or the king, but was surprised to see Trevor standing there.

"My lady," he gave a quick bow. "I didn't mean to startle you."

"I'm sorry," she replied. "I'm not usually easily startled." She glanced quickly at the door Mikal had left through. Maybe it was the echo of the old woman's warning in her ears, but something about Trevor at that moment made her very uneasy. It was a very different feeling from the warmth he'd given her that day on the green.

He followed her eyes to the service door. "Are you expecting someone?"

"Yes," she answered, speaking louder and with more confidence, hoping to catch the captain's ear. "Captain Mikal escorted me here for a meal. He should be returning momentarily."

"I see." She felt like Trevor's eyes were boring right through her. "Do you dine here often?" He faltered. "At the castle, I mean."

"No, this is the first to my memory." She strained to hear booted footsteps approaching.

"I see," he repeated. He saw the tension in her eyes and posture and realized she was uncomfortable. "Forgive me," he said, "I do not mean to intrude. I merely saw a familiar face and wanted to say hello."

"Oh, hello," she laughed weakly.

The footsteps finally made it to the doorway, and Mikal entered the room and paused when he saw Trevor on the opposite side. "Good morning, sir," he said formally. "May I be of assistance?"

Trevor's dark eyes sparked with fire briefly and then turned a cooler brown again. "I doubt it," he grumbled. Then he spoke louder. "I just stopped to say hello to an acquaintance I noticed from the hallway." Serena noticed his choice of words and wondered how he saw her face when her back was turned to him.

Mikal rounded the table to stand beside Serena. "The young lady is familiar to you?"

"Yes, we've met briefly recently—once in the market and again on the square."

Serena nodded in agreement, but her face still held some tension and Mikal's instinct was to protect her from whatever part of the carpenter's presence made her uncomfortable. "So, you've given your greeting. Is there anything else?"

Trevor shrugged. "No, I guess not."

"I rarely see you inside the castle. What are you working on here, carpenter?"

"Maintenance," Trevor answered quickly.

"Of course." Mikal turned his attention to Serena. "The cook said our meal will be served in a quarter hour and thanked us for our patience."

"Thank you, Captain," Serena relaxed a little.

Trevor was still standing near the main doorway, and he cleared his throat. "Might I inquire why you are here, Serena?"

Mikal glared at him. "I don't believe that's any of your business, sir."

Serena gently rested her hand on Mikal's arm. "It's alright, Captain. My answer isn't much of one. His Majesty invited my mother and me, and so here we are."

"Your mother, too?" Trevor looked toward the hallway nervously.

"Yes, she's currently with the king. They'll be joining us shortly."

Trevor stared at her for a moment before speaking again. "A friend of King Liam?"

"I guess so," she answered quietly.

The captain put his hand over hers, still resting on his arm. "Any other questions?" he asked sternly.

"Did you hear the noise from the woods this morning?" There was a bit of excitement in Trevor's voice.

Mikal asked, "Noise?"

"I did," Serena answered. She tightened her grip on the captain's arm slightly.

Trevor asked, "Do you know what it was?"

"Mother said it was a banshee."

Mikal looked down into Serena's face and was surprised to see that she didn't seem frightened by the thought. "Did you say a banshee?"

"Yes."

"As in a phantom that screams?" Mikal recalled the stories his grandmother told of a family ghost that screeched an unearthly cry when someone in the family was near death, whether or not the death was expected.

"Yes," Serena confirmed.

Trevor's voice was a little more controlled when he asked her, "Did you see it as well?"

"No," she shook her head and paused momentarily. "At least, I don't think so. I saw movement in the woods across the river, but I didn't see detail, and that easily could have been a deer. It's an omen, right?"

Trevor answered, "Yes, an omen of the worst kind. She's a family spirit who warns of impending death."

Mikal commented, "There are fates worse than death, or so I've been told."

"I guess you could be right, depending upon what you fear. Most average men fear death," Trevor told him.

Mikal asked, "What's there to fear about death? It happens to all of us, eventually."

Trevor answered, "Maybe it's the fear that it will happen too soon? Before we get to set things right with the world?"

"Live life as though you'll die tomorrow, and you'll have reason not to wrong anyone, and therefore, no need to set them right again," Mikal told him.

Trevor thought for a moment. "Maybe it's the fear of not seeing your children grow?"

"I wouldn't know," Mikal answered matter-of-factly. "I have no children."

"So, you have no fear of death?" Trevor asked incredulously.

Mikal answered, "It will come whether or not I fear it, so I will not fear it. Fear is an energy not to be wasted on unpreventable things."

Serena had been watching the exchange with curiosity. "So, what _do_ you fear, Captain?"

"Failure," he answered.

"Failure?" Trevor repeated.

"In my position, failure is a fate worse than death because in my position, failure means I've let others die in a way I could have prevented."

Serena asked, "You don't fear your own death, but you fear being responsible for the deaths of those in your charge?"

"Yes," Mikal answered, "I think that sums it up."

Trevor scoffed. "Yes, it does."

Annoyance crossed Mikal's face. "What, pray tell, do you fear?" he asked Trevor.

"A different sort of failure," he said as he turned and walked into the hallway and out of sight.

A knot formed in his stomach as Mikal watched the carpenter leave. If Trevor Ash was in the town when Serena heard the banshee—and Mikal was sure that was the case—how did he know the banshee was in the forest? The cook bustling into the room through the servants' entrance with a tray full of covered, silver dishes interrupted his thoughts.

She was a tall, round woman with a square jaw. She wore her black and silver hair pulled haphazardly into a topknot. Her dark eyebrows and thin lips gave her a harsh façade, but when she spoke, her voice was surprisingly warm and friendly. "I have a lovely meal prepared for the king and his guests." She looked around the room. "He's not arrived, then?"

Mikal shook his head. "Not yet."

"Well, he knows that hot is the best way to eat it, so he is to blame if it's not to his liking." She shrugged and set the tray on the table. "Please, have a seat." She gestured to the chair nearest Serena, and the young lady obeyed.

Mikal surprised her by pulling the chair out for her. Serena felt awkward about the noble act. It was a rare thing for her to dine with a man, and rarer still to be treated like a lady. He took the chair opposite hers, and the cook set a dish in front of each of them.

"Please do not wait for King Liam. He would want you to enjoy this the way it should be—piping hot!" She gave a nod and waited.

Serena watched Mikal lift the silver cover off the dish in front of him. Underneath was a bowl of oatmeal topped with fresh berries and an apple-filled pastry beside it. Of all the possible favorite meals of a king that Serena imagined, oatmeal had never crossed her mind. He was truly a down-to-earth royal.

Mikal smiled at her and pointed to the dish in front of her. "Go ahead, my lady. It will please Jeryl," he pointed to the cook, "for us to eat now."

Again, Serena obeyed, and was happily surprised to find the oats had been sweetened with honey in addition to the berries. "This is quite good! Thank you," she said to Jeryl, who smiled, nodded again, and left the room.

"I am concerned," Mikal was almost whispering over his pastry, "How exactly do you know Trevor Ash?"

Serena swallowed her bite, and answered, "We bumped into each other in the market a few days ago. Literally, I mean. I turned around, and he was right there." She held her hand up close to her face to show his proximity. "The next day, I came into town for fresh rolls and saw him again on the green, where he was placing a new bench." She thought for a moment and asked, "Why does he concern you?"

"He has a bit of a history. The king asked the guard to monitor him."

"Mother said he has a history, too. I wish I knew what that meant."

"I will let your mother fill you in when she is ready because I only know what has been told to me—hearsay, really."

Serena leaned toward him and whispered loudly, "Hearsay is more than I know."

The sound of footsteps approached the main door behind her, and she heard the swish of her mother's skirt. Serena followed Mikal's lead as he rose from his seat to greet the king and her mother. The king casually motioned for the two to be seated. "Do not let me interrupt, Captain," he said and led Briget to the chair next to Serena, pulled it out for her, and then took his place at the head of the table. "I see the cook beat me here."

"By only a few minutes, Sire," Mikal answered.

Liam smiled as he lifted the lid off his dish. "I see she used fresh apples this time. Wonderful!"

The four ate in silence, and when the plates were empty, Briget placed her hand on Serena's and said, "I want you to go home ahead of me, dear. The king and I have more to discuss. It will do you no service to wait here. There are things to be done at home."

"But the chores are done," Serena insisted.

"Not those things," her mother answered softly. "Other things." Briget gave her daughter's hand a gentle squeeze and Serena understood. *Practice.*

"Yes, Mother."

The king looked at Mikal. "Captain, please see that Serena gets home safely in my carriage. Then, send it back for her mother. Use as many men as you see fit."

"Yes, Sire." Mikal understood the unspoken part of his orders immediately. The two women were being placed under his protection.

When they finished eating, King Liam and Briget excused themselves and started down the hallway back toward the library. Serena overheard the king say, "I wish you would reconsider my offer. Life in the castle isn't so bad."

A million possible reasons for that statement rushed through Serena's mind. Why would the king offer them a home in his castle? Why would her mother decline the invitation? Maybe he proposed marriage. He'd been a single father since Serena could remember, and her mother had been a widow for a decade, which was plenty of time to mourn her husband and rear her daughter. Serena chuckled at the thought of her mother, the humble gardener and healer being queen.

Mikal caught the soft sound she made and noted the amused look on her face. "What is so entertaining, my lady?"

Embarrassed, Serena shook her head. "I'm sorry. I couldn't help but hear the king's last remarks in the hallway. The thought of Mother living in the castle tickled me. It doesn't fit her personality."

Mikal smiled. "I see." He stood from his chair and made his way around the table to help her from hers. "As I understood his hopes before I left him to retrieve you this morning, he was going to offer a home to both of you."

Serena, standing, froze in her place for a moment and then turned to face the captain. "I don't understand. Why?"

"The king and your parents were close friends when you were a child. Your mother and father were his most trusted advisors."

"Both of them?" she asked. Serena had heard her father died in service to the king, but the details had been kept hidden from her. She had always thought the memories were too painful for her mother to share.

"That is my understanding, yes," Mikal offered. "The king is concerned about a change in the atmosphere of late. He wants to protect his friends, you and your mother included."

"I know the change you mean. I have sensed it, too, since the blacksmith's death."

"I don't want to say too much, but I will say that as of a few minutes ago, I have new orders for my part in this."

"Captain, I admire your honor," Serena said, recalling their conversation with the carpenter.

"Miss, I appreciate the compliment, and I hope I shall never fail you."

"So, I am in your charge?"

"In so that the king has asked me to look out for you and your mother since you will not be moving inside the castle gates."

Serena thought for a moment. "My mother can be stubborn, but she usually has good reason."

"I doubt she needs to be stubborn in this matter. The king can offer better protection within the castle."

"Since you take your position seriously, I have no doubt we'll be fine in our own home."

"If that is how you and Briget want it, then I am at your service until the king bids me stand down." He offered his arm to escort her to the carriage. "I will send you home with an escort, and when your mother is ready, I shall escort her myself."

"Many thanks to you, Captain, and to the king for his concern."

...

Trevor Ash left the town walls behind him at a fast pace toward the river. He found a narrow plank bridge just below the rapids and crossed to the hemlock forest on the other side. Then he continued until he found himself across the river from Serena's property. There, he sat down on the trunk of a fallen tree and began tracing an image in the dirt with his finger.

He heard the wind blow through the leaves in the trees above him. The birds went silent, and the crickets stopped chirping. A low moan emanated from deep within the forest. Trevor sat still and waited.

A shadow formed twenty feet in front of him and seemed to rise from the ground. It gradually took the form of a female with long scraggly hair and a gray skeletal face—an animated version of the crude drawing in the dirt in front of him.

The moan grew louder and surrounded him until his senses were drowning in the melancholy noise. Words formed, although the wraith's lips did not move. "What do you want?" she hissed. "Why do you beckon?"

Trevor stood and asked, "For whom do you cry?"

"Not for you."

"What family do you claim?" he asked.

"It is not yours."

Trevor grew angry at her indirect responses. "Answer me!" he shouted.

"Or what?" Her voice was a gravelly whisper, but louder than a waterfall in his ears. Her hollow eyes grew darker.

"I shall have my answers!" He yelled over the wind, which was howling through the trees.

The banshee laughed—a cackling hiss that faded to a moan. "You shall!"

Then she was gone. The wind ceased. The forest was silent.

Trevor left the woods, more frustrated than he'd felt in a year's time. The only answer he found should have been consolation enough: the banshee was not of his family, so it wasn't his death she foretold. Somehow, though, that knowledge did nothing to settle his mind.

...

Serena was sitting on the edge of her bed when her mother arrived home in the company of Captain Mikal and two other guards. Mikal gave the man who had escorted Serena permission to return to the castle, and then he took the other two for a patrol around the property. Serena could hear their conversations concerning security measures outside her window. As the men's voices grew distant, she heard her mother enter the house.

"Serena," Briget called.

"In my room, Mother," she answered.

Briget came into her small bedroom with a serious look on her face. "I'm sure you have questions."

A million questions, Serena thought, but she only nodded.

"Well," Briget started, as she sat on the bed beside Serena, "you may ask them. I will answer as well as I am able."

Serena noted her mother's choice of words, and she felt Briget sensed time was running short. All the insinuated secrecy concerned her more. "Why do I not recall visiting the castle when clearly I have?"

"You were too young to recall."

"Why did you tell me only that father was an advisor to the king, when today it became clear that you were, too?"

"I was once, but most people did not realize it. Most people assumed I was only there as your father's wife. It turned out safer for us to let them believe that."

"How?"

"Your father was killed..." Briget paused.

"In service to the king," Serena sighed. "I know."

Briget placed her hand on her daughter's knee. "Yes, but that was not what I was about to say. Let me finish."

Serena's eyes grew wide, and she stared at the floor in front of her instead of facing her mother.

"Your father was murdered by three wizards because of what he could advise the king. He knew who was faithful, loyal to Liam. He knew who was conspiring against him."

"How?"

"Your father could read people—could read their souls better than anyone."

Serena lifted her eyes to gaze into her mother's. She'd never heard this part of the story before.

Briget continued. "The way you've learned to read people's energy, to understand them, and help heal them is the same thing. Only you focus on their physical body. Your father's focus was on their spirit and their character. He was a master at it, and no one could deceive him. The king relied on him to survive the dark times."

Serena began to comprehend the implications of that talent. "So, the king's enemies must have hated him."

Briget nodded. "If they could hide from Waylon, they were fine. He had to see them to read them. Otherwise, their energy was more like a shadow of danger lurking in the dark corners of his mind. He knew it was there, but he couldn't identify who it belonged to."

"I think I know what you mean," Serena told her.

"You should," Briget said. "You have the same potential."

"I do?"

"Yes," her mother nodded. "It's the same idea, but a different practice and much more difficult to hone than what you already do."

A thought crossed Serena's mind. "Then why haven't you told me this before?"

Briget dropped her eyes to the floor in what seemed like shame. "Maybe I should have, but I had hoped to never need to."

Serena tried to wrap her head around all the day's new information. There was so much she didn't know about her parents and so much she should have known. "Mother," a new question tumbled out of her mouth, "What did you do for the king?"

Briget lifted her gaze to meet her daughter's. She took a moment to form her answer carefully and finally said, "I took care of those your father identified as enemies."

Serena just blinked. *What was that supposed to mean? Did she kill them? Care for them? Banish them?* There were way too many possibilities, and some were unpleasant visions of a woman she was realizing she only thought she'd known all her life.

Before she could ask for clarification, there was a knock, and they heard the front door open. "My ladies?" The captain's voice called.

Briget stood. "Just a minute, Captain."

Serena touched her mother's arm and whispered, "Wait. I have something to tell you."

Briget paused. "What is it?"

Serena kept her voice low. "At the castle this morning, I had my arm in the captain's, and I took the opportunity to practice reading him."

Her mother's eyes widened. "Did he know?"

"No, I'm sorry. I didn't ask permission as I should have, but I think it made a difference somehow."

"What do you mean?"

"What I saw, I saw through his eyes."

"That's interesting," Briget said thoughtfully.

"I've never done that before." There was a hint of excitement in Serena's voice. "What does that mean?"

Her mother looked at the bedroom door. "It means he deserves to know what you did, if he can keep it a secret."

"Secret?"

"Yes, dear, because it means you're more like your father than we thought."

...

The sun was high in the sky when Trevor Ash locked himself in his room. Full of tension, he barred the door, shuttered his window, and lit a candle on the table across from his bed. He leaned over it and whispered again and again, "Red, red, red." To his frustration, nothing happened. He threw his hands in the air and said a little louder, "Where are you?" Still, nothing happened. No answer came.

Defeated, he went and sat on the bed. The day was becoming a waste. The banshee had not given him anything useful. The encounter with Serena had been awkward under the watchful eye of the captain. The fact that she and that mother of hers were in the castle only created more questions. "Damn!" He said under his breath. "Damn, damn, damn!"

The candle across the room flickered, and the flame began to dance.

"Red," he tried again. "Red, red, red," and the flame stretched several inches higher without the aid of a draft. He noticed the bottom of the candle began to glow and gradually changed from white to pink to bright, bright red. "Finally!" he whispered. The room was bathed in the same shade until he even thought his skin glowed with it.

The same deep, male voice from his dream filled the room. "You should not summon me during the day."

"I had to," Trevor pleaded. "I need your guidance."

"What have you learned?"

"Very little," he answered and proceeded to explain the morning's events.

When he finished, the deep voice had an air of annoyance. "This could have waited."

"I couldn't wait."

"You've always been too impatient. Your haste could be your undoing. Your foolishness could ruin everything we work for."

"I'm tired of waiting!" Trevor growled. "Nearly nine years, I waited a prisoner, and now a year of servitude has passed. I do not like my situation. I'm ready for a change. I'm ready to act..."

"You are ready when I say you're ready."

Trevor growled, "Then, you should say it now."

"Prove your value, Trevor Ash. Then, I will call you ready." With that, the room darkened again, and the candle's base returned to white. The room was quiet and painfully normal. Once again, Trevor sat in frustration. The day would hold no answers for him.

...

Captain Mikal stared at the young lady standing before him. Her light brown hair seemed to shimmer in the sunlight that streamed through the window behind her. Serena's olive skin peeked out through the lace on the long sleeves of her dress. He had not really looked at her until that moment, and he was surprised by her natural beauty and taken completely off guard by what she had just confessed. He blinked twice and tried to gather his thoughts. "Did you just say that you saw my youth through my own eyes?"

Serena nodded. "Yes, I did." Her eyes were fixed on his as she tried to read his reaction to her unexpected confession. All she saw in them was confusion. "Well, not all of your youth," she added, hoping to ease his mind a little.

"What exactly did you see?" he asked.

"I saw what I interpreted as two brothers and a sister," she tried to choose her words carefully. "You lost her while she was still young, and I'm sorry for that."

The captain swallowed hard, but said, "Go on."

"Next, I saw you on a rise, standing next to the king, overlooking a fierce battle. Actually, I saw the king and the battle through your eyes."

"That's enough," Mikal said in a hushed voice. "I believe you." He was too shocked to know if he should be angry at the intrusion into his most intimate memories. He was afraid to ask what else she had seen. He had no real secrets to hide, but some personal moments should be kept private.

Serena could feel his emotion. "I saw nothing that would embarrass you," she explained. "Only important moments in your life that anyone around you would have witnessed."

"Nothing of a romantic nature?" he asked.

"Oh, no, nothing like that!"

He sighed in relief. He did not want a lovely, inexperienced young lady under his protection knowing about the indiscretions of his youth. "How did you see these things?"

She answered honestly. "I really don't know. I've never done it—well, I've never seen first person like that in my life!" Serena looked at her mother who was washing lettuce in the basin across the room. "Mother, do you know?"

Briget put down the giant leaf she held and wiped her hands on her apron. "You come by it naturally, my dear." Briget looked at Mikal. "She has always been able to read the physical body, which has helped her become a wonderful healer. I've been training her to change her focus, but she's only practiced on me, and I knew when she was doing it. Apparently, her skills made a giant leap forward with you today. My guess is your guard was not up, and it made things easier for her."

Mikal looked back at Serena. She expected anger from him over her intrusion. Instead, to her surprise, he gave a quick bow and said, "Then, my lady, I'm happy to be of service." Then he added, "But please, don't do it again. If you want to know anything about me, just ask. I will keep no secrets from you." And in his heart, he truly meant it.

...

Her footsteps echoed loudly through the castle halls as Princess Shay marched toward her private chambers. The red-haired, mustachioed guard ahead of her bowed low as she approached. "Your Highness," he greeted her with the only acceptable greeting by her standards. She barely acknowledged him as she passed, but two steps beyond where he stood, she turned to see him still bowing.

A smirk crossed her red lips. "Stand up! You can be of service to me for a change. What's your name?"

"Tom, Your Highness," the young guard straightened.

"Fetch the carpenter for me—the dark one." She turned and marched on.

The guard stood motionless. Shay turned back to see him staring at her. "Are you deaf? I meant now."

"But I am not to leave my post."

"By whose orders?" she demanded.

"My captain's, Your Highness."

She tilted her head like a dog trying to understand a new phrase. "He may be your captain, but I am your princess. I suggest you follow my orders if you wish to continue to serve my family."

"Yes, Your Highness," he said and bowed again. The young man understood the insinuation: one day, she would take the throne. Her reputation was the first lesson he had learned when he received his first assignment as her chamber guard. Captain Mikal had whispered to him, "You may need a protector of your own if you cross her. Stay quiet, do your job, and bow low."

Now Tom had to choose between his orders or her command, and for his own safety, he chose wisely and headed toward Dame Critchen's boarding house.

...

A cool breeze fluttered the fabric of their skirts as Captain Mikal watched Briget and Serena gather vegetables from their garden. He stood in the shadow of their cottage, out of earshot but close enough to respond quickly if his skills were needed. The sky was darkening sooner than normal for a late summer evening. Clouds were creeping in from the north and bringing a chill with them. He told himself the changing weather was to blame for his sudden uneasiness, but he wasn't convinced.

Briget spoke in hushed tones to her daughter as they worked. "Be quick, Serena, we need to go inside soon."

Serena glanced toward the house and smiled at the handsome captain standing watch. "I saw that," her mother teased. Serena blushed and moved faster to fill her basket. "It's nice to see you take an interest in a good man."

"Oh?" Serena asked without looking up from her work. "Why do you say that?"

"I see the way you smile at him. You've connected with him. He feels the connection, too."

"Of course he does! I told him about it."

"No, even before you told him, he felt it."

Serena snorted. "How do you know?" She realized immediately that was a silly question given whom she was asking.

"His energy changed the minute he looked at you this morning," Briget told her. Serena grinned coyly. "You did feel it," her mother confirmed.

"I thought I imagined it."

"No, it was real. That would be why you saw through his eyes. His immediate connection with you let his psychic guard down."

"But most people don't know about psychic protection."

"Know it consciously or not, the ability is natural to everyone, but not all use it. Many must be trained. The captain works closely with King Liam. I would expect he has had training in this matter."

Serena looked toward the house again, but the captain was not standing in its shadows this time.

"Where did he go?" She stood up straight and scanned their property. "The others are gone, too."

Her mother also straightened to look around. Not seeing the three men, she closed her eyes and focused on the surrounding energy. "Not good," she whispered.

"What is it, Mother?"

Briget turned to face the woods to her right. "They're there!" She pointed. "Something approaches and they've gone to see what." She grabbed her daughter's arm suddenly, and Serena nearly dropped her basket of vegetables. "Let's go! To the house!"

Serena did not ask questions and followed her mother's lead. She had learned as a small child there would be better times for talking. A rumble came from the trees behind them that sounded like thunder but did not emanate from the sky. She heard the guards' voices yelling but couldn't make out their words as she and Briget made it to the front door.

Once inside, Briget shuttered the windows. Serena threw her basket on the table and rushed to lock the doors. "The back door only," her mother shouted over the noise. "Leave the men a way in!"

Serena wondered what they were hoping to keep out. She heard the wind rise and whip around the walls of the house. The rumbling was closer, and she heard rain pounding on the roof. *Could it just be a storm?*

Even with the shutters closed, she could tell it was dark as midnight outside.

Serena held her breath and listened for some sign of the men. Barely over the wind and under the rumble, she heard their yells approaching. Her mother opened the front door, and the wind slammed it into her. She winced but stood firm as the three guards, soaked to the bone and scraped up, ran inside. The captain was last in and helped Briget shut and bolt the door.

"What is it?" Serena yelled over the roar.

"Tempest," one guard answered.

Briget took Serena's hand and led her to the center of the room. "Focus," she demanded.

"On what?" Serena asked, confused.

"The energy between us. Make a bubble!"

Serena immediately understood. She lifted her hands toward her mother, and Briget matched her motion. There was about six inches of space between their palms.

The men moved closer, and the captain motioned to the other two to create a circle around the women. They obeyed. Serena could feel Mikal standing close behind her as she envisioned a bubble of white light forming between her and her mother's hands.

"Now expand it!" Briget yelled. The circle of light increased in size until it compassed all five of them in the middle of the room. The three guards could see it with their own eyes as the wind intensified and tore at the roof. Shutters rattled and tore at their hinges. The back door opened wide. A fierce wind rushed in and tore through the house, upending everything inside, shattering glass and dishes. The noise was deafening.

But inside their sphere of protection, all was calm.

After a few minutes, the roar outside died. Everything became still, and the sunlight returned, dimly since it was nearly sunset. Briget and Serena lowered their hands, and the white light surrounding the little group faded quickly.

Mikal was the first to speak. "Is everyone alright?" All nodded. He walked to the front door, unbolted and opened it to peer outside. The storm was gone, but not gone as if it had continued on its path. It was gone as if it simply vanished ten feet past the cottage. He motioned the other two guardsmen to follow him outside to investigate. Then, he glanced at the two women and ordered, "Stay here."

Outside the younger guard with fiery red hair and a hint of stubble finally spoke, "What in the realm was that?"

"It looked like a storm to me," the older guard answered. He was a larger man with gray-speckled, short hair and a goatee.

"Not that. That!" The younger one pointed at the cottage. "What those two..." he grasped for the word, "witches just did!"

Mikal hushed him quickly. "Quiet!" He lowered his voice. "Tod, they are not witches," he stated matter-of-factly. "They are energy workers and very important friends to our king."

The older guard looked over his shoulder toward the cottage. "My only question is why the king thought they needed an armed guard. I'm pretty sure they were the ones doing the protecting just now."

Mikal was quiet for a moment as he surveyed the damage to the property, the abrupt end to the storm's path, and the sky. There wasn't a cloud in it from horizon to horizon. Then he spread his arms wide and answered, "This is why. That storm was not natural. The king knew these women would be targeted."

"Not natural?" Tod repeated. The captain pointed to the sky in the direction the storm had been moving. "Do you see that? Not a single cloud! Nothing to hint a powerful whirlwind passed over just moments ago."

The young guard swallowed hard at the reality. "Sheesh! You're right, sir."

"And the damage," Mikal continued, "is limited to the path through the woods, their garden, and the width of the cottage. Then it ends here."

"Targeted," the older guard observed. "Amazing!"

The captain looked at the younger one and pointed toward the barn. "Grab a horse and go to the king. Explain what you witnessed and ask for further orders."

"Yes, sir!" The guard ran toward the barn.

"Wait!" Mikal yelled behind him, and the young man froze in place. Mikal walked closer to him and spoke softly. "Be calm. Do not race through the town. Do not rush through your story. Remember that you address King Liam, and tell no one else about this. Am I clear?"

"Yes, sir." The young man turned and hurried toward the barn.

The captain turned back to the other guard and said, "Let's go inside, Erik, and help them clean up. There's nothing to be done out here with sunlight fading fast."

"Yes, Captain."

...

Tom questioned his decision to leave his post as he left the castle to find the carpenter. The princess may be dangerous, but how could he propose marriage to Rebecca if he lost his job for insubordination? He prayed Captain Mikal was as fair-minded as he seemed.

Hoofbeats clamored on the cobblestone road behind him, and Tom spun around to see his twin brother, Tod, trotting toward the castle. Tod slowed the horse at the sight of Tom on the street.

"Brother?" Tod greeted him. "Why aren't you at your post?"

Tom grumbled the words, "Princess Shay's orders." He nearly choked on them. "And you?"

Tod's excitement got the best of him, and he jumped from his mount to whisper to his brother, "I bring strange news to the king himself!"

"What news?"

"A storm of magical origins struck our assignment! The ladies—magical themselves—did more to protect us than we them!"

"You jest!"

Tod remembered his orders and started walking his horse to the castle gate. "Can't talk. Must go!"

Tom watched his brother round the corner before continuing his own assignment—to find the "dark" carpenter and bring him to the princess's chambers. There were so many things wrong with this errand. His eyes were focused on the ground when the dingy, worn boots of a laborer appear in front of him. He stopped quickly to avoid a collision and raised his eyes to see the man standing in his way.

"Pardon," Trevor Ash said earnestly. "I didn't see you there."

Tom was taken aback. "Nor I, you," he answered as recognition hit him. "Are you the carpenter?"

"Yes, sir," Trevor bowed slightly.

"I was just on my way to find you."

"It seems I've saved you the trouble," Trevor said, tilting his head. "How may I be of service?"

"The princess has requested your presence."

"Oh?"

"Yes."

"Dare I ask why?" Trevor feigned surprise.

"You may dare, but I didn't." If Tom's face had not been so serious, Trevor would have thought he was joking.

"I see," the carpenter dusted off his pants. "Shall I change? Put on something more presentable?"

Tom shrugged. "It's best not to make her wait."

Trevor smirked. "Well, that's a relief! I have nothing better to wear."

That time, Tom cracked a smile. "Come along," he said, and they walked toward the castle in the evening's growing darkness.

...

Briget had spent most of her daughter's lifetime insisting on living simply. They did not have expensive dishes or drink ware, and that was a good thing because all of it shattered in the storm. She stood in the kitchen area and surveyed the damage by candlelight.

Captain Mikal's whisper about the storm's magical origins echoed in her head. It was happening too soon. She had feared the wizards would find a way to weaken or break her binding spell, but she thought it would take decades—not just one decade—but many.

Briget was starting to question her decision that morning to decline the king's earnest invitation to move into the castle. She and Serena had protected themselves and their guards, but her home was in terrible shape. If there was one attack, there would be more.

Serena, Mikal, and Erik were doing their best to straighten the living area and pick up the fragments of pots and ceiling that the storm left behind. Serena wondered how the outside of the cottage must look. At least, when she looked up, she couldn't see any moonlight, which meant the roof was still mostly intact.

Briget motioned toward the far part of the room, "Just sweep it all to that wall over there. I'll deal with it in the morning. We need a clean patch of floor for sleeping."

"Sleeping on the floor?" Serena asked. "The guards will have to sleep on the floor?"

"No," Briget answered, "all of us."

"But Mother," Serena started.

Her mother gave her a sharp look that told her not to argue. "There are only two bedrooms, which are in the same shape as this room, and worse—they are on the forest side of the property."

The captain nodded his agreement. "You are correct, madam, they are not safe for you."

Serena saw their point. "Oh, I understand now. I'm sorry. I'm just not used to having to think like that. Strategically, I mean."

Briget crossed the room and took her daughter's hands. "My sweet daughter! I tried to make a life for you in which you'd never have to think that way." Briget lowered her eyes. "Unfortunately, I fear that by sheltering you, I've denied you some important skills that you're going to need."

"Don't worry, Briget," Mikal said. "I'll make sure she won't need them now."

"Captain," Serena started.

"Call me Mikal," he told her gently, "unless you prefer formal titles?"

Both ladies shook their heads.

"I'm Erik," the other guardsman offered. "At your service."

Serena nodded at him and then redirected her attention to the captain. "Mikal, please don't misinterpret my meaning, but I would rather learn what I need to know to think for myself than to have any man think for me."

Mikal couldn't stop the grin that crossed his face. "Of course, I understand, and I apologize. I did not mean that you couldn't..."

"I know you're honorable and a naturally protective person, but I need to know I can stand on my own."

"Yes, Miss," he agreed.

"Until today, I thought I had a grasp on reality. I thought I knew everything I needed to know about life." She looked at her mother accusingly. "Today, I learned that I'm woefully ignorant. I know too little about my parents, too little about myself, my own gifts, and too little about the world outside these walls."

"Serena," her mother tried to interrupt.

"No," she raised her hand. "I'm done with being sheltered; it's kept me naïve, not safe. I need to know everything!"

That last part stung Briget, but she knew it was true. The past had caught up to her and hiding anything from her daughter now would only put her in jeopardy. She sighed, "You're right."

Mikal and Erik exchanged glances and returned to sweeping the debris from the area where they planned to sleep. Briget walked her daughter to the other side of the living space and whispered to her, "When we have more privacy, I will tell you our story."

...

Trevor Ash followed the red-haired youth through the castle corridors to the princess's chambers. "Inside the castle twice in one day," he thought. "I could get used to this."

Tom led him to a hall that ended at a large, ornately carved mahogany door. "Stay here," he told Trevor and pointed to a spot on the floor about ten feet from the door. Then, he walked to the door and knocked.

Trevor obeyed and tried to envision what was on the other side of the door. He didn't have to wonder for long.

Tom was surprised to see Princess Shay open the door, dressed completely differently than she was just a half-hour before. Instead of her usual formal attire that she wore whether she needed to or not, she wore her purple wool riding cloak with the hood pulled over her blond hair and equestrian boots. She said nothing but looked past Tom at the carpenter standing in the hallway. "So, you found him," she finally said under her breath.

"Yes, Your..."

"Back to your post," she snapped.

Tom silently retreated to stand next to Trevor.

"You," she said, pointing at the tanned, long-haired, rough-looking carpenter. "Come here."

Trevor shrugged casually at the guard and obeyed. She opened her chamber door wide enough to let him pass her and then said to Tom, "Tell no one." With that, she turned back to her room and closed the door behind her.

...

Erik's gray-blue eyes were focused on Briget as she lit candles around the room. The glass of her lanterns had been shattered in the storm, but the candles were still usable. He thought about his odd assignment—protecting two unusual women who appeared powerful in their own rights. Watching them create... what _was_ that? A shield of energy? A protection spell? Whatever it was had him intrigued. The captain said they weren't witches. Briget herself called them energy workers. Was that not the same thing?

"Don't stare so hard," Mikal whispered next to him. "She might take offense." He handed Erik a stack of blankets Serena had pulled from an old chest in her room. They smelled like cedar.

Erik took the bedding. "I'm sorry, Sir. I'm just trying to make sense of all this."

The captain spread a large square blanket on the floor in front of them. "It's simple, really," he kept his voice low. "Briget is an old, dear friend of the king's. She helped him in the past, and today, promised to help him again. Ten years ago, it was she and her husband. Serena was young—just nine years old and had no idea her parents were advisors to King Liam. Now with her father gone, it's her turn to assist her mother in aiding the king."

"But how did they, and how will they help him?"

"You saw today that they have unique talents."

"Yes, sir." Erik couldn't help but glance back at Briget. "Unique is a good description."

Mikal chuckled. "Well, that was just a hint at what they can do. They can manipulate energy in all sorts of ways, but they only do it for the purpose of aiding others. Serena has become known in the town as a gifted healer. Briget, on the other hand, does her best to keep her head down. She would rather people forget about her."

Erik was beginning to understand. "If that storm truly was unnatural, someone remembers her."

"That," Mikal replied, "is why the king fears for their safety."

"Ironic they protected us, isn't it?"

"Yes, but don't be fooled. The same weapons that can harm us can harm them. It's the things you don't see coming that can do the most damage."

Erik nodded. "Right, so our job is to watch their backs so they can watch the king's."

"Exactly."

"Sir," Erik whispered, "how exactly did Briget help the king?"

"She bound the wizards," Mikal answered directly and then crossed the room to barricade the back door.

...

Princess Shay's chambers were unlike any other part of the castle. She had covered every surface in art, fine fabrics, or ornately carved decoration. It was a space befitting the royal daughter of the king. Liam spared no expense to keep his only child happy. The knowledge that her mother's death stemmed from vengeance against him only counteracted his guilt about indulging his daughter's every whim.

Standing in the center of Shay's bedroom, the carpenter looked completely out of place in his dirty work clothes. She regarded him carefully and finally spoke. "We must get you new clothes if you are going to escort me."

Shocked by the comment, Trevor asked, "Why? Where are we going?"

"To visit old friends, of course!" She laughed. "Do you really think I have need of a carpenter in my chambers?"

"I thought the princess would do with me as she pleased—the same as in the past."

She scoffed. "I have more important tasks for you, Trevor Ash."

...

Deep in thought, King Liam paced the floor of his throne room. The young guard, Tod, stood back and kept silent. His story of the unusual storm seemed to rattle the king. Liam had not been surprised at the attack, but the timing—how fast it came—was alarming. He had hoped it would be days, even weeks, before Briget was targeted. Truly, he had hoped the attack would never come, but his gut had told him otherwise.

Finally, the king broke his silence. "And you say the captain is sure it was an attack?"

"Yes, Sire, he was convinced of it."

"And what do you think?"

"I've never seen anything like it, Sire. It did appear to aim straight for the cottage."

"I trust the captain's judgment. Please, return to your post there, with my gratitude for the update, and let them know I have rooms ready for their arrival in the morning." The king nodded in assurance with that last part.

"Sire," Tod asked pensively, "what if they don't want to come to the castle?"

Liam smiled. "I assure you, they will. Briget may be stubborn, but she's not careless when it comes to her daughter's safety."

Tod bowed. "Thank you, Sire," he said and left quickly.

...

In the shadows of the castle, a large dark bay stallion awaited the princess. The carpenter would have to make do with a small brown mare. It was just one of many ways Shay reminded those around her who was in charge.

Trevor did not need reminding. He was accompanying the daughter of the man who had imprisoned him for nine years on an errand late at night. He knew Shay would just as quickly throw him to the wolves to save herself as she would speak his name without a hint of hatred. He had no idea what mission she was on, but he suspected she was an ally for the moment.

Shay had a history of aligning herself with anyone that might usher in the reign of the new queen, which could only happen with the death of the beloved king. All her father's affection was unreturned; Shay only thought of her own power.

They left the town through a small passage in a side wall. The watchmen nodded silently as they passed. Either the two men were already in her employ, or they were afraid of her reputation. They did not raise one eyebrow between them at the sight of the princess and the former prisoner leaving town together under the cloak of darkness.

Trevor's horse kept pace with the larger one, but he made sure to stay just behind Shay to her left as a dog would heel its master. Once, years ago, his powers made him her equal and his arrogance rivaled hers. No longer was this the case. He was bound by a spell that kept him from doing harm to anyone, including himself. Yes, he was as powerless as a goldfish and that night, he was swimming in the cat's water bowl.

They traveled in silence away from the town and the river, riding toward the distant mountain range on an overgrown hunting trail. After what seemed like hours to Trevor's mind, they came to an opening in the woods. Although he saw no one, his senses told him there were people nearby. He began to fear an ambush as he felt many eyes watching them. Princess Shay stopped her horse and raised her hand in a motion for him to do the same. His anxiety increased and his mind spun with questions. *Why would she pause here? Why would she bring me? Does she know others are nearby? Is this a plan or an ambush? What is going on?*

All he could hear was the pounding of his heart in his ears when five cloaked figures stepped out of the shadows surrounding them.

...

The knock on the door had aroused all of them, but Briget and Erik pretended to sleep on the floor.

"Who is it?" Serena called from inside her front door. Mikal stood beside her with his sword ready.

"Tod, my lady." The voice on the other side answered.

Mikal recognized his voice and lowered his weapon. He gave Serena a nod and she stepped back so he could open the door. Tod entered quickly, surveyed the room, and nodded toward Briget and Erik.

"Did I wake them?" he whispered.

"Not asleep," Briget answered and popped her head up with a smile.

Tod bowed, "My lady."

Mikal told him, "We've dispensed with the formalities, Tod. Since we're all to be cozy together tonight, we've decided to use first names."

"I see, sir." Tod walked a little farther into the room. "The king was displeased to hear of the trouble we had this evening. He again extended his invitation to be his guests in the castle and said your rooms are already prepared."

Briget sat upright on the floor, started to speak, and then stopped herself. She stared at Serena for a moment, and Serena stared back at her. Then Briget shrugged in defeat. "The king is most generous. We will have to take him up on his offer this time."

"How did he know she'd say yes?" Serena asked.

Tod answered, "Because he knew she'd want what's best for you, miss."

"Then, it's settled. We'll leave at first light." Mikal sheathed his sword. "Erik, please take watch. Tod and I will rest."

"Yes, sir." Erik stood and offered his spot on the floor to Tod. "Your turn."

...

The five cloaked figures stood, arms crossed silently threatening Shay and Trevor. Without his magic, Trevor was terrified. He was unarmed and untrusting of his companion for the evening. He looked at her for guidance, but she did not even glance his way.

The man closest to her spoke first. "Princess, you know to come alone. We have our rules."

Shay's voice was soft, cool, and confident when she replied, "I assure you he is no threat. In fact, you will be happy he's here."

The man raised an eyebrow under his hood. "How so?"

"This," she finally turned her attention toward the carpenter, "is Trevor Ash."

Trevor attempted to look as calm as Shay sounded, but he was close to trembling with fear. He began to think the heartless princess was about to hand him into slavery, or worse. He had made more enemies than he could count in his youth. What if the men had a vendetta?

"Is he now?" their apparent leader asked. "*The* Trevor Ash? The youngest of the three wizards? I thought he was imprisoned?"

Shay nodded. "He was in the dungeon for nine years. I convinced my father that since he could do no harm, he should be given a chance to prove himself reformed, and he has been a carpenter to the king ever since."

Trevor was sure he didn't hear that right. She convinced the king? She was the secret benefactor? That wasn't possible. It made no sense. Trevor sat dumbfounded.

Another hooded man to their left sneered. "So, what do we want with a powerless wizard?"

"We need another man inside," Shay answered sharply. "I can only do so much. We need someone who is not constantly being watched like I am."

Trevor wanted to laugh. She obviously didn't know that the commander of the king's guard had just warned him that his every move was being scrutinized and he was possibly a suspect in the blacksmith's death. No, that knowledge would render him useless and expendable to her, so he held his jaw tight and stared into space.

The leader of the group stroked his beard. "I see your point," he said. "A carpenter in the castle may prove exceedingly useful in the long run."

"Now that it's settled, Ranald," Shay redirected, "why did you call this meeting?"

Shock ripped through Trevor's mind. Ranald? The warlord? The man who had once given him and the other two wizards orders was the one who wanted most to see the virtuous King Liam overthrown. Trevor was surprised that despite the darkness and through the whispers, Ranald didn't recognize him.

"Someone attacked the seer and her daughter this evening."

"Unplanned?" Shay scowled.

Ranald nodded grimly. "Let's just say our secret weapon prematurely deployed."

"So, you can't control all the elements as you promised you would."

"Oh, I have control," he assured her. "That is the last time it will happen. Let there be no doubt."

"What kind of attack?" Shay asked.

"An unnatural force of nature. Their abode was heavily damaged, but they survived unscathed."

Shay shook her head. "How unfortunate."

"This means we should advance our timeline. I'm sure reaction to this incident will be swift."

"Understood," she nodded.

"Good luck, dear Princess," Ranald said just before he and the other four men appeared to fade into the trees behind them.

Chapter 4

Day 3

As the sun rose, Briget and Serena were collecting what was left of their belongings. The storm had broken anything that it could, but fabric items survived. The two were folding and stuffing clothes, sheets, and blankets into a trunk to take to the castle.

Captain Mikal came in from patrolling the property to survey the damage and saw them packing. "That won't be necessary, you know," he said, gesturing to the trunk. "The king will provide anything you need."

"This is all that we need," Briget replied, "our own things."

"He's not sending a carriage this morning. We are to take the horses so they can be stabled with His Majesty's."

"But..." Serena objected.

"We can return for the trunk later, but I want to move the two of you to the castle at once. Tom and Erik are saddling your horses now."

Serena asked, "Why such a rush?"

"After looking at the damage outside, I am more convinced than ever that what happened here was not natural."

"What did you see?" Briget asked.

"The path of that cyclone started just a few hundred feet into the woods and made a straight line toward your home. It abruptly ended just past the house. We witnessed for ourselves how long it sat over the cottage after moving quickly toward it. It just sat over us and did its worst before disappearing."

Briget took a deep breath and released it slowly. "I have known of only one man who could create a storm out of thin air."

Mikal and Serena asked simultaneously, "Who?"

"Kent DeGrane," Briget had a far-off look in her eye.

"It couldn't be," Mikal said.

"If the bonds have been broken, it could."

"Would you know if that were the case?" Mikal asked.

"No, he's been away so long that I can't read his energy." She looked up to meet the captain's intense eyes. "He's still far away, geographically. He's not near Myribell. I can tell that much."

Serena didn't quite know who they meant, but she had a feeling. "Who is Kent DeGrane?" she asked.

Briget turned to her sadly. "One of the three wizards who caused so much trouble a decade ago." She counted them off on her fingers. "Kent DeGrane, Coy McAdams, and Trevor Ash."

Serena's heart fluttered. "Trevor the carpenter?"

"The same," Mikal assured her.

No wonder, Serena thought. No wonder he seemed so different. No wonder her mother warned her to be careful of him. The history that her mother had mentioned was far more dangerous than she imagined.

Serena knew little about the three wizards, but she knew they had wreaked havoc until the war ended, they were enemies of Myribell, and her parents ended their reign of terror. Just the day before, she had learned that her father's death was at their hands, although her mother had not elaborated on the details.

Her head told her not to ask more questions, but her heart had just one left. "Is Trevor still bound?"

"Yes, dear," Briget nodded. "But that doesn't guarantee that he's trustworthy."

Serena nodded and frowned. Her world felt upended. Her home was in ruins. Nothing would ever be the same.

...

The sunlight filtered through the windows of the shop where Trevor and others worked, turning logs stripped of their bark into works of art, doors, furniture, and anything else asked of them. Trevor absentmindedly sanded the seat of a new chair for the banquet room while the events of the previous night replayed in his mind. The conversation after the meeting with Ranald shocked him the most.

They rode for a time in silence on the way back to town, but Trevor's curiosity made him break that silence. "Why did you do it?"

"Do what?" Shay answered his question with another and an irritated tone.

"Convince your father to set me free."

"Obviously, I had a plan for you."

Fair enough, he thought. "Why did your father do it?"

"Because he's weak when it comes to me. He always has been," Shay answered without ever looking over her shoulder at Trevor behind her.

Somehow that answer wasn't good enough for him. "To set me free—an enemy of him and his people—the man should have condemned me to death instead of life in the dungeon—to set me free and give me a chance to prove myself reformed and worthy of my freedom—there must be more."

"Why? Why must there be more?" She still did not look back.

"It makes no sense otherwise."

Shay stopped her horse and turned in her saddle. "Fine," she glared at him. "You want the whole truth? Then you shall have it."

"That's all I ask," he said softly, noting the ice in her eyes.

"When his only daughter asks for the sake of his granddaughter that the father of that child be freed, he caved with the hope that somehow all would be reformed and his world would be set right for all time." The princess faced forward again and kicked her horse into a trot.

It took a moment for Trevor to process what she said, and longer for him to decide that she was telling the truth. He had a daughter, an heir to the throne of Myribell. How did he not know of her? How did the people never speak of her? And most importantly, when would he be permitted to meet her?

...

As the captain requested, Serena and her mother arrived at the castle on their own and with just a small bag of personal items on each of their backs. They traveled lightly and made their way through town and into the castle quickly. Everything felt differently now, and as they passed under the castle gate, Serena marveled at the massive foundation stones and the weight of the years they had witnessed.

Mikal and his men accompanied them the whole way, which made the townspeople stare and wonder why the two women suddenly needed an armed escort. Briget nodded and smiled at the familiar faces they passed in an effort to limit any rumors that might start at the sight of them.

Briget and Serena were helpful and compassionate healers. People celebrated their generosity and loved their warmth toward everyone they met. Even so, the sight of Captain Mikal, Erik, and Tod—three of the king's personal guards—escorting the ladies to the castle was sure to drum up whispers and speculation.

Serena remembered the morning after the blacksmith's mysterious death. There was so much talk! So many people were making wild guesses and innuendo based on superstition, suspicion, and fear. What if they thought her mother and she were being arrested for his murder? She looked at her mother with concern in her eyes.

Briget read her mind, as she often did. "Don't worry, Daughter. What they don't know won't hurt us," she said with a wink.

Mikal overheard Briget's assurance and pulled his blue roan gelding closer to Serena's palomino mare. "Don't worry about what they think. The truth has a way of getting out."

Serena nodded. "Thank you both." She thought for a moment and then added, "But do we really want it to?" She leaned on her horse toward Mikal and whispered, "What if the one who killed the blacksmith thinks we are taking the fall for him? Could that flush him out?"

Mikal only half-heard what Serena was saying. Her soft voice and her closeness made him momentarily fuzzy-brained. He felt dazed and then annoyed with himself. Now was not the time to let his guard down, but her proximity was just too much. All he could muster when he realized she had just asked him a question was, "We'll see." Then, he quickly positioned his horse ahead of hers just in time to enter the castle's main gate. His head cleared as soon as he escaped her gaze, and he cursed under his breath at what he knew could be a weakness.

As they dismounted their horses, Mikal caught sight of Trevor walking toward the castle. "What's he doing here?" he asked Erik.

"I have no idea, sir," Erik answered quietly.

Mikal watched to be sure the ladies did not notice the carpenter. He worried Briget would be upset by his presence, and he was unsure how Serena would feel. She almost seemed intrigued by the man. She ought to be disgusted by him. After all, if it weren't for those three wicked men, her father would still be here to look after her.

"Find out, Erik," Mikal whispered. "I'd rather him keep his distance, and I'm sure the king would agree."

Erik nodded, tied his horse, and followed Trevor into the castle. The carpenter walked with purpose, but he appeared to be lost at the same time. Erik held back to observe him glance through open doors and change directions twice. The castle halls could be confusing to those unfamiliar with them, but that confusion helped with security. Trevor obviously did not know where he was going, which gave Erik reason to question him.

"Halt, Carpenter!" Erik boomed.

Trevor froze immediately and then turned slowly to face Erik.

"What are you looking for?" Erik asked him.

"The way to the chambers of Princess Shay."

That answer shocked Erik. "What? Why?"

"She sent word that she has need of me, but did not send an escort to guide me like last time."

"What need does she have of you?"

Trevor thought quickly, but not clearly. "Broken bedpost, sir."

Erik scoffed. He knew Shay's reputation. The answer could be truth, or it could be a terrible joke. Unlike the guardsmen stationed in Shay's wing, Erik had no fear of her. "Follow me," he told Trevor, and the carpenter did as he was told.

...

Serena and Briget accompanied Mikal and Tod up a spiral staircase to the entrance of the north wing of the castle. Then, they traversed one windy hallway to another until they came to a simple pair of doors opposite each other. Mikal motioned to the one on the right. "This one is Briget's chamber." Then, he pointed to the one on their left. "That is Serena's."

Tod strode up and opened Briget's door, glanced around the room inside, and then stepped aside with a gesture to let the lady know she could enter safely. Then

Mikal mirrored Tod's actions at Serena's door. She walked into the room and was speechless. Mikal followed her in.

The room was much larger than the door made her think it was. In fact, it was nearly the size of their modest cottage. There was one stained glass window high above eye level that was filled with light blue and gold glass so as to allow as much light into the room as possible while still keeping it private.

The bed under the window was big enough for an entire family to sleep in. It was fitted with four posts and a canopy that blocked it well from the window's light. The captain walked over to it for a closer look. He wanted to be sure there were no surprises hidden in its shadows.

A large wardrobe stood against one wall all alone, and a desk and chair fitted with a lantern, writing implements, and paper sat in the corner. In between, there was a lot of empty space.

Serena noticed a door on the wall opposite the bed. She pointed at it with a questioning look. "Private bath and water closet," Mikal told her. He looked around the room once more. "The king said that you and your mother have free access to his private library any time you want. If there is anything you need..." He paused at the frown on her face. "My lady, what is wrong?"

Serena realized she was frowning and forced a smile. "Nothing, Captain." She gestured at the space around them. "It's all lovely."

"But?"

"It's just not very cozy, is it? Actually, it's quite empty." She thought back to her home, the tight little space full of comforts and soft textures that welcomed her in after a long day.

Mikal understood. "It's not home, I know."

"It's only temporary, right?" Serena's eyes sparkled with a hint of tears.

"Of course," Mikal assured her. He glanced around the room again. "Maybe I can find some additional..."

"No," Serena interrupted. "Do nothing on my account. This is perfectly fine. I do not want to cause any trouble."

No trouble at all, he thought. The least they could do was make things comfortable for the ladies whose home had been badly damaged, presumably because of their relationship with the king.

...

Trevor didn't recognize the part of the castle he followed Erik through. It seemed to him they should have traveled up a stairway or two at some point. Instead, they were deep inside the ground level far from where they started when they came to a door with an iron cross nailed to it. Erik pushed open the door and motioned for Trevor to enter first. The carpenter expected a chapel of some sort, but came face to face with three more of the king's guards, and more surprisingly, the king himself. Trevor immediately knelt at the sight of His Majesty.

Erik bowed. "I'm sorry, Sire. I didn't realize you were here."

Liam waved his hand in a gesture that said there was no harm done. He looked closely at the man kneeling, head down, before him. "Is this our wizard turned carpenter?" he asked.

"Yes, Sire," Erik confirmed. "He was wandering the castle halls with uncertainty, so..."

"What were you looking for, Trevor Ash?" Liam asked him.

Trevor lifted his gaze to meet the king's eyes, but hesitated with his answer.

"Come now," the king said with gentleness in his voice. "There are no secrets inside my castle. None hidden from me, anyway."

Trevor gulped at the irony, or was it the truth? Did he already know his own daughter was plotting against him? He decided to be honest. "The princess's chambers, Your Majesty."

The three guards stared blankly, but the king regarded him seriously. "I see. Does she know you are seeking her?" Liam asked.

"Yes, Sire," he lied and hoped Shay would sensibly back him up if asked.

"She should have sent an escort for you in that case," Erik said from behind Trevor.

"Last time, she did," he answered. "I guess she expected me to remember the way, but this castle is a puzzle to me."

The king chuckled. "It was built to confuse those who do not belong."

Trevor lowered his eyes to the floor. "I obviously don't belong."

"Well, Carpenter," the king said as he approached Trevor and put his hand on his shoulder, "stand up. Let me guide you through these halls."

"Yes, Sire." The shocked carpenter rose.

"Shall I accompany you, my king?" Erik asked.

The king answered, "Yes, but out of earshot. The young man and I have a private matter to discuss."

Erik obeyed and followed about twenty paces behind them.

"Trevor, you have been spending time with my daughter again, correct?" King Liam asked bluntly.

"Yes, Sire," he added quickly, "but not like last time. I haven't touched her, nor she me."

"I understand," the king nodded. "Has she told you the good news?"

"Good news?" Trevor acted surprised at the thought.

Liam imagined Shay had already mentioned the child, so he didn't sugarcoat the conversation. "That you're the father of her daughter, of course!"

Trevor gulped. Fear of the king's understandable anger gripped him, and he stopped walking. "I'm sorry, Your Majesty. I was young and foolish."

"And full of yourself, too," Liam added. There was no rage or hatred in his gray eyes—only compassion. "Apology accepted," he said and started walking again.

"She told me that is why she asked you for my freedom," Trevor offered.

"Is that how she remembers it?" The king had a tone of amusement. "Interesting."

"Sire?"

"I suppose I should fill you in regarding the circumstances as they once were and are now." They rounded a corner and entered the throne room. To Trevor's surprise, Liam did not take his place in the ornate chair at the focus point of the room. Instead, he led the carpenter to a round table with five chairs surrounding it and offered him a seat. Erik motioned silently to the king that he would stand guard in the doorway to keep the discussion private, and the king nodded his approval. He then took a seat opposite Trevor and told his story.

"I was quite delighted when my daughter was born. She was breathtaking from the moment she arrived. I immediately knew I was in trouble because she had me wrapped around her finger from day one. Her mother was so pleased that I was happy with a girl. So many kings waste their energy fretting over whether they'll have a male heir to the throne. To me, all life is precious. Boy or girl mattered not. She was healthy and beautiful.

"Her mother did not do well in childbirth. A few days after Shay came to us, she succumbed to fever and died. It saddened her to leave us, and in the end she made me promise to raise our baby as a princess should be."

The king leaned across the table and lowered his voice. "I admit that I had no idea what she meant, but I made the promise, anyway."

"I did not like to hear Shay cry. Ever. I would try to hold and comfort her, but she would have none of it. She'd just cry louder. So, I would give her a toy to distract her. She'd bore of the items quickly, so it was always a new toy. I realize now that was not the best strategy, but it kept her quiet and happy, at least while she was a small child.

"I spent what time I could with her, but running a kingdom requires long hours, especially when at war. By her teen years, she had become too accustomed to my absence and very demanding of everyone around her. In short, she quickly grew into a tyrant. By the time you met her, she had a reputation for causing trouble for anyone who crossed her path. As much as I tried to explain to her that everyone should be treated well because we are all human souls, she would not listen. She had somehow bought into the belief that her title made her better than everyone. I have no idea where she got that idea. By now, you know that is not my philosophy. I believe a king, while he is a ruler, should also live to serve his people. My goal is for everyone in my kingdom to have a chance at prosperity."

"I have noticed, Sire," Trevor assured him.

"Anyway, the two of you... consorted and created a new life." He cleared his throat. "I have to admit that learning that my own daughter had literally laid down with an enemy angered me greatly, and more importantly to her, it hurt me deeply."

Trevor shifted in his seat nervously. He started to speak, but Liam raised his hand to silence him and kept talking.

"Do not worry. I am no longer angry. You must understand that I consider all life sacred and all children blessings, at least, as long as they behave as such."

"Shay wanted nothing to do with her child. When I learned that she was searching for a way to terminate the pregnancy, I locked her in her chambers. To make a long story short, I confronted her, learned that you were the father, and made plans to end the Three Wizards' War on Myribell once and for all—all within an hour.

"Do you ever wonder why you were captured and not exiled like the others?"

Trevor thought back to the endless days in his cell. "Occasionally, I did."

"Well, the answer is simple: I wanted my granddaughter to have two parents." Liam shook his head sadly. "Unfortunately, her own mother wants nothing to do with her. Ever."

"Where is she, Sire?" Trevor's heart ached for the little girl he'd never met.

"She is being raised to share my values by a woman I trust with my life," was all the king would tell him. After a pause, Liam added, "If you make the right choices, Trevor Ash, you may meet her and spend time with her. That is why I released you. That is why you work for me."

Trevor tried to smile through the mixed emotions swirling in his mind.

The king continued, "I believe you can be a good person and even a good father, despite your history. You have the potential to redeem yourself to me, my kingdom, and my granddaughter, but you must consistently choose light over darkness every day."

The sound of Erik clearing his throat from the doorway interrupted Liam. He glanced toward his guard, who motioned that someone was approaching. The king stood and finished with, "I trust that you understand me, Trevor."

"Yes, Sire," he answered meekly. While he was not lying, he was not making any promises. The king had hopes for him, but the princess had plans for him. One wanted him to master his fate, while the other wanted... well... what exactly did she want? He knew she was using him for her own gain, but what then? After she had the throne, would she keep him as a lover? Make him king? Throw him to the howling wolves that ran through the forests at the mountain's edge?

Erik's voice broke the train of thought that was bouncing out of control. "It is just Captain Mikal, Your Majesty."

As he entered, Mikal raised an eyebrow at the word "just" as if it hurt him. "Well, thank you for that introduction, Erik." He looked at the king standing next to Trevor. "What have we here?"

"Erik is going to escort him to Shay's wing," Liam answered. "It seems she has decided that she requires a carpenter."

That he would still be allowed to go to the princess's chambers after all the king had just told him shocked Trevor. He took the hint with a bow and followed Erik out into the hallway.

Mikal watched them leave before addressing the king. "Sire, we have Briget and Serena settled into their new rooms."

"Very good!" the king smiled. "Did they find everything satisfactory?"

"Mostly," Mikal tilted his head thoughtfully, "although I doubt either would ever complain."

"What makes you say that?"

"Serena mentioned how large her room is. It does look quite empty and stark compared to their cozy cottage. Of course, she's probably just homesick already."

Liam tapped the table beside him. "Do you think we should add more decoration? How about a nice couch or some tapestry?"

Mikal chuckled. "I'm no decorator, but anything to soften the space would probably make her—or them—more comfortable."

"Then do what you can. I'm sure we have the resources to make our dear guests feel more at home."

"Yes, Sire." Mikal turned to leave.

"Aren't you going to ask what the carpenter was doing here?"

Mikal paused and shook his head. "No, I figured you would tell me if it were my business."

"It is your business," the king assured him. "I challenged him to make the right choices if he is interested in becoming part of his daughter's life."

"So, he knows about her?"

"He knows *of* her, but no details. He must prove himself."

"Understood."

"I fear that will prove too difficult for him, especially since my daughter has taken a new interest in him."

"I agree," Mikal said.

"She is up to something. Keep a close eye on them both. Make sure your most trusted men are watching quietly. I know her influence her has grown. I know she hates me; although I'll never understand why. Sadly, I know I can't trust her. I can only hope to trust those who have pledged their devotion to me."

Mikal noticed the word "devotion" as opposed to "allegiance," which was in the oath each member of the guard must take. "I understand," he assured Liam. "Do you need anything else?"

The king thought for a moment before asking, "Are you returning to the guest chambers?"

"If you wish, Sire. I was hoping to round up some comforts for them first."

"Please, stop there first, and ask Briget to meet me in my library."

"Yes, Sire." The captain obeyed. As he walked the castle halls back to the guest rooms, he thought of how he could brighten Serena's room, and he surprised himself with the thought that he hoped to improve her life.

...

The red-haired young man leaned against the stone wall of the hallway leading to Shay's rooms. His staff was resting on his forehead, and his mind was on other things like dinner, payday, and the new barmaid, Rebecca, at his favorite tavern. She was a beauty with her brown hair, green eyes, and tight bodice. He hoped she'd be there the next time he visited.

The sounds of footfalls on the hard floor shook him from his thoughts, and he looked up to see the older guard bringing the carpenter toward him. Tom quickly stood upright. "Hello, sir!" He greeted Erik, his senior in rank.

"Good morning, Tom."

The younger guard looked at Trevor. "The princess wishes not to be disturbed."

Erik responded loudly, "But this young man insists she summoned him." He looked beyond Tom to the doorway to her chambers. "Isn't that right, Trevor Ash?"

Trevor nodded meekly. Knowing they would catch him in a lie, he silently prayed she would not let him down.

Tom realized that Erik was trying to get the attention of the princess through the heavy doors, so he tapped his staff on the floor, and the sound echoed through the hall. "I am sure her orders were to be left alone today." His voice matched Erik's volume.

Trevor started to sweat.

One of the large doors swung open, and the princess, with her hands on her hips, stood before them. "What is this commotion?" Her eyes landed squarely on Trevor, and her lips parted as if she were about to speak, but she said nothing. She only stared with fire dancing in her eyes.

Erik finally spoke. "Your Highness, Master Ash claims you sent for him, in need of his services. Is that correct?"

She continued to stare but said nothing as if she were cautiously considering her answer and enjoying watching Trevor break.

Erik put his hand on Trevor's shoulder as if to turn him around. Fear flashed across Trevor's face at the touch, and he cringed.

"I do have need of him," Shay finally said. "Leave him here."

Instead of turning him, Erik gave Trevor a playful push toward the princess. "Here you go!"

With both hands still on her hips, Shay snorted. "You both may leave!" She told the guards.

Erik shook his head and looked at Tom. "Why don't you take a break? I'll mind hell for an hour."

"I said both," Shay insisted.

Erik did not move his gaze from the younger guard but answered nonchalantly, "So you did."

Shay stamped her foot like an angry toddler, and the noise echoed down the hall. Tom looked scared, and Erik patted his shoulder. "Like I said, I'll stay here." Then, he looked the princess directly in her still fiery eyes, and said, "I take my orders from the king."

Trevor walked toward the princess too slowly for her liking. She stepped forward, grabbed his arm, and yanked him hard through the doorway. The doors slammed shut.

Erik grinned. "I guess she didn't appreciate my temperament today."

"Or anyone's. Ever," Tom added.

"Run on, now, Tom. Go get some food while you can."

"Sir, will she be mad with me?"

"Isn't she always mad?"

"Yes, sir."

"Then, why worry? Nothing will change. Besides, I'm the defiant one in her eyes. You're only following orders."

Tom nodded, handed Erik his staff, and hurried down the hallway. He wanted to put as much distance between himself and the irate princess as possible, even for an hour.

...

After Briget assured Mikal her room was quite satisfactory, she found her way to the king's library. Tod had gone to the kitchen to request a late morning meal, which meant Mikal was alone with Serena.

He watched her put the few clothes she'd brought from home into the wardrobe and noticed the colors were subdued and natural looking. In fact, what she was wearing was a faded brown full skirt with a bodice that looked like it had once been a burgundy color—possibly even vibrant.

"It seems unusual," he observed aloud, "that a guest of the king..." He stopped midsentence, realizing that what he was about to say might offend her.

Serena shut the wardrobe and turned to face him. "What?"

He swallowed hard and rethought his phrasing. "I know this is just a temporary home for you, but you didn't have the opportunity to bring much with you. Do you think those clothes will be enough?"

"I hope so," she answered. "They're all I have."

Mikal tilted his head to the left thoughtfully. She'd seen him do that a few times and thought how it reminded her of an inquisitive puppy. "Do you mean," he asked, "that's all you brought, or that's truly all you have?"

"It's truly all I have," she answered. "Mother and I live simply, and we work the land ourselves. We have no need for more than this." Serena noticed the concern on his face and understood. "Oh, I see. Guests of His Majesty don't usually dress like farm maidens, do they? I bet they come with ball gowns and new skirts and frilly shirts." Her eyes flashed a little. "Well, apparently, Mother has never been one to behave like a courtesan or dress like one."

"I'm sorry."

"Don't be."

"I meant no disrespect," Mikal said quietly.

"I know."

"You do?"

"At the moment, Captain, I feel like I know you better than I know my own mother."

He winced, "Call me Mikal."

"Mikal," Serena repeated with a nod.

He attempted a smile, but was unsure of what to say next. Questions arose about how he thought she knew him so well, but he feared the answers. Rather, he was sure he knew the answer, and it scared him.

She felt his curiosity and answered without his having to ask out loud. "Yesterday, when I saw through your eyes, I also felt your emotions. You're a brave man with a powerful love of family, and you're loyal and honest. The king holds you in high regard; your men look up to you, even the older ones. You have a good mind for strategy, a clear head, and an understanding of the world that I admire."

Mikal was speechless. No one had ever described him to himself and used so many of the words that he typically associated with a description of King Liam. He finally found the words to say, "Thank you, Serena. I can only hope that I am half the man you take me to be."

...

"What in all the realm were you thinking?" Shay's eyes sparked red flames, or at least, that's how Trevor saw them as she lectured him for his carelessness in coming unbid to her chambers. "You told my father and his personal guards I asked for you? Are you insane?"

"I..." Trevor tried to reply, but she wasn't waiting for an answer.

"What if I wasn't even here? What if I were with someone else with more pressing business? What if I simply called you out for the liar that you are?" she paused.

"None of that happened," he said quietly.

"Any of it could have!" Her voice was loud enough to be heard by Erik still outside the large doors of her room. "What did my father say about this?"

"Nothing."

"You must be lying."

"No, he said nothing about this," Trevor motioned to the space around him. "He did say something about *this*, though." He pointed back and forth between the princess and himself.

Shay let out an exasperated sigh. "What about it?"

"He warned me to be careful of you if I ever want to meet my daughter."

She threw back her blond hair and laughed. "Ha! That's too precious! The overprotective grandfather."

"I can understand his reasoning," Trevor kept his voice low, but even. "His daughter is not what he'd hoped for, so his granddaughter gives him a second chance."

Shay froze and glared hard at the man standing before her. "You think I don't know this? Do you think I don't see his plans?" She started pacing in front of him. "He means to bypass me and give the throne—everything—to her. The little runt I never wanted. The child of the weakest wizard, who right now is following a servant around the back rooms of his castle, calling her 'mommy' and eating her table scraps."

Trevor stood silent, processing what she told him and feeling the sting of "the weakest wizard."

"Do you really want to meet her? This daughter of yours?"

"I do."

"Then, do as I say. The king is not much longer for this world, and all will answer to me soon."

Trevor could only nod.

...

The king's smile had always been warm, but Briget was surprised at how youthful it was. Only the lines around his eyes gave a clue to his age. She watched while he sat with a suntanned child on his lap the same way he used to hold Serena while thumbing through volumes of history and archives in his private library.

The little girl was about nine years old and seemed intrigued by the fancy script on the pages. She studied them with her large, deep brown eyes and kept sweeping the bangs of her long black hair away from her face. Briget could tell the child had a special affection for the king, and the feeling was mutual.

"Well, my dear Eleanor," the king said as he closed the book in front of her, "I think it might be time for you to return to your mother to help her prepare the noon meal."

The little girl looked up at him with pleading eyes and asked, "Just one more book, please?"

"I'm sorry," the king shook his head, "Didn't you just say that before this one?" He tapped the closed book.

The girl nodded. "I guess I did." Understanding that her time in the library had ended, she hopped off Liam's lap, gave him a quick kiss on the cheek and ran toward the hall that led to the kitchens.

"Such a sweet child," he said as he watched her disappear down the hall. "Always a joy to have her visit."

Briget smiled and nodded. "She seems very smart for her age, too."

"Eleanor reminds me of your daughter more than mine. I truly believe the key is more in nurture than in nature. Given her parents' history, I would have expected a troublesome child, but instead, she has the disposition of an angel."

"I'm glad for you. She obviously adores you."

"Now," the king changed the subject, "about the issue at hand. Who do you think was behind the attack on your home?"

Briget's smile faded. "The only one I know of who ever had that kind of power over nature was Kent DeGrane."

"I was afraid you'd say that." He thought back to the oldest of the three wizards. Before the war's final battle, the man looked ancient; exile and binding left him horribly scarred from head to toe. The evil energy he had unleashed through his very hands would forever mark his skin. Waylon was his last victim. The memories tore at Liam daily, and he could only imagine how Briget was feeling. "I am so sorry, my dear. This must be incredibly painful."

She put a hand on his shoulder to assure him and replied, "It could be worse."

"How so?"

"Serena could have been harmed, but she wasn't. Our cottage can be repaired. Our things can be replaced, but she is truly all I have."

The king nodded. "Yes, I'm grateful for the safety of both of you." He took her hand from his shoulder and kissed the back of it gently. "So how can we be sure Kent is behind the attack?"

"I don't know," Briget answered. "He's not geographically close enough for me to sense him, and if the bounds aren't broken, it couldn't have been him. That attack was meant to cause harm, and he's bound from harming anyone."

"So, he's not nearby, and he shouldn't be able to pull off an attack like that?" Liam shook his head. "Then it must be someone else."

Briget sat in the heavy wooden chair beside him. "There needs to be a way to see where he is and test him. That's the only way to rule him out."

"Test him?"

"Give him a reason to harm someone. Knowing him, it wouldn't take much. He's quick to anger and slow to forgive. Just the mention of my name might be enough."

"If he has broken the binding, that might prove terrible for whoever finds him." The king rubbed his chin in thought. "There are few people strong enough to send against him if he has his powers back."

"They must have protection against the dark arts." Briget tapped her finger on the table. "Who else in the kingdom knows energy work?"

A look of enlightenment crossed the king's face, but pain quickly replaced it. "Other than you and Serena, I can think of only one."

...

Two large men dressed in laborer's clothes heaved the enormous rug into Serena's bedroom. With one on each end, there were easily fifteen feet between them. Both looked at the captain for direction when they reached the center of the room.

"Lay it there, right in the middle," Mikal told them.

They followed orders and unrolled the most beautiful tapestry with colors that reflected those of the stained-glass window above her bed. Immediately, the room appeared ten times brighter and felt slightly warmer.

Serena beamed with delight. "It's beautiful!" She exclaimed from her viewpoint on the other side of the rug from Mikal.

"I'm glad you like it," he said. "There's more to come, if it pleases you."

"You really don't have to..."

"I want to," he interrupted. "And if you'll accompany me on a brief tour of the castle, these men will finish more easily." The captain held out his hand, inviting her to take it.

Serena walked quickly around the rug to him and put her arm in the crook of his, and Mikal chuckled. "What?" She asked.

"It's a rug. It's safe to walk on it."

"Oh, um..." She blushed. "It just seems too pretty to tread on."

"It can be cleaned. Please, don't concern yourself with that. Use it," he insisted.

"Yes, Captain," she nodded to him as they left the room.

Mikal led her down the castle corridors, explaining each room or hall as they passed. There was the formal throne room, the king's personal library (with a shut door for a private conversation between the king and Briget), the formal waiting areas, grand ballroom, grand dining room, formal meeting rooms, private meeting rooms, the king's chambers, the princess's chambers, where surprisingly Erik was standing guard...

They paused there, and Mikal lifted an eyebrow to Erik. He answered only "No worries," and waved his hand in a gesture that said, "ask me later," without another word uttered. The captain nodded, and the pair continued their tour.

As they passed the familiar informal dining room, Serena asked, "Is this where we should come for meals?"

"Yes, this works unless the king has other plans." He added, "But on days like today, there's no need to wait for the king. Just enter the room and ring the bell next to the servant's entrance. Someone will come to your aid and prepare you whatever you want."

The idea was daunting to Serena. No one had ever waited on her until the day before in that very room. "What can I have?"

"Anything you crave—within reason, of course." Mikal saw the concerned look on her face. "What's wrong?"

She blushed and answered, "I've never had options like that. I have no idea what I'd ask for."

He patted her hand resting on his arm. "I'm sure you'll be fine. Our kitchen staff can make the simplest to the most gourmet meals imaginable." He paused and thought of his own lunchtime hunger. "In fact, if you are hungry now, we could practice."

"Practice?"

"Sure. Why not?" He led her back down the hall to the little dining room. The places were already set just as they had been the day before. This time, instead of leaving Serena to visit the kitchen, Mikal rang the bell as he had instructed her to do.

Just a few seconds later, a little girl with dark hair and tan skin bounced into the room through the servant's door. With a look of surprise, she studied Serena and asked Mikal, "What can I do, Captain?"

"Ellie, meet Serena. She and her mother are guests of King Liam for a while, and she'd like to have some lunch."

Eleanor smiled and nodded. "What would you like, Miss Serena?"

"Well, Ellie, I don't know. I'm new to all this. At home, I usually have some bread and cheese for lunch."

The child laughed. "But you're in the castle! Bread and cheese is a snack. What do you like?"

Serena looked from the child back to the handsome captain standing beside her. He shrugged. *No help at all,* she thought and sighed. "I guess I like fresh fruit, fresh bread, and..."

"Fresh cheese?" Eleanor guessed.

Serena couldn't tell if the child was teasing or serious. "Well, I really eat almost anything except mushrooms."

"I'll tell Mom to make you something extra special!" She said and then looked at the captain. "And you, sir?"

Mikal pointed to Serena and answered, "I'll have what she has—something extra special!"

"Alright then!" Eleanor said and skipped back through the servant's door.

"She is just adorable!" Serena said.

"Yes, she is," Mikal agreed. "Very bright, too."

"Her mom is the cook?"

"Yes."

Serena thought for a moment about the only cook she had met so far. That one looked too old to have such a young child. "Not the one I met, though."

"Actually, yes," Mikal replied. "She's adopted. It's amazing how much joy she's brought to the kitchen now that she's old enough to visit and help there. Everyone adores her, especially Jeryl, her mother."

"That's really sweet. Does Ellie know she was adopted?"

"Jeryl has raised her since her birth but has been very open about the adoption. Eleanor still calls her 'Mother' and loves her like a biological daughter should love her parent." He paused. "The only thing Ellie doesn't know is who her biological parents are."

"Obviously, it doesn't matter. She seems well-loved and well-adjusted." Serena observed.

"Yes, she is. Even the king adores her." Mikal said, and then he walked her to a chair at the table. Serena sat, and he seated himself across from her. He studied her for a moment as she looked at him with a slight grin. Finally, he tapped his index finger on the table and said, "You should learn to defend yourself."

Puzzlement crossed her face. "I'm pretty sure I can defend myself. You saw that yesterday."

"I mean physical self-defense. Have you ever hit someone?"

"Of course not!" The very idea insulted her. "My life is about healing, not hurting."

Mikal spread both hands in the air in front of him in a gesture that said, "hear me out," and smiled. "I know, but what if someone attacks you? What would you do with only a fraction of a second to respond?" She stared at him blankly, and he could tell she was thinking it through. "In under a second, could you make the bubble you did yesterday?"

"Not quite."

"And if you didn't see the attack coming?"

Serena dropped her eyes to the table between them. "I don't know."

"You've always been sheltered, never threatened, right?"

"I guess so."

"Until yesterday," Mikal added.

She sighed and lifted her eyes to meet him. "That is correct."

"Today, your world is different. You know someone wants to harm you and your mother. Today, you should understand why you need to learn to defend yourself."

He was persuasive, but after thinking for a moment, she still replied, "No, I could never hurt anyone."

"Not even if his goal was your death?"

"No, my soul is at peace."

"That's very noble, but you might not be so sure if the situation arose," he said.

"Excuse me?"

"Nature has ensured that we automatically act for self-preservation. All of us have that instinct, and you may find that when physically threatened, the reaction is reflexive."

"Maybe I'm not made like everyone else." She hated the point he was making. She despised the thought of violence. There was no way she would ever hurt someone intentionally.

He grinned at her grimace over the conversation. "It's true. You differ from anyone I've ever met. However, as far as I can tell, you are still human."

Serena tried to hide her smile at the way he said she was different. There was an undertone in his voice that she knew meant something more than his words. "I can practice using energy as a shield. I'll get faster." She was trying to convince herself as much as him.

"What if the threat is to someone you love?" Mikal leaned in for emphasis. "What if your mother was about to be seriously harmed? God forbid, of course. But the two of you are targets now, so we must consider these possibilities."

She shifted in her seat. "I can protect others the same way and focus my energy elsewhere. It doesn't have to be around me."

"Really?"

"Sure."

"How does that work? Have you tried it?" He was truly interested. The idea of protecting others from any distance can be highly valuable in battle.

She put her hands in front of her face a few inches apart with her elbows on the table and said, "Yesterday, Mother and I focused the energy between us as a bubble and made it grow to encompass all of us, because we were standing together, right?"

"Right," Mikal answered as he watched a tiny pinpoint of light appear between her palms. "The light is just focused, positive energy," she explained as it grew to a ball that was about a few inches in diameter. "As I envision the bubble growing, it attracts more positive energy to it." She spread her hands a little wider, and the ball of light grew some more. "Now it's big enough to use as an example. Easy to see, right?"

Mikal nodded in agreement. "But do you have to hold it in order to control it?"

Serena shook her head. "Watch." She moved her hands around the sphere as if it had solid physical form, and it remained floating right where it started. Then she moved her hands away from it and rested her chin and her palms. She looked through the little light and smiled at Mikal briefly. Next, she put her hand behind the ball and pretended to give it a push. He watched her eyes as they followed the circle of light across the table toward him. It spun in the air close to his chest.

"Alright," he started.

"Wait," she told him, and she spread her hands arm's length apart and nodded toward the captain. Immediately, the bubble grew and encapsulated him.

This time, inside the light, he noticed a warmth that permeated his entire being. It wasn't so much a temperature as it was a kind of calm contentment he remembered feeling when he was a child resting in his mother's arms. The feeling made him want to close his eyes and breathe it in deeply. He didn't recall feeling that way when the storm was tearing at the cottage, but maybe he hadn't had the chance. He wasn't exactly in the mindset of experiencing anything but adrenaline when the house was shaking all around them.

Serena watched Mikal's response to the light. She could feel it calm him, and he smiled at her through it. She returned the smile and waved her right hand slowly through the air in front of her. The sphere of light faded, but the sensation stayed with him for the rest of the day.

Just as the light dimmed, Jeryl arrived with two covered dishes on a tray. She paused at the entrance and watched the room appear to darken as the two lunch guests seemed to gaze into each other's eyes. She cleared her throat, and both glanced at her, startled. "Am I interrupting, Captain?" she asked.

Mikal shook his head. "No, madam." His face told her otherwise.

...

"Briget," the king pleaded, "it's too dangerous. You can't leave the castle."

She shook her head. "No, it is too dangerous not to leave the castle. I must meet with him."

"I can have him brought here." Liam stood and pointed at the floor. "He can come to the castle."

"That won't work," she insisted. "He likes his secrecy. You just said so. He won't want to come, and forcing him won't help our case."

Liam dropped his shoulders in defeat. "You're right. He won't come. I'm not even sure if he'll help. Our relationship is tenuous at best."

Briget began pacing the floor in front of him. "How long has he been here?"

"A few years."

"And why do I not know of him?" She answered herself before the king could. "Oh, right, secrecy. He's cloaked himself from the rest of us." She glanced at Liam and added, "Or just me."

"Briget," he tried to speak, but to no avail.

"Secrecy. Why is he in this kingdom now? What brought him here? Why stay? Was he running from... where is he from?"

"Voorstland."

She stopped pacing and looked at Liam. "Where is that?"

"Across the sea to the north."

"It's an actual place?"

Liam chuckled. "It's on my maps."

Briget shrugged. "What do we know about it?"

"It's cold, frozen, really mountainous. They export lots of precious metals, like gold and silver."

"And who rules there?"

"I've heard it's some sort of utopian society. They keep to themselves mostly. There are a few appointed ministers who deal with the outside world."

"More secrecy."

The king shook his head. "I think it's more about distrust. They are wealthy. They export riches. Who knows how much they keep? They are peaceful enough, and in order to do business with them, other governments do not pry and do not threaten them."

"Do you do business with them?" She crossed her arms.

"No." Liam noted her body language. "We have no need to import riches. We have enough of our own. Why do you ask?"

"I don't like the sound of it, and I wonder why an energy worker would leave a wealthy utopian society and hide out here in our kingdom."

The king saw her point. "He said he preferred our climate. I couldn't argue with that."

"Maybe you should have."

"My dear," Liam walked to her and took her hands in his, "if you don't trust him, and you obviously already do not, then please just stay in the castle and forget about him."

Briget looked her old friend in the eyes. She understood his concern and felt his love, but she could think of no other way to make sure the stranger did not make the attack. "I can't. If it was not this wizard from Voorstland, then it can only be Kent.

Either way. We'll find out who we're dealing with." She paused. "What did you say his name was?"

"I didn't," Liam answered. "He said they called him Krayvyn, and it's not spelled as it sounds, so don't take it to mean what you'd expect."

"Noted." Briget tapped her right temple with her index finger. "How far is he?"

"A half day's ride by carriage."

"So, a bit faster on horseback?"

Liam nodded. "I will only accept this excursion, if you take my personal guard."

"Only one," she told him, "any more may alarm him."

"Yes, fine." He nodded again. "Take Captain Sage."

Briget considered it and shook her head in disagreement. "He seems to have taken an interest in Serena. I prefer they not be parted."

"Really now?" The king stroked his chin. "I didn't see that coming."

"I did from the moment they met."

"Is the interest mutual?"

"I believe it is, but Serena is not used to attention. I'm not sure how she'll handle it."

The king smiled at the thought of a romance between the two. "She is a smart girl. I'm sure she will be just fine. In fact," he tapped the table beside him, "we can observe tonight."

"Tonight?" Briget asked.

"Yes, yes, we will have a formal dinner in the main hall in honor of our lovely guests." He pointed to her and moved closer to take her hand in his.

"Oh, Liam, no!" she protested. "We have nothing to wear. It will be an embarrassment to her."

"Nonsense," he told her. "I have seamstresses who can put together marvelous designs in just hours."

"It's not our style. We live simply," Briget continued.

"You are guests in the castle, my home. Here you will live like the royal family. When it's time to return home, you can leave anything you want behind or take all of it with you, but please, grant me the opportunity to treat you and Serena like the ladies you have always been." Liam gently kissed the back of each hand. "Waylon would make an exception under these conditions. You know he would."

Briget couldn't argue; the king was right. Her husband didn't mind the pageantry of court if he thought it was called for, and he would have loved to see Serena in a formal gown, looking all grown-up. A tear fell from the outside of the corner of her eye at the thought of Waylon missing Serena's first state dinner.

Liam wiped her cheek and hugged her. "Alright," she whispered. "Yes, but no new dresses. I'm sure you have some already made here in the castle that will fit us. I want no fuss."

Liam broke his hold and stepped back to look at her carefully. "I guess we can compromise. I'm sure we can find you something."

"And tomorrow morning, if you'll allow it, I shall have Erik escort me to visit Krayvyn from Voorstland. We can leave early and be back by nightfall."

"Erik, you say?" Liam nodded. "He's almost as good as Mikal in battle and just as loyal. I'll agree. I will give him his orders this evening."

"Thank you, Liam." Briget curtsied gracefully. "Now if you'll excuse me, I must break the news to my daughter that she will have to wear those horribly uncomfortable undergarments that accompany formal gowns." She winked, and the king laughed.

...

The smooth round wooden ball in Trevor's hand was heavier than it looked. It had taken a great deal of effort to snap off the top of Shay's bedpost. He tossed a few inches in the air and caught it again as he left her chambers. He was carrying more than that with him as he left. He had marching orders from the princess to learn what the mother and daughter team of energy workers or healers or whatever they were masquerading as were doing while in the castle. Unfortunately, her highness didn't say how he was to find out their plans. She had only, "Do this and you'll be one step closer to meeting your daughter."

The older guard was still waiting in the hallway. Trevor wondered how much, if any, of Shay's rant he had heard. The chamber doors were large and heavy, but they hadn't stopped the princess from hearing the guards earlier, and she sounded twice as loud to his ears when she berated him for his stupidity.

Erik tipped his head toward Trevor. "Ah, you survived, I see."

"Yes, sir."

"What's that in your hand?"

Trevor looked down at the wooden ball. "Part of her bed. It really was broken," he said.

Erik glanced back at the chamber doors. "With her moods, you're lucky she didn't clock you with it," he said quietly.

Trevor rubbed the top of his head. "I'm beginning to see that."

"So," Erik straightened up and his voice took on a more official tone. Where to now?"

"The workshop, I guess. I need to make a replacement."

"And how do you plan on getting there?"

The question confused Trevor. "Sir?"

"I am to stay here until her personal guard returns, so I cannot show you out as I should. So, the question is, do you know the way out?"

"I... I think so." Trevor's voice wavered as he realized the opportunity the guard had just handed him.

Erik studied the carpenter for a moment and pointed down the hall. "Take this to the end, then to the right until you come to the first stairway. Take those stairs down and make another right. Just keep walking until you smell the stables, and you'll know where you are."

"Thank you, sir."

"You're welcome. Now don't get lost."

Trevor gave a short bow and walked briskly down the hallway and to the right as he was instructed, but when he found the stairs, he paused. He listened for footfalls and watched for a sign that someone might be following him. When he was satisfied that he was truly alone, he kept going, tiptoeing past the stairs, and continuing toward the area he thought would be the kitchens. If anyone would know about the latest news or rumors, the service staff would.

...

When Serena and Mikal returned to her room, she was stunned by what she saw. Sitting atop the beautiful rug was a blue velvet and mahogany love seat flanked by two formal, high-backed velvet chairs and tall wrought iron candelabras. It was at once elegant and luxurious, befitting the castle.

The walls bore more tapestries in the same blue and gold shades, and a large mirror now stood next to the wardrobe. The room looked completely different, and it was breathtaking.

"Oh, Mikal!" Serena gasped. "It's..."

"Too much?" There was a hint of nervousness in his voice.

"No," she said and looked at him standing beside her, searching her eyes for approval. "It's amazing!"

He sighed in relief. "Your mother's room received a similar treatment, I believe."

"Oh, I do hope she loves it as much as I do." Serena rushed to the love seat to try it. The velvet was plush, and the seat was well cushioned—soft but firm enough to hold it shape. "How beautiful! I could sit here all day." She smiled at him, still standing in the doorway. "Don't just stand there. Come in! Try it."

Mikal loved the sparkle in her eyes and the childlike enthusiasm in her voice. He wanted to join her, but he hesitated. There was that feeling again and that loss of control. The thought of being close to her on that seat made him breathless. A soft voice behind him startled Mikal, and he was a man who was never caught off guard.

"That's just lovely!" Briget said from the doorway to her room across the hall. "Captain, was this your doing?"

He turned toward her and saw genuine delight on her face, which surprised him, given her apparent disdain for the royal treatment. "Yes, madam. I thought you'd appreciate a more comfortable space."

"Mother!" Serena called from her room. "Come look!"

Briget obeyed and walked in to see her daughter bouncing lightly on the loveseat. "It is quite nice, my dear," she said. "And I have another surprise for you."

"What is it?"

Briget glanced at the captain and back to her daughter. "We are to be guests of honor at a formal dinner in the Grand Hall this evening."

Serena's face paled. Mikal noticed and turned somber in response. "But," she said, "I have nothing to wear."

The captain stepped further into the room and started to say, "I'm sure we..."

Briget raised a finger to her lips, and he stopped. "The king is taking care of that. He has promised that someone will be along with the dresses for us to try on, and they will be altered in time for the banquet."

A look of relief crossed Serena's face, and Briget noted the tension leaving Mikal's. He truly cared for her daughter, and she was pleased. "Yes," Serena said, "that will be good."

"In that case," Mikal said with a quick bow, "I will take my leave now."

Serena stood, smiling. "Thank you for the tour, Captain."

"It was my pleasure, my lady."

...

Colors of sunset decorated the Grand Hall; deep violet, fiery red, and sapphire blue, with hints of gold sparkled everywhere. The finest silver the continent offered adorned the tables. Truly, Myribell had wealth, although the king rarely flaunted it. But on this night, Liam wanted to celebrate with his guests and his kingdom in all its glory. He wanted the citizens to appreciate how blessed they all were to live in a peaceful and prosperous land where no one needed to go without. Pride was not usually a sentiment he allowed himself, but on this night, he was proud of his world. For he knew soon all he held dear would be in jeopardy once again, and he hoped it wouldn't be long before he knew the names of those who threatened to end his peace.

A young woman wearing an apron with her hair pulled back entered the hall and cautiously approached the king as he oversaw the final preparations. "Sire?" she said, "Princess Shay sends word that she will be late to the dinner."

Liam greeted her with a smile tinged with bitter amusement. "Let me guess. She can't find anything to wear, despite having more gowns than all the ladies in the realm combined."

Shay's messenger shook her head. "Something like that."

Liam patted her on the shoulder. "Did she expect a response?"

"She did not say."

"Did she tell you to return after delivering this message?"

"No, Sire."

"Then," Liam nodded, "you are dismissed, and if you have something you'd rather wear to the celebration, I suggest you go change. Most of the young ladies who aren't serving tonight are already preparing themselves."

The girl smiled. "Thank you, Sire. I will." She curtsied and bounded out of the room.

"Don't you still need to get ready, Sire?" Mikal's voice asked from the servants' entrance.

"Yes, but it only takes a moment, and it takes the ladies so much longer."

Mikal crossed the hall slowly, admiring the decorations. "You've outdone yourself."

Liam smiled. "I have cause. Briget and Serena haven't been in the castle since Serena was a small child. This is a sort of welcome-home dinner."

Mikal paused to process what the king had just said. "Sire?"

Liam pursed his lips and shook his head. "I didn't think before I spoke, Captain." He tilted his head toward the main door. "Walk with me. I must go to my chambers to don the royal colors."

"Yes, Sire." Mikal obeyed.

As they walked through the hallways, Liam cleared his throat. "How do our guests like their new appointments?"

"I believe they like them very much," Mikal answered. "Serena was as close to giddy as she'd allow herself to be. Briget appeared to approve of hers as well."

"Good, good." The king nodded. "Excellent job, Captain."

"Sir, if I may ask," Mikal started, "what did you mean by welcome home? Have they lived here before?"

Liam shook his head slowly. "Not exactly, but they could have." He stopped and looked in both directions down the hallway to ensure no one was near, and then the king lowered his voice to almost a whisper. "They *could* have."

Mikal knew that only family and servants lived in the castle, and he doubted the king would ever count Briget among his servants. "What is Serena to you, if you'll pardon such a direct question?"

"The only way to get a direct answer is by asking the correct direct question," Liam replied. "I trust you understand that this is not to be repeated. All who know are sworn to secrecy."

"Yes, Sire," Mikal assured him and placed his right hand over his heart. "You have my vow."

Liam leaned closer, eyes bright and voice at a soft whisper. "Serena is my niece."

Mikal raised an eyebrow and tilted his head to one side. "What?" He finally managed to ask.

Liam nodded in assurance. "She is my niece."

"So, Briget is your sister?"

"In-law, yes," he answered quietly and looked around again. "Waylon was my older half-brother." Liam could see Mikal trying to piece everything together, so he continued. "You see, Mikal, my mother was married before she met my father. She had one son with her first husband before he passed. That son was Waylon, and he was only a year old when mother caught my father's eye. She initially rejected his advances and the whole idea of life inside the castle. Eventually, he won her over, and she became queen. I was born two years later."

"Why doesn't everyone know you have a brother?"

"Mother did not want him raised in the castle. His father's people took him in and taught him what he needed to learn. You see, from early in his childhood, they recognized his innate abilities."

"I understand," Mikal said.

"He came to visit often but was publicly treated as a family friend. Privately, he was family, and we were close. He was my best buddy and my big brother. As we grew older, he also became my top advisor. He met Briget during his studies, and she was of the same mindset that my mother was about life inside these walls."

"How so?" Mikal asked. He couldn't imagine why the castle could be so disdained.

"They thought of it as both a loss of freedom and a life of distraction from spiritual things. I must say that without their influence in my life, I might be more like my daughter than I am—selfish and petty. They kept me grounded and focused on what matters most—the good of the kingdom."

They started walking again. "So, you see," Liam finished, "Briget and Serena are very special to me. They're all I have left of my brother."

The whole idea saddened Mikal. He had heard how Waylon died protecting the king. Knowing they were brothers added a new layer of tragedy to the story. "I will protect them with my life, Sire."

"I know," Liam said. "That is why I gave you this assignment." He paused, "You should know, Captain, that if something were to happen to me, it is in my will that Serena takes my place until Eleanor is of age. My daughter does not deserve the throne. She has not proven herself a good ruler by my family's standards."

A shock ran through Mikal at the thought. "Sire, nothing will happen to you."

"I know you will not fail me, but I also know I will move on to the next world, eventually. We all do."

"Does Serena know?"

The king shook his head in the negative. "Her mother has not told her."

"But..."

"It is not our place to tell her. Briget will when the time is right."

They arrived at large mahogany doors that opened to the king's chambers. "I trust you'll not tell her. I can see you admire her and that pleases me, but you must not even hint that you know these secrets."

Mikal smiled weakly. "Of course, Sire. Thank you for your confidence."

Around the corner, hiding behind a half-closed door to an unused room, Trevor Ash smiled.

...

All who lived in the castle, on the grounds, and many of the families in town attended the ball that evening. The king of Myribell opened his hall to any citizen who enjoyed a wonderful celebration, and for all who did not dine in the Grand Hall, there would be fireworks after sunset.

With the mysterious death of the blacksmith still fresh on the minds of many, Liam took the opportunity to focus their collective energy on the positive. The kingdom had all it needed and wanted. No citizen went hungry, and anyone who wanted to work could work. There were so many reasons to be thankful that he proclaimed a day of feasting in thanksgiving to the Creator. While there was no official religion of the realm, most who lived there believed in a divine being who blessed their land with peace and prosperity.

Guests wandered into the Grand Hall, dressed in their finest clothes cut of velvet, silks, and chiffon. The women wore corsets and jewels; the men wore doublets. A celebration of this size was so rare that no one missed the opportunity when the time came.

Captain Mikal Sage knocked on the doors of the guests of honor while Erik and Tod stood nearby. All three were dressed in their full military regalia of navy and black. Pins and ribbons on the chest of their coats clued strangers into their statuses. The captain wore an eagle in flight made of gold above all his other markings, symbolizing the utmost trust of the king.

To his surprise, when Serena's door finally opened, it was her mother that greeted him. She wore an emerald green velvet gown trimmed in a gold cord with roses embroidered the full length of the fitted sleeves. The color made her tan skin glow, and a simple emerald pendant necklace added to the intensity. She was stunning and as royal as anyone who had ever slept in the palace.

"My lady?" Mikal greeted her.

"Hello, Captain."

"We are here to escort you to the celebration."

Briget nodded and stepped around him into the hallway. Serena appeared at the door, and Mikal's heart came to a full stop.

"What's wrong?" Serena asked, concerned that his face suddenly lost color. The healer in her reached for his hand and felt his heartbeat start again, faster than she had expected.

Mikal blinked twice and realized she held his hand. He smoothly turned hers over, raised it to his lips, and gently kissed it. "I'm sorry, Serena," his voice was nearly a whisper, "You are quite literally stunning."

Serena blushed slightly and thanked him. He stepped back to look at her again. Her dress was sapphire-blue velvet fitted with a corset, showing more of her chest than she would normally be comfortable with. The sleeves were a sheer material of the same color, and her flowing skirt had a hint of silver jewels sparkling near the bottom. Her hair was half up with the sides pulled back leaving little curls to frame her face. Mikal had never seen anyone so breathtaking. Even Erik and Tod wowed when she stepped into the hallway.

The five of them began walking toward the Grand Hall when Mikal paused. "Wait," he said, "I nearly forgot. Serena, I have something for you." They all stopped to watch him pull a small box out of his coat pocket. He opened it, and Serena gave a slight gasp.

Briget peered over her daughter's shoulder to see a dainty chain running through a familiar pendant shaped like a silver key, the head of which was a round, brilliant blue sapphire surrounded by tiny diamonds. Two coin-sized silver disks stamped with the inscriptions *Strength* and *Trust* nestled in the box on either side of the necklace.

"I couldn't!" Serena told him.

Mikal shook his head. "This is from the king himself, chosen especially for you tonight. He asked me to present it on his behalf and said that it had a special meaning to your father and that your mother would understand."

Serena turned her head to see a smile on Briget's face and tears in her eyes. Speechless at the sight of the necklace, all Briget could do was nod.

"Please," Mikal said, "Wear it tonight for him."

Serena thought for a moment and then nodded reluctantly. "Alright, for him." In her mind, *him* meant her father; although, she guess Mikal was referring to King Liam. She turned her back to Mikal and lifted her hair off her neck so he could carefully place the necklace on her. The weight of it surprised her, and she guessed stones were heavier than they looked.

Briget wiped her eyes as she watched. She recognized the necklace as being Waylon's mother's, and she understood why the king had sent it. Her husband would have been so proud at that very moment.

"Now," Mikal's voice shook Briget from her thoughts, "shall we?" He held his elbow out for Serena to weave her arm through. Erik did the same for Briget, and Tod led the way to the celebration.

...

The Grand Hall was full of dinner guests. Serena guessed there must have been at least 300 attendees, all well dressed and enjoying the formal sit-down meal. Knowing Briget would not want a spot at his table, Liam had one set for the guests of honor just in front of him at the far end of the hall. He sat with a few advisors on each side and an empty chair directly to his left. His daughter, who should have occupied it, had still not arrived. Liam did not look concerned by her absence and seemed to be enjoying a lively conversation.

Briget, Erik, Mikal, Serena, Tod, and his brother Tom ate their fill and enjoyed the country's finest wine. Serena and Briget kept theirs to just one glass so they could keep their wits about them. Serena had learned early in life always to keep her psychic guard up in large gatherings. More than one drink would make it difficult.

The servers were clearing the tables when the musicians started playing. Tom and Tod excused themselves and walked to the center of the room, faced each other, and bowed. Then each twin pulled a kerchief from inside his doublet and tied it over his own eyes.

Serena looked at Briget for guidance, and Briget returned her puzzled expression. Mikal noticed the exchange and whispered, "You'll enjoy this."

Now fully blindfolded, Tom and Tod drew their swords and bowed toward each other again. Someone in the room gasped as their blades clanged, arced, and clashed again in smooth movements. The two circled as if dancing, striking and blocking in incredible anticipation of each other's movements. Their audience held rapt as they sparred.

Serena had heard that twins held a special bond and could read each other's minds. She wondered if this show was evidence of a soul connection or just a well-rehearsed exhibition.

When Tom and Tod were finished, they removed their blindfolds and bowed to the king. The room erupted in cheers and applause.

King Liam stood and raised his hands above his head, and the guests hushed quickly. "My friends," he said in a voice that echoed through the Grand Hall, "I am so happy you could join us in this celebration of thanksgiving. Our kingdom wants for nothing. Our tables have plenty. Our people have shelter, clothing, and more—prosperity!" The room erupted in applause. "We've gone too long without a celebration such as this, but I assure you all that daily, I say a quiet prayer of gratitude for all our blessings." Another round of applause filled the room. "And now, we dance!" The musicians played louder, and the people moved toward the space at the end of the hall that was reserved for dancing.

Mikal stood and asked Serena if she would favor him with a dance. She looked to Briget, unsure of herself, and Briget nodded. "Let him lead, Daughter, and you'll do well."

Serena took his hand and followed him across the length of the hall, past the empty tables, and finally to the dance floor. She was lost in the moment, enjoying the warmth of her hand in his, excited and nervous all at once when Princess Shay was suddenly in front of them. Mikal, Serena, and it seemed everyone in the hall stopped, frozen.

Shay's eyes flashed with anger and feigned pain. She definitely found something to wear. It was an ice-blue gown trimmed in white lace and embroidery. Her hair fell in blond ringlets down her bare shoulders, and her cheeks flushed with rage.

Serena sensed the rage was insincere, a ruse to scare everyone into silence so that she could have the attention she deserved. However fake her anger may have been, it was squarely and uncomfortably directed at Serena.

Mikal gave her hand a squeeze to reassure her he was there. To his surprise, she gave a quick squeeze back, then let go. He watched for the telltale sign Serena was about to use her ball-of-light defense, but she lowered her hands to her sides, relaxed. He saw her shoulders rise and fall as she took a deep breath and waited.

Shay's bright red lips finally formed words. "What is this peasant doing in my gown?" Her eyes bore into Serena, but she spoke as if talking to someone, anyone else. No one answered, but she didn't pause long enough to notice. "Who told you that you could wear my clothes, thief?" Serena said nothing and only stared back at her.

From halfway across the hall behind Serena, Liam's voice echoed. "I did."

Shay's eyes never lifted from Serena, but she spoke to her father. "You would sully my favorite ball gown by allowing a farm maid to wear it?"

"Enough!" he bellowed. "You will show some respect for our honored guest. You should be honored that she would wear your castoffs."

"Honored," she paused, and her eyes narrowed, "that a common witch would wear my clothes?" There were a few gasps from the still unmoving crowd on the dance floor. "And her mother," Shay continued, "did she also steal my mother's clothes too, or has she wiled her way into more than just an old dress?"

Serena glanced at her mother briefly. Briget only blinked. Words would never shake her, especially the words of a ranting brat. Serena finally spoke loud and clear, matching Shay's volume but keeping her tone cool. "Would you really like the dress back? It had to be fitted to my waistline, but I'm sure they'll let it back out again." Shay only glared at her. "Perhaps," Serena continued, "I should take it off right now. I'm sure at least one chivalrous man in the room would lend me his long coat so that I could escape the scene somewhat modestly. If it will please Your Highness to see me strip of your gown here for all to see, for everyone to witness that you, who have more dresses than all the ladies of the kingdom combined, could not bear to see just one discarded gown worn by a humble servant to the king. Well, if that would please the princess, I shall take it off immediately."

The entire room was silent. Mikal was stunned at Serena's bold choice of words. Briget saw the wisdom in her daughter's challenge. Shay proved herself petty and selfish, and Serena pointed it out without calling names or lowering herself to answer being called a witch. Mikal removed his coat in case Shay might call Serena's bluff, and he worried she was not bluffing at all. Serena saw the motion from the corner of her eye and nodded in his direction. "Chivalry is not dead. Thank you, Captain." Then she looked at Shay. "Princess, it's your call."

Shay's face was turning a shade of crimson, and everyone around her stepped back reflexively, except the captain. He took a step closer to Serena and wondered how long the king would let the showdown last.

"You would like that, wouldn't you?" Shay finally answered, "but I'm sure you don't need to coat to hide behind what you have. When you have magic like the kind you used to sneak into the blacksmith's home in the dead of night and choke the life from him without ever being seen." Some bystanders gasped. Serena cocked her head to one side and closed her eyes.

Shay continued. "That's right. Don't be fooled by this humble servant act. She and her mother practice magic in their home. They have the ability to do great harm, and now they've tricked their way into the castle and charmed our king into opening his home to these vipers."

The sapphire stone on Serena's necklace began to glow from within. She felt the weight of it change, and a warmth radiated into her chest. That sensation was peaceful and calming, even while Shay made her outrageous accusations in front of everyone who mattered. She put her hand on the stone and took a deep breath. The warmth filtered through her, and she opened her eyes to see its brilliant color clearly. It reminded her of the sky at nightfall with stars twinkling inside it. Shay pointed at the glowing key-shaped pendant.

"I bet that's mine, too, stolen from the family vault."

Serena shook her head calmly. "It is not yours. It was my grandmother's."

"You lie!" the spoiled princess yelled.

"I have no reason to lie," Serena said calmly, her voice nearly a whisper. "You however, have reason, although unknown fully to me, to arrive at a celebration and cause a scene, accuse my mother and I of foul deeds and hope someone will believe you." Her voice remained calm, but its tone brightened a bit. "Look around you,

Princess. These people know me for who I am." She pointed to a young lady on her left clinging to her husband's arm. "Maria came to me with a broken ankle three weeks ago, and she is here, ready to dance tonight." She motioned to an older gentleman behind the princess. "Joseph nearly died from a fever last year, and mother and I brought him back from the brink." Shay did not turn her head to see Joseph nodding adamantly, his gray curls bouncing around his temples. "We are energy workers, Your Highness. We use our gifts to help people, not to harm them. We are here at the gracious invitation of King Liam, who offered us shelter after a storm badly damaged our home."

The anger remained in Shay's eyes, but her rant was over. King Liam appeared between Serena and Briget. Mikal was still close on her other side. The king finally spoke. "Captain, you may put your coat back on. Our dear Serena won't be needing it." Mikal obeyed, and Liam continued, "Daughter, I have failed you as a father. When you were born, I wanted to teach you what it takes to rule our kingdom—love, patience, compassion, and strength of character. Instead, you have somehow come to embody everything that it takes to ruin a kingdom. Tonight, your little tantrum here has proven that you do not have what is required to rule."

Shay looked like she had been punched in the gut. "But, Father," she started.

Liam raised his hand to silence her, "You were born into our royal family, but the throne of Myribell is not a birthright, even to the child of the king. The throne must be earned by proving yourself time and again. Every chance you've ever had, you have proven yourself utterly unworthy of ascension." He let his words sink in. "You are not the heir to the throne. You are merely my daughter. Because I love you, you may live in this castle, but because I love these people," he gestured to everyone around them, "you will never be queen."

Shay glanced at the guests around her and tears filled her eyes. They would never fear her or bow to her again. They had no reason to respect her, and she had nothing left to lord over them to get her way. In just a few sentences, the king had stripped her bare of everything. She turned away from him and marched out the door without saying a word.

All stood in awkward silence until Serena whispered to Liam, "I am sorry, Sire."

He turned to her and gently grasped her shoulders. "No, my dear, I'm sorry to put you through that, but it had to be done. You will never be disrespected in my castle again. You and your mother may call this home for as long as you live, if you like." He looked down at the necklace, which was dimming. "You were right about that," he said. "It was your grandmother's, and she would be overjoyed at the young woman you've become." He turned to the guests, still gathered around them. "Now, please, get on with the celebration. Musicians, play. Play!"

The music began on cue, and couple by couple, the crowd danced again. The king guided Briget, Serena, and his trusted guards away from the guests so they could huddle up and get their orders. "Tod and Tom, please go see where my daughter ran off to. My guess would be that she retreated to her chambers to sulk, or she's off to the stables for a midnight ride."

Tod asked, "Where does she go on her rides, Sire?"

"She meets with our enemies to tell them what a horrible father I am."

Shocked, Tod asked, "How do you know this?"

"Your brother has followed her."

Tom nodded. "And this time, do we follow or engage her?"

"Just find out where she went in the castle and report back," the king said, and the brothers departed immediately.

"My orders, Sire?" Erik asked.

"Rest well. You will escort Briget on an errand outside the walls tomorrow. I'll give you further instructions at daybreak."

"Yes, Sire."

Briget smiled, "And I will rest well, also. I've had enough excitement for one night. I'd like to retire now."

Liam kissed the back of her hand. "Please, sleep well, my dear. I'll see you off in the morning." Then he faced Serena, who stood eagerly awaiting her orders from the king. "Serena and Mikal, you go enjoy yourselves."

"That's it?" Serena asked, sounding disappointed.

"Isn't that enough? At least one of my honored guests needs to stay and enjoy her party."

Mikal laughed, "Sire, I expected a bit more of a challenge, but I'll be happy to make sure she does her share." He winked at Serena.

"Please, Daughter, this celebration is for us. Dance, enjoy the fireworks, and appreciate how lucky we are to be friends of our king." Briget kissed Serena's forehead. To Mikal she said, "I recommend you do the same."

He nodded to her. "I will do my best, my lady."

Mikal led Serena back to the dance floor, and they joined the others in a formal waltz. Joseph and his wife appeared beside them, and he said to Serena, "You were right, young lady, we know you. The kingdom knows you and your mother. We could never believe such lies."

"Thank you, Joseph." She smiled at his kind words, and the older couple waltzed away.

"I told you," Mikal whispered, "the truth has a way of getting out."

Serena remembered his words and grinned. "So it does."

Tom was the first of the brothers to return to the king's side in the Grand Hall.

"The Princess is not in her chambers, Sire. Tod is checking the stables."

Liam nodded, "As I suspected." He watched his guests dancing for a moment as if lost in the music.

Tom asked, "Sire, what is next for me?"

The king looked at him for a moment. "Do you not have a lady to dance with?"

"Not here, Sire."

"Then I suggest you go find one." Liam paused thoughtfully, then added, "But first, please tell the fire masters that their orders are to begin at sunset."

"Yes, Sire." Tom bowed and hurried away.

...

Down in the stables, Tod crouched behind bales of hay and watched the princess bark orders to the poor, scrawny stable boy that she had forced into working during the party. The teenager struggled to get her saddle over her stallion but eventually managed to complete the task and step out of the way without being trampled as a princess mounted and rode like the devil toward the castle's side gate.

"The king was right," Tod thought, "she rides out to tell our enemies of his actions."

...

At eight o'clock, the dinner guests spilled out onto the balcony of the Grand Hall, which overlooked the town on the south side of the castle. More citizens gathered on the streets below and looked to the sky, waiting for the fireworks to begin. Still others crowded at windows. All were abuzz with the tale of the princess's downfall, and no one seemed upset by the news. Most thought the celebration was that much more fitting for the day.

The king guided Serena through the crowd to the balcony's edge, with Mikal and Tod following closely behind them. "The benefit of being king," Liam said to her, "is that we always have the best view."

"I see." She marveled at how lovely Myribell looked in the twilight.

He pointed to the center of town, and the crowd gradually quieted after seeing the motion. "Watch there for the display," he told her. Then, he raised both hands above his head as if calling forth some great power. Trumpeters blew the celebration call, and at the sound, the fire masters on the village green lit the first rockets. The display was truly spectacular. The king stood with his arm around Serena for the first few minutes while she watched the explosions of colorful sparks. She barely noticed when he left her, but a few minutes later, a touch on her shoulder got her attention. The king was gone and the new arm around her was a warm, almost hot, familiar touch. She turned her head to see Mikal beside her, smiling as he watched the show, and she let herself relax into his hold.

When the last spark faded, the crowd dispersed, but the two of them stayed on the balcony, enjoying the mild night, the slight breeze, and each other's company. Serena stared at the town below her and considered just how quickly her life had changed. Until a few days before, her world comprised her mother, their little farm, occasional trips into town, and using her abilities to heal anyone who came to them in need. It was a small, sheltered world, and she had been quite content.

For better or worse, now she found herself in a much larger world, and she felt like she could have belonged in it all along. It included more people than she could count. Of all of them, only one had really changed her perspective, and he was the handsome, trusted captain beside her. She tilted her head to look at him, and he saw the slight smile cross her face.

"What?" he asked.

"I admire your..." she trailed off as her nerves got in the way.

"My what?"

"Your honor, loyalty, integrity, and... well... just everything."

"I am humbled by your admiration," he said.

"Oh, yes, and your humility. I mean, truly, I've never met anyone like you before. You amaze me."

"The feeling is mutual."

"It is?" asked Serena.

"Of course. You are such a wonderful, selfless person— strong, wise, bold, and yet somehow still quite innocent." He paused for a moment and searched her brown eyes. "My only concern is how I feel so off balance when you're standing close to me."

"You do?"

"Yes, and yet, I always want you close to me," and then he kissed her. It was a quick, gentle kiss with just enough pressure to show he meant it, but he didn't linger in it. He smelled of the outdoors—clear night air and cedar.

"Off balance? That doesn't sound good for a captain of the guard," Serena teased. Her face was warm, and she wondered if she was blushing.

"I'll make it work. You are my charge and my priority. I am the luckiest man alive."

"How so?" she asked.

"To be ordered to spend my time with you," and he kissed her again.

Chapter 5

Day 4

THE SUN WAS SHINING, and the songbirds were in full chorus at the king's stables the next morning. Horses whinnied from their stalls in greeting to Briget. When she arrived, Erik had already had their horses prepared. And the king was instructing him where to go while wiping down his mount after an early morning ride. They ended their conversation and said a merry "Good morning" to Briget, but she could tell from their eyes that both were in serious moods. Erik had wanted to bring Krayvyn to the castle for questioning, thinking that he would keep Briget safer, but the king did not want to upset the strange sorcerer unnecessarily. He insisted it would be a quick visit, and Erik could easily handle the errand.

Liam did not believe Krayvyn posed a threat. He only wanted to allow Briget the opportunity to ease her mind. On the other hand, Erik had a knot in his stomach that he hadn't felt in years. "Good thing," the king had told him, "It will keep you on your toes."

They mounted their horses, said goodbye to Liam, and left the safety of Myribell behind them in the early morning light. The journey was no longer than three hours by horse and they made light conversation along the way. Erik remained on edge even the whole way, and Briget was well aware of his nerves. She had not mentioned it to him, though, because she felt a similar sense of dread.

They arrived at the cabin on the edge of the forest that marked the kingdom's border. Erik looked around carefully from atop his horse. The cabin looked just big enough for one person to sleep in and still had room for a sink and a privy. The garden behind it was about twice the size of the home, and there was a small gray mare tied to a tree beside the structure. A voice from inside called out. "Welcome, Briget of the Order of the Mystic Moon!"

Erik immediately placed his hand on his sword's hilt. Briget saw the motion and raised her hand toward him in a sign that meant "wait." He let himself appear to relax, although he was ready to spring into action.

Briget answered, "Good morning, sir. We've not had the pleasure of meeting, so forgive me if I'm not as familiar with you."

A tall, slender man with light blond hair appeared in the doorway. He wore brown pants and a black tunic. His long hair pulled loosely back, exposing high cheekbones and icy blue eyes. "No forgiveness is necessary," he told her. "I am a stranger in your realm, and I would not expect you to know me." He stepped forward toward them and bowed fully. "I am Krayvyn of Voorstland."

Briget dismounted, removed her riding glove, and offered her bare right hand. Krayvyn shook it gently. "You know who I am," she said, "but I should introduce my security detail. This is Erik." He promptly dismounted. "Erik is a member of the king's guard, here only to guide me safely on my journey to meet you."

Krayvyn held out his hand to Erik. Briget nodded approval, and Erik shook it, not warmly. "To what do I owe the pleasure of your visit, my lady?" Krayvyn asked.

Briget answered, "I recently learned that the realm had a visitor who is an exiled wizard. I must say, my curiosity got the best of me."

"Ah," Krayvyn smiled slightly. "Curiosity does that." He paused for a minute and added, "Where are my manners? Please, would you like to come in for a warm drink or some fresh fruit from my garden?"

Erik looked to Briget for any sign of hesitation, but there was none. "Yes, sir, I believe we would enjoy that," she answered. They followed him inside and were surprised by how much larger the cabin looked from within. Krayvyn put a pot of water on the top of a wood stove, and they seated themselves around a circular table with three chairs.

The deceptive feel of the house and the perfect number of chairs had Erik's nerves on edge. As much as he tried to follow Briget's lead and act casually, he was stiff and anxious, as if he were preparing for battle. Briget, on the other hand, relaxed in the wooden chair and glanced around the cabin. "Was this already here? Did you build it?" she asked.

Krayvyn smiled proudly. "It was here and in poor shape, long ago abandoned. I enjoyed fixing it up."

"You did a fine job," Briget complimented.

"It didn't take long. Well, not very long because I had little else to spend my time on, so I put all my energy into making my new home livable."

Briget nodded, "And I can tell you have a lot of good energy."

Erik caught the double meaning. Briget was telling him she felt safe there. Yet, he still could not shake the feeling that danger was close. As a seasoned soldier, he knew better than to fight it. She was too important for him to let his guard down.

"Did you expect the worst?" Krayvyn asked her.

"I wasn't sure what to expect," she replied. "My home was attacked supernaturally two days ago, and I wanted to be sure of who might have been responsible."

Her honesty did not surprise the blond wizard. Her order was known for honesty, integrity, and great power. She was grayer than he had pictured her, but as lovely as he had been told. He could tell she was keeping as much of her energy in check as possible so as not to attract unwanted attention. For several years, he had been doing the same. "I assure you, madam, that is not how I use my energy."

She nodded. "I can tell. I feared the worst when I learned you were here in exile, and I don't know what might have caused that fate for you. Still, I can tell you would never intentionally harm anyone who did not give reason."

"You are correct," he confirmed. "My pledge is to only use my talents to help those who cannot help themselves."

"That is a very honorable pledge, sir," Erik said.

"It is said," Briget explained, "that with great talent or power comes great responsibility. A wizard must make a pledge regarding his purpose for the use of his power, and then he must live by all the days of his life."

"And if he doesn't?" Erik asked skeptically.

"He will die by it in a karmically acceptable way," Krayvyn answered Erik's next question before he could ask it. "In my case, for example, that might mean being rendered completely defenseless, and then slowly torn to pieces or burned to ash."

"Harsh," Erik whispered.

"Fitting," Krayvyn corrected. "I am sworn to only use my power for one purpose, and if I abuse it, I will be severely abused for it."

Briget asked, "Do you mind telling us what brought you to our kingdom?"

"A much nicer climate and a chance to live peacefully." Krayvyn avoided her true meaning.

"I see." She accepted his evasion. After all, if he didn't tell the king himself, why should she expect anything else?

...

"The carpenter says he has not seen your daughter, Sire." The bearded guardsman told the king as he led Trevor into the throne room. "He says she's not visited since last night."

Trevor interjected, "She's not visited ever, Sire. I assure you she doesn't even know which room is mine."

The king nodded patiently. "I am not surprised." He looked at his guard and pointed to the door. "You may leave. Thank you."

"Yes, sir," the guard said and left quickly.

Trevor bowed. "Forgive me, King, but why did he bring me here if he was going to tell you my answers, which you seem to have expected?"

Liam moved closer to Trevor so Trevor could hear him whisper. "Your answers were only half the reason I sent him for you."

Trevor blinked blankly. "You have a job for me?"

"You could say that," the king answered. "The princess left last night, angry and likely not in her right mind. I'm sure you've heard by now of our interaction last night."

"Whispers, Sire."

"She will not be my successor. Her behavior is undeserving of the throne, and last night she forced my hand. I publicly denounced her for the way she treated our guests." Liam paused and studied Trevor's face. "So, do you realize what this means?"

"That I don't have to fix her bedpost?" Trevor asked innocently.

"Well, there's that. More importantly, it means that your daughter is next in line, assuming my family remains in power until she is of age." Liam continued to watch Trevor's face for traces of understanding and recognition. He expected to see a moment of epiphany, but the carpenter never showed it. "You realize Trevor Ash, that makes you the biological father of the heir to the throne of Myribell, right?"

Trevor averted his eyes and glanced around the throne room. Then he finally spoke. "I guess I should be happy for this child I've never met."

"Your child," Liam stressed.

"I'm sorry, sir. Until I meet her and look upon her with my own eyes, she is not real to me."

"In that case, I shall arrange it. Return here midafternoon, clean and smiling." Liam's tone was stern, but there was a hint of happiness in it.

"Yes, sir," Trevor bowed and exited.

Tod stepped out of the shadows on the far side of the room after Trevor left. "Are you sure this is a good idea, Sire? If he's plotting with the princess, won't Eleanor be in danger?"

Liam sighed. "She'll be in danger anyway. Enough people here know who she is. While I don't think they'd intentionally throw that sweet child to the wolves, it would only take a slip up to reveal to the wrong people. At least, if he meets her in my presence, I can watch his eyes for his intentions."

"That is true," Tod conceded.

"I would like for Serena to meet Eleanor as well, at the same time. She can help me read Master Ash."

"Shall I fetch her, Sire?"

A soft voice from the doorway asked, "Can I be of service?"

Startled, the men looked up to see Serena and Mikal at the entrance to the throne room. He was in uniform, and she wore riding pants and a cotton tunic. Her hair was haphazardly pulled back with a piece of cloth. She was the grounded, earthy girl they all knew, very different from the glamorous lady of the night before. Yet, she still somehow looked radiant. Liam was surprised to see the pendant necklace still on her neck.

Tod chuckled. "My lady, thank you for saving me the trouble."

Serena gave a slight curtsy. "I came to thank the king for a lovely evening last night."

"You are most welcome, my dear. Did you talk with your mother before she left this morning?"

Serena shook her head and blushed slightly. "I'm embarrassed to admit that I slept rather late this morning."

"Nonsense," Liam said, "you may rest in this castle. There's no need to be embarrassed."

Captain Mikal stiffened. "Of course, Sire, if she can't rest well here, I don't know where else she could." He looked at her, and she was still blushing. "Not every lady has an armed guard making sure she sleeps undisturbed."

"Good job, Captain," Tod smiled, but his grin faded after a sharp look from Mikal.

"It was not me. I was off duty and slept well enough in my own quarters," Mikal assured them.

"Of course," Tod said. "I meant nothing by that."

"Of course," Liam interrupted, "Serena, I had hoped your mother would have spoken with you, but there will be time for that when she returns this afternoon." He pointed to the necklace peeking out from the V-shaped neckline of her tunic. "I see you're still wearing the necklace."

She touched it reflexively. "Yes, sir," she paused. "I didn't sleep in it, though."

Liam told her, "You could sleep in if you wanted to."

"But I'd be afraid to break it."

Liam shook his head. "You wouldn't. As long as you wear it, I believe it is unbreakable." Mikal popped one eyebrow at that statement, and Liam continued. "How did you know it was your grandmother's?"

"The energy felt very similar to my father's, but more maternal and protective," she answered. She wanted to tell them how it felt when she was facing down Shay, but she was not sure how.

"I swear it glowed last night when the princess was—" Mikal paused, trying to find the right non-accusing words to describe the king's daughter, but Liam saved him the trouble.

"Was being a royal brat." Liam finished and shook his head. "Technically, you don't have to call her the princess anymore," he said. "Soon you may call her the enemy."

"I am sorry, Sire," Serena put her hand on his shoulder. "I truly am."

"Me, too," he told her and patted the sweet hand as she imparted some healing energy. "She made her choice long ago, and you were merely the innocent catalyst. Indeed. I am beginning to think she wanted it to happen that way," he gently lifted her hand and held it with both of his, "because you were exactly where you needed to be when we all needed you to be there."

Serena wasn't sure how to take that, so she only nodded in response, and then she remembered the Tod had been told to take her to the king. "Sire, did you need me for something?"

"Oh, yes," he nodded. "I would like for you to meet my granddaughter this afternoon."

Serena glanced around. "Your granddaughter?" she repeated.

"Yes, her name is Eleanor, and she's a very bright, lovely child. Very unlike her mother."

"It shall be an honor to meet her."

Mikal spoke up, "Sire, Serena has asked me to escort her to the cottage to gather a few things she feels her mother and she will need. I wanted to check with you first."

"That explains the riding clothes," Liam observed. "Can you be back here in this room by midafternoon?"

"Yes, of course," Serena assured.

"Then I have no objection. You are in very capable hands." He nodded at Mikal.

"Thank you, Sire," she said.

...

The visit with Krayvyn had gone well, Briget thought. He was definitely not the wizard behind the cyclone, but that knowledge was not as soothing as it could have been. Instead, it further opened the possibility that Kent was somehow behind it, which meant he was no longer bound and once again a great danger.

She looked at Erik beside her, still on edge as he had been all morning. Had he sensed the same growing danger she was considering? The horses' ears twitched, and she felt hers tense underneath her. Erik's gelding stopped suddenly, and he instinctively drew his sword. They paused for a moment to listen but heard nothing.

Briget clicked her tongue on the roof of her mouth, and her mount took a step forward but stopped again. She was reaching over to touch the horse's head when the noise started. It sounded as if all the surrounding trees groaned in unison. Then, with a loud chorus of creaks, they all began to sway violently as if the earth was quaking underneath them. The horses whinnied in fear, and Briget's reared, but she held tight and did not fall. "Steady, Gabrielle," she said as calmly as she could. Erik's horse couldn't decide which way to run as he held the reins tight to keep control.

Then, one by one, the trees closest to the road fell, creating a tight circle, trapping in the travelers. The branch of one knocked Erik off his horse as it fell, and he struck the ground with a thud that was barely audible over the crashing wood.

Briget could see him on the ground and worried the horses might trample him. She grabbed his reins as they flopped around the panicked animal and yelled "freeze!" The horse literally froze in place. Her own horse stilled quickly, but only at the tone of her voice and not the command. The trees were silent now, caging them in tightly, and there was nowhere to run. She slid off Gabrielle and rushed to examine Erik. He was breathing but unconscious and bleeding. The branch that knocked him to the ground now trapped him there. She looked around for something to leverage the weight and noticed her horse was sniffing the air. Then she smelled it too. Dark Magic.

...

"Yuck!" Serena disapproved of the scene inside the cottage. At first, she thought it was the way they had left it in their rush to the security of the castle, but upon closer inspection, she realized it was worse. Much worse. She gasped loudly.

"What is it?" Mikal asked, peeking around her from the doorway.

She stepped further into the house. "Someone's been in here."

He looked at the corner where they had piled the broken items, and there was nothing but a scattered mess. "Vandals," he guessed.

Serena walked into her mother's room and returned quickly, "Ransacked," she said as she rushed into her own room. The items they had packed neatly into trunks to take with them were thrown across the beds on the floor of each room. "Who would do..." She couldn't finish her thought.

"Who would want to?" Mikal thought out loud. He watched Serena's face flush with anger. "Do you have any idea?"

She shook her head and went back into Briget's room. He followed since she seemed to be on a mission this time and watched her start sifting through the scattered items from the trunk. "No, no, no," she repeated.

"What?" Mikal asked. "What are you looking for?"

"The book," she whispered loudly, as if afraid someone else might hear her secret. "The whole reason we came."

"What?" Mikal asked and started searching with her.

"Not just any book. I think it was my father's. I saw it in my dream last night, and I thought for sure Mother would have packed it."

Mikal hesitated. "Do you know for sure it exists? I mean, have you only seen it in a dream?"

"No," she said, "I mean yes. Yes, it exists. The dream reminded me. It was like a flashback or a memory of when I was small."

"Alright, what did the book look like?"

"Old, dusty with a dark purple almost black leather cover. Inside, I saw a page that had the same design as this necklace." She pointed to the one around her neck, but the words weren't the same. She knelt on the floor, piling items haphazardly as she sifted through them. "I know it's important. I have to find it."

"If it is that important, maybe it's what they were after," Mikal suggested.

The idea knocked the wind out of Serena, and she slumped over on her knees, defeated. "No, it can't be gone."

Mikal knelt beside her. He felt her anguish and took a deep breath. "You're right; let's keep looking," he encouraged. From his vantage point on the floor, he could see a shape beneath the bed. "Wait a minute," he reached under and pulled out a small leather-bound book. "What is this?"

For a moment, Serena's eyes brightened, but soon she realized it was not her father's book. "It's not the one—too small, too brown." She took it from his hand and looked at it carefully anyway. "I've never seen this one," she finally said as she untied the leather closure and opened it.

On the first page was a very intricate drawing of a crescent moon hanging over the castle of Myribell. Mikal watched over her shoulder as she turned the page, and the next one was a similar drawing but with a different castle and a half-moon. On the third page, yet another castle with a full moon. "What is this?" she whispered.

"A sketchbook, maybe?" Mikal suggested.

The fourth page held the answer and begged more questions. "The Ledger of the Order of the Mystic Moon," was all it said in fancy script.

...

The sharp smell of smoke and sulfur permeated the air around Briget, but she didn't panic. He would enjoy that too much. Instead, she quickly placed light energy around Erik and hoped his injuries weren't life threatening already. A small frog jumped onto the stack of downed trees in front of her and seemed to be questioning what had just happened. She only shook her head and tried not to think about the odor burning her nostrils.

A voice from behind her, deep and raspy, announced his presence. "My dear Briget, what an awful spot you're in."

She turned slowly and continued to focus light energy toward Erik. His protection was all that mattered at the moment. "Good afternoon, Kent. You know I've been in worse."

"Yes, but never as alone as you are now."

She forced a smile and confidently answered, "I am never alone."

The scarred wizard did not look around. He understood her meaning to be symbolic of her trust in the Order. "Trust me; you are." He raised his left hand and five cloaked and hooded men on horseback appeared behind him. "As you can see, I am not."

"What do you intend to do with us?"

"Not him. Just you," Kent said sharply. "I need him to let your king know he failed in protecting his best asset. I mean, assuming he ever regains consciousness. That looks like a rather nasty cut on his head." He sneered.

Briget moved toward Erik. If she could touch him, she could heal him. Kent was acutely aware of that fact, but would he let her? She took a step toward Erik.

"Don't even," he hissed.

Knowing that Kent meant for Erik to survive gave her another option. She glanced behind her to see if the small frog was still on the tree trunk. He was, and he was seeing everything. Briget faked a sneeze in the frog's direction and hid the words "caught you" in it. The frog immediately turned to black wood, inanimate and blending into the bark of the tree. Then she turned back to Kent and said sarcastically, "Aren't you going to bless me?"

He scoffed. "Hardly." Then he looked at the man to his left. "Bring her."

...

"We should return soon," Mikal told Serena as she flipped the pages of the ledger one by one. Her eyes were seeing, but her mind was not quite comprehending the names and dates on the pages. "Serena," he struggled to get her attention with a smooth voice, so he tapped her lightly on the shoulder.

"What?" she asked him almost inaudibly. Her eyes were glassy with tears.

"We need to leave soon."

"Oh." She closed the book and clutched it close to her chest.

"We can bring it with us. Maybe your mother can answer your questions, or the king." Mikal didn't know what secrets the ledger held, but he guessed they were shocking to the sweet young lady in front of him. He stood and held his hand out to help her up. "What else here should we take with us?"

She shook her head. "I don't know. The book from my dream isn't here." She looked around the room slowly. In the quiet, she heard her mother's voice in her head saying, "Bring the bag." Serena didn't think twice as she grabbed a small leather pouch from beside her mother's bed and moved into the kitchen to pull a handful of herbal medicines off a little shelf.

"What is that?" Mikal asked.

"A healer's kit." Serena held it out for him to take from her.

His face showed surprise, but he took it. "The king has a doctor in the castle."

Serena cut him off. "Not the same." She took a cloth sack of clothes that had escaped the destruction from her bedroom and her favorite shawl. "Alright, let's go," she said with a sudden sense of urgency. "We wouldn't want to keep the king waiting."

...

Erik lay bleeding and barely breathing below the cage of downed trees. Krayvyn approached slowly, carefully looking for signs of a trap. He had watched the men leave with the king's sorceress from afar, but he could not hear what was said. The pale wizard was concerned that the guard who was left for dead had already passed to the other side. He scampered over the fallen trees with the agility of a squirrel and was relieved to find the man had a pulse. He twittered like a bird, and his mare trotted down the path toward him.

Now that he was sure Erik was still alive, he looked more closely at the two trapped horses. One of them seemed to have been turned into a statue. The other seemed unusually calm for the situation. He could only guess that someone had used magic to keep the first horse still, and he was sure he couldn't undo the spell. So, he examined the second horse for injuries and found none.

With the extra horse trapped in the magical cage, he had transportation to bring Erik to safety. The trick would be moving the large guy from under a fallen tree onto the horse. He knew the guard was truly defenseless, and so he used the most guarded and trusted skill set he had. Within a few moments. A battered, slightly ashen soldier was lying across Gabrielle and on the path back to the safety of Myribell, with Krayvyn silently leading the way.

...

Mikal and Serena rode in silence back to the castle. He could tell her mind was focused on that ledger, and he wondered if she realized that her family tree was far more complicated than she had ever imagined. The fear of her asking him about it kept him from initiating a conversation. He decided to consider the silence a blessing and focus only on her safety, which brought questions back to his mind. Who ransacked the cottage, and what were they expecting to find? Did they find it? Was it the book from her dream or the ledger in her saddlebag, or just more mundane items like money and jewelry?

...

The smell of dark magic continued to burn Briget's nose. She listened as she rode on the back of one of Kent's henchman's horses. She tried to keep as much space between her and the cloaked man in front of her as possible without falling off the animal. His energy was sickening, and she could only imagine the kind of abuse he had suffered at some point in his life that would lead him to a life of following the orders of a dark wizard. A youth filled with love and laughter would never lead to an adulthood of greed and destruction. That is, unless the child was born with evil in his heart. *People don't change easily, for better or worse,* she thought.

On the trail ahead, she could hear songbirds in the trees, but they silenced as the group approached. A shadow cast them in darkness as if the midday sun did not exist, and she fought hard to keep her own light dimmed. The only way to win against Kent was to learn exactly who he was conspiring with. What greater demon had he pledged what was left of himself in order to loosen her binding spell? There was a shadow of doubt in her mind that maybe the magic he seemed to exhibit was not his own. He was not fully free of the binding, or he would have simply destroyed her upon sight.

No, he was taking her because he needed her alive for now. Her death would leave the binding permanent. Only alive could he try to force her to undo what she and Waylon had done.

Briget saw a break in the trees ahead of them and knew they were nearing the far boundaries of Liam's kingdom. Although they were a bright blur beyond the meadow, she recognized the towering cliffs of the White Mountains. She closed her eyes and projected a sigh as far as she could, and hoped a kindred soul would receive it.

...

Jeryl and Eleanor sat at the meeting table in the throne room, studying a map of the kingdom. The child was quickly picking up place names and historical facts about her homeland. "What is this called?" Eleanor asked, pointing to a jagged line on the northwest edge of the map.

Jeryl answered, "That is also a boundary line. It is jagged because it borders a mountain range."

Eleanor studied the line for a moment and pointed to a spot on it. "A friend is there."

"No," Jeryl corrected the child gently, "We know of no one who lives there. It is a no man's land."

"But that's because she's a woman," the girl insisted.

Jeryl decided not to argue the point with an imaginative nine-year-old. Instead, she pointed to a wavy line on the other side of the map. "Do you remember what this is?"

"Yes," she answered proudly. "It is the Blue River."

The king's cheerful voice echoed through the room. "Such a smart child." He strode to Eleanor's side and patted her on the head softly. "You amaze me daily, my dear."

"Thank you, Sire." She beamed. Jeryl noticed the carpenter lingering in the doorway. The king had forewarned her that the time had finally come for Trevor to meet Eleanor. But he would only introduce him as a friend so as not to confuse the child. She nodded to Trevor and motioned for him to enter, fighting the urge to lecture him about lurking in doorways.

Liam took the lead. "Eleanor, I have someone to introduce you to. His name is Trevor, and he works for me."

The girl considered the stranger carefully before saying hello. He stood before her with his hands behind his back. Her eyes showed caution, and her tone was polite. "Are you a woodworker?" Her directness surprised everyone.

"Yes," Trevor answered. "I am. How do you know?"

She pointed at his feet. "You have sawdust on your shoes and oil stains on your pants."

Embarrassed by his appearance, Trevor immediately bent over to dust off his shoes with one hand but stopped when the king cleared his throat. He straightened and apologized. "I'm sorry. These are the least scruffy clothes I have."

Eleanor's warm smile lit up her face. "I don't mind. You smell like cedar. I like that smell."

Liam watched as a child melted her father's heart. He had hoped for as much.

Trevor moved his other hand from behind his back to show a small, carved wooden horse. "I have a gift for you."

The child took the miniature and examined it, delighted. "Thank you!" She exclaimed as she hugged it and grinned.

Echoing shouts from the hallway interrupted the meeting. "Sire. Come quickly!" Another yelled, "You're needed in the stables."

Liam nodded to Jeryl, a sign to take the child back into the kitchen. He pointed to Trevor. "Come with me," and Trevor obeyed, smiling at Eleanor's response to his gift.

They met two guardsmen in the hallway, who described the urgency. A stranger had just brought Erik, unconscious, on horseback through the gates. He was asking for the king and refused to explain himself until His Majesty's arrival. As they rushed through the hallways and down the stairs to the stables, Trevor slowed his pace and fell back. He wanted room to run if his worst fears were realized.

When he rounded the corner to the stable entrance, Liam saw two forms on horseback entering. Mikal and Serena were returning from the cottage. He followed Mikal's line of sight to a group of men gathered around a large soldier lying on a pile of soft hay. Erik was indeed lifeless and pale.

"Send for my physician," the king ordered, and one man went running.

Mikal jumped off his horse quickly and paused, only to help Serena from hers. By the time she turned to grab the healer's kit, he was already on the ground beside his friend. "What happened? Who did this?"

All eyes turned to the tall, blond stranger who had brought him home. Krayvyn looked the king in the eyes. "I found him the way the dark wizard left him."

From behind the group, Serena asked, "Where's my mother?"

Krayvyn tried to see the young lady from behind the men crowded around Erik. "Are you the daughter of Briget?"

Serena moved quickly around the men to see the stranger who addressed her. As she did, she glanced between them at Erik. "I am," she confirmed. "Where is she?"

"I am sorry," Krayvyn answered, "the dark wizard took her."

Serena's face betrayed her deepest fear. "Who?"

"She is alive," he assured her. "I do not know his name. He came from the northwest and trapped the two. He took her on horseback and left her bodyguard for dead."

Serena turned her attention back to Erik. He looked oddly gray and badly injured. "How was he injured?"

"A tree, well, more than one actually, fell. The wizard used the trees as one would use iron bars to trap a bear." Krayvyn pointed to Serena. "You can help him, can't you?" His tone was not so much a question as it was an observation.

"Yes, of course." She turned her full attention to Erik and asked the crowd to stand back. The king tapped Mikal on the shoulder and nodded. They all stepped away from Erik and toward Krayvyn.

Liam started a barrage of questions. "Which direction did they go? Was he alone? Did you get a good look at his face? Was Briget injured in any way?"

Mikal added, "And who are you?"

Krayvyn gave a quick bow. "I am Krayvyn of Voorstland. I live near the border woods by the generosity of your king." He nodded at Liam. "Your soldier and Briget visited me this morning. He was very on edge the whole time. I thought it was my presence that bothered him, but after they departed, I sensed danger was tracking them. He's quite intuitive for a soldier."

"Yes, he is," Liam agreed.

"I decided to follow him at a distance, and by the time I almost caught up to them, I heard a terrible ruckus ahead of scattering birds and falling trees, so I held back out of sight. The forest smelled of dark magic. I watched them leave with Briget on the back of a henchman's horse. The dark one fully hidden in a hooded cloak, but for his scarred hands, led the way back toward the northwestern border. When they were clear, I approached the timber cage to find him in terrible shape. I feared at first that he was dead."

Serena listened to the blond man's story as she opened her healer's kit to find what she needed to help the fallen guard. His head was bleeding, and his breath was faint. She could see a large gash across the top of his head—swollen with bruising around it—and she marveled that the heavy blow didn't kill the man instantly. She pulled a short wand from her bag that was about the length of her index finger and had two polished stones, one bound on either end by copper wire. The pink stone was thuline, which would help with regeneration, and the orange stone was carnelian, her favorite for restoring vitality.

She reached back into the bag and felt around until she touched a hexagonal clear quartz wand. She would use that one first. Now, she needed to focus, so she turned to the men questioning Erik's savior and hushed them. "I need silence, please. Either save the conversation for later or leave and continue it somewhere else."

Liam understood and followed her direction. "Yes, my dear," he told her. "I shall ask them to follow me quietly outside. Please, call if you need us."

The men followed the king through the stable doors and out of sight, but Mikal held back. "Can I help you?" he asked.

Serena looked at him with compassion in her eyes. He couldn't help much, but he wanted to stay. "Stand back," she whispered, "be silent, and let your only thought be that he will be fully healed."

"I will."

"Repeat it in your mind with every breath. Intention is the key."

Mikal inhaled deeply and tried to clear his mind of any doubt. *He will be fully healed. Erik will be fully healed,* he repeated silently.

Serena took the clear quartz wand in her left hand and held it horizontally over Erik's head. With her right hand, she swept the air over and around his head, neck, shoulders, and chest as if clearing invisible cobwebs from the space around him.

He will be fully healed.

Next, Serena moved the quartz to her right hand and tilted it toward the wound on his head. She moved it closer until the tip of the wand was nearly touching the clotting blood. Slowly and deliberately, she began to twist the crystal between her thumbs and index finger.

Amazed, Mikal saw the tip of the quartz that was close to the wound become dark red, as if filling with liquid. The color spread through the crystal until it reached where her fingers touched it. He tried to refocus his thoughts on his intention.

Serena slowly moved the newly blood-red quartz away from Erik's head and placed it, pointed tip down, into the dirt beside her bag. Then she picked up the double crystal wand with her right hand and twisted it as if it were a tiny baton in the air in front of her. Mikal swore he saw the pink and orange stones begin to glow like the sky at sunset. When they did, she moved the wand closer to Erik's wound and repeated out loud, "He will be fully healed," three times.

The glow from the stones grew so bright that Mikal had to look away. It was like staring directly into the sun. He could see the brightness high in the dark corners of the stable. Then suddenly, the light winked out. He was afraid to look back. Afraid the magic failed. But he heard a deep voice say gently, "Hello, my lady." Erik's eyes were open. The blood was gone, the wound was a big scar, and he was smiling at Serena as a waking child would at his mother.

"Hello, my friend," she replied sweetly. "We've been waiting for your return."

"I think I got held up," he said as he tried to lift himself into a seated position. Instantly, Mikal was beside him to help him. "I was someplace peaceful, but quite plain."

Serena smiled at him. "You will be there again one day, but hopefully not for a very long time."

Mikal asked, "What do you remember?"

"The forest turned dark. The ground quaked, and the trees fell around us." Erik thoughtfully touched his head. "Then it all went black." He gasped, and a terrified look crossed his face. "Briget! Oh, sticks! Where is she?"

Serena hushed him to calm him down. "Your head hurts."

"Yes." Erik nodded weakly, "A bit."

"I thought he'd be fully healed," Mikal said.

Serena nodded. "He will be. With that last bit, it takes some time. Now it feels more like you drank too much wine last night, right?"

"Yes," he nodded again, "far too much."

"He needs water and rest," she assured them.

"But where's your mother?" Erik asked again.

"Krayvyn says she is alive," Mikal answered for her. "We will find her soon."

"The big man is awake," Krayvyn observed from the doors to the stable. Liam, a few other men, the king's doctor, and Trevor, who had come out of the shadows to rejoin the group, followed him. Krayvyn looked at Serena. "Your skills are more than impressive, young lady."

She nodded and thanked him. "You're a fire wizard?" she asked.

He looked startled by the question, so she rephrased it. "Your element is fire, sir?"

"Yes," he confirmed, "how did you know?"

"The ash on his skin was not dark magic," she answered and looked beyond him to the others. "Our friend needs a bath."

"No wonder I smell smoke," Erik said.

"The scent will fade," Krayvyn told them. "It was the only way I could think to move a large, truly helpless man."

Erik's face showed offense at first, but his expression softened when he understood. "Thank you, sir, for not leaving me to suffer my wounds."

"What wounds?" the physician asked. "I was told a man was dying."

Mikal stood as the king helped Serena to her feet and said, "Wonderful work, young lady. Thank you."

"You're welcome, Sire."

The physician, confused, said, "I don't understand. Where is he?"

Erik raised his hand. "Here. I'm sorry, Doc, but the energy worker beat you to it."

Mikal suggested, "Maybe you should accompany Erik to his room and give him a once-over. She said he needs rest and water."

"And a bath," Erik added. The physician nodded, helped Erik up, and the other men laughed.

Having seen the results of Serena's talent and noted the strange blond man claiming his own powers, Trevor turned to leave, but Mikal stopped him. As everyone else dispersed, only Liam, Mikal, Serena, Trevor, and Krayvyn remained.

The king spoke first. "After talking with Krayvyn, I am certain the dark wizard who kidnapped your mother is Kent DeGrane. My question is how?"

Serena only rubbed her forehead. "Isn't he the one she and Father bound?"

"Yes," Liam answered and changed his focus to Trevor. "As is this one."

Trevor visibly shook under the heavy stares of the group. With a hard swallow, he only mustered a shrug in response to the unspoken questions.

"What do you know of this, Trevor Ash?" Mikal broke the silence.

"Nothing," the carpenter stammered. "I spent a decade in prison for my part. I've not seen Kent since my capture." His voice cracked under the stress.

The king asked directly, "Have you since attempted to use magic for any purpose whatsoever?"

"No, Sire," Trevor lied. "Why would I jeopardize the new life—a new start you granted me?"

Serena closed her eyes and focused on Trevor's energy, and he noticed immediately. She felt a wall go up between them. He might not have used magic for evil recently, but he could still manipulate his own energy.

"And as I told you earlier," the king replied, "doing so will compromise your chances with your daughter."

The words took Serena by surprise, but she held her questions for later.

"I understand, Sire," Trevor said.

Krayvyn spoke next. "If indeed Briget bound the wizard, he will need to keep her alive."

"She did," the king confirmed.

"Alone?" Krayvyn asked.

"No, she worked with her husband to do it."

"Waylon?" Krayvyn questioned. "Is that right?"

"Correct," Liam answered.

It was too much for Serena just to stay quiet. "How do you know my parents?"

"Only by reputation," the blond wizard answered. "The Order of the Mystic Moon is known everywhere."

The answer only spurred more questions from Serena, but the king raised his hand in a gesture that stopped her before she could start. "Let us go somewhere a bit more private to continue this conversation," he said. Then he pointed at Trevor and added, "That includes you, Carpenter."

...

The White Mountains were not named for snow covered peaks. Although winter's touch often painted their tops, the narrow range between the kingdoms was filled with milky white quartz crystal that lay just below the ground's surface. Anywhere there was little to no vegetation to hold the soil in place, outcroppings of the stone shone through and glinted in the sunlight. The effect was almost blinding, and yet somehow, the darkness that traveled with Kent's most unmerry band of brooders dimmed even the mountains' glow.

The horses should have paused at the entrance to the trail that led up into the range. They should have sensed the intense energy the place held. Instead, each one fell into a single file line with his rider on his back and never broke pace.

Briget guessed they were either shielded from the intensity or so accustomed to it that the feeling of it meant nothing to them. As for her, she felt it as a tingle on her skin and a slight pressure in the center of her back. It was neither positive nor negative, but even in its near perfect neutrality, it could still be almost overwhelming. The quartz absorbed energy just as easily as it radiated it.

As an energy worker, Briget could use quartz to heal others by asking it to absorb negativity. Then, she would leave the laden stone in rich soil under a full moon to cleanse it. The full moon bathed these mountains monthly, and under the stars, they reflected the power of the universe every night.

After another hour of following the trail deeper into the mountains, Kent raised his hand in the signal to stop. They were pausing in a small meadow with green grass, a few trees, and a patch of wildflowers near the far edge. The space seemed peaceful and almost comforting to Briget.

The rider in front of her stiffened despite the calming scene. She felt his energy shift focus and watched as a shadow seemed to darken the grass in the center of the field. It was a circle at first, and it spread out, developing what looked like spiraling arms that whirled slowly around it. The darkness grew like a tree from the ground up and reached nearly twenty feet high in less than a minute. She watched in amazement as the darkness blocked her view of the field beyond it. The swirling blackness beckoned, and Kent nudged his obedient horse to move closer. To Briget's surprise, horse and rider continued right into the shadow and disappeared completely. The next rider did the same, and one by one, they all followed. For the first time, she felt concerned for the situation as the man she rode with dug his knees into their horse. The animal jerked forward and trotted into the darkness with a snort, and they, too, were swallowed whole.

...

King Liam led Mikal, Serena, Krayvyn, and Trevor to his library and shut the heavy oak door when they were all inside. Then he motioned for them to gather around the large table where a map of the kingdom was spread out. Pointing his finger at the map, he looked at Krayvyn and said, "Please show me where you found Erik."

The wizard leaned over the parchment and stroked his chin. The details of the topography and roads were hand drawn and incredibly accurate. He found the road that passed his house and followed its curves and bends back toward the castle with his finger. "Here," he pointed. "It was only about a mile from my home."

The king looked at Mikal and said, "That is your first stop."

"Yes, sir." Mikal nodded. "Whom shall I take?"

Serena realized they were planning a rescue mission. "I'm going," she said confidently.

"No," Mikal disagreed.

"Yes," she told him with a forcefulness that surprised even her. "My mother is missing, and I can help find her."

"It's too dangerous," he snapped. Then he gently put his hand on her shoulder. "My job is to protect you, and you're best protected by staying in the castle." He looked at the king for an expected nod of confirmation, but there was none.

Liam's eyes were contemplative as he mulled over the situation. Finally, he spoke. "The young lady is well skilled at protecting herself." He saw Mikal was about to argue and held up his hands to stop him. "She knows her mother better than any of us. She connects with her on a level that needs no words. That connection will aid in finding her. Is that not true, Serena?"

She nodded. "You are correct, Sire. Mother can guide me from afar when she is ready to." Of course, the question in Serena's mind was when her mother would make contact.

Liam said to Mikal, "You will need at least two of my most trusted men, and Erik is not up for the task."

Mikal nodded. "I'll take the brothers, Tom and Tod."

The king nodded. "You will also take the carpenter here." He pointed to Trevor, who had been doing his best impersonation of a fly on the wall.

Shocked, Trevor asked, "Sire?"

"You know Kent DeGrane better than any of us. He ran while you were captured and left you to your imprisonment, so I presume you have no trust of him, do you?" He studied the man's face as he asked the question.

Trevor's answer was indirect. "You're right. He left me to rot."

The king noted the evasive wording and nodded slowly. "So, Mikal, you will have two soldiers, Serena, and Trevor in your party. I will have the staff prepare horses and supplies immediately." He walked to the corner of the library near the door and pulled a rope hanging from the ceiling. Within moments, a servant arrived to take his orders to the stables and the kitchen staff.

They allowed Trevor to go to his quarters to prepare, but the king asked Mikal and Serena to stay behind for a moment. Krayvyn stood silently, waiting to be dismissed, but was not. When the four were alone, Mikal asked, "Sire, if I may say so, I do not trust Trevor Ash."

"Nor do I," Liam replied. "He hasn't earned our trust. I am giving him the chance to do so or show himself as untrustworthy once and for all."

"But doesn't that throw the safety of the rest of us into question?" Mikal asked.

"I have faith that you and Serena can use your unique talents to figure him out on this journey and leave him outside the gates if you feel it fitting upon your return," the king answered.

Mikal and Serena glanced at each other. Serena wasn't feeling overly trusting of anyone at that moment. She was trying to understand what she had seen in the ledger and trying to figure out who knew what about her family history. After a moment of silence, she allowed herself one question, "Sire, is there a bit of family history you'd like to share with me?"

The king's eyes widened and for a moment, he looked stunned. Then he took a deep breath and exhaled. "I don't believe so," he replied, and shot a glare at Mikal, whom he thought must have betrayed his trust. Mikal shook his head slowly, as if to say, "it wasn't me."

"Why do you ask?" Liam questioned her.

Serena pulled the ledger from a small bag, hiding under her travel cloak, and answered, "Because I found this at home."

Liam squinted his eyes at the leather-bound book. "What is..." He paused as a flash of recognition hit him. "May I see that?"

Serena handed the ledger to him carefully, as if it might disintegrate. "Sire, our names are both in it," she whispered.

Krayvyn broke his silence. "Is that..." thinking better of what he was about to say, he stopped short.

The king shot him a sideways glance, and then slowly opened the book. "The records of the Order of the Mystic Moon," he answered. "I had wondered if it was still in good hands." He smiled at Serena. "I see it is."

She shifted her weight on her feet nervously and asked him, "Am I to believe what I read on the seventh page?"

Liam carefully turned the fragile pages and studied the one in question for a moment. Then he closed the book and returned it to her without lifting his gaze from her. He said to Krayvyn, "Will you please do me the honor of remaining in the castle while our little search party carries out their mission?"

"If you wish, it will be my honor," the wizard answered formally.

"Mikal, please show our friend to the guest quarters on the third floor in the north tower."

"Yes, Sire." Mikal bowed and escorted Krayvyn out of the library.

When they were alone for the moment, the king motioned to a chair at the map table. "Please sit, Serena." Serena quietly obliged.

Liam rested his hand on the back of another chair and took a deep breath. Finally, he spoke softly to her. "My dear, in answer to your question, yes, it is true, but before you judge too harshly, I'd like to tell you about what is not in that book." Serena nodded and folded her hands over the book in her lap. Liam continued. "Your father and I were half-brothers by birth, full brothers at heart. He, your mother, and you have always been welcome to live in the castle, but this was not the lifestyle they enjoyed and not a place to raise a child as special as they knew you to be.

"They wanted more experience in the world for you than life inside these walls would allow. Here you would have been niece to the king and a member of the court with a life of privilege and expectations... and certain restraints. You could never have had the opportunity to develop your natural talent for energy work and healing. You would have been expected to learn only how to be a proper lady-in-waiting for the princess, your cousin.

"Your parents were wise to raise you far differently from the life my daughter experienced. I thought that rearing her as a princess meant giving her all she desired. Instead, I failed her as a father by spoiling her. The more she received, the more she demanded until nothing was ever good enough for her, not even my unconditional love."

Liam paused for a moment, but Serena could not respond. Her mind was too busy processing all he was telling her. Princess Shay was her cousin. Did Shay know? Had she known and attacked her at the ball, anyway?

The king's voice interrupted those thoughts as he continued. "At any rate, my daughter has proved herself a lost cause and you my dear, you are far more worthy of a crown than she could ever be."

"A crown?" Serena repeated. "No, I'm a farm girl and a healer, not a princess."

Liam raised his hand to quiet her. "Yes, and you are humble and thoughtful—two requirements of an outstanding leader." He sighed and locked eyes with his niece. "Your mother should be telling you much of this, but I cannot blame her for not having done so yet. Nor can I wait any longer." He lowered his voice to almost a whisper. "Serena, until my granddaughter is of age, you are next in line for the throne. It is the truth that you technically cannot be queen since you are not in my direct line, but you can act as regent and rule until the child is ready to be crowned."

Serena sat in shock at the very thought, and then a few things dawned on her. "The child Eleanor is Shay's daughter."

"Your intuition is spot on, as usual."

"She's so young." Serena's mind raced. The king must live until the little girl could ascend. King's niece or not, Serena wanted nothing to do with ruling a kingdom. Her mother was right to think that life in the castle would not suit her. There were too many rules and expectations and servants. "You are raising the next queen as a servant?" she asked.

The king nodded. "She has learned the humility and compassion that were beyond my daughter's comprehension. She is bright and joyful and will grow to become a great ruler one day."

"Sire, nothing can happen to you. She is not ready, and I cannot rule the kingdom."

He sat down in the chair and faced Serena. "My dear, I am not planning to burden you with my death. I only aim to prepare you for what may come. If you and Mikal retrieve your mother and return here safely, we will easily defeat Kent and his co-conspirators, but if anything goes wrong—if they manage an uprising to usurp my throne," he searched for the right words but only managed, "they will have it only over my dead body. And if that is the case, you must take my place or Myribell will be lost." His eyes were gray and tired at the very thought of losing to the evil wizard and his warlord comrade.

"Then we must not lose. We must find Mother and defeat that monster." Serena's own words surprised her. She had never wanted to fight anyone. She was a healer above all else. Destruction was not in her disposition. But the idea of the king, Eleanor, and her fellow citizens suffering at the hands of evil men assaulted every fiber of her being. They could never be allowed to win.

Liam took her hands in his and whispered, "I know you can do this, and now you understand why you must."

"Yes," she nodded.

"Your father would be proud of you," he told her with softening eyes. "As would your grandmother." He pointed at the necklace Serena still wore. "Your father made this for her. As long as she wore it, the pendant protected her from harm. And now it is yours, and it will do the same for you."

"But she died anyway," Serena pointed out.

"Yes, she did. The charm protects against outside harm, not old age or illness. We all must pass eventually."

Serena touched the pendant thoughtfully. "I can feel her energy within it. She sort of spoke to me through it last night."

"I know," Liam confirmed. "Her love and your father's love will come through and guide you when you need it most. Do not take it off, no matter what. You are too important to lose in this battle."

She said with a heart full of wonder and dread, "I will wear it always for you, Sire."

"Do it for yourself, too. You must accept your fate and all that it entails." A tear glistened in his eye.

This new burden would be a heavy one, and she had to carry it alone.

...

The horse carrying Briget and the rider in front of her relaxed after passing through the strange portal. They seemed to be underground in a cavern, but it was brighter than she expected in a cave. She blinked her eyes and saw a glimmer coming from the walls. It was a milky white glow. *We're inside the mountain*, she thought.

One by one, the band dismounted, but Briget did not move. Kent approached and offered his scarred hand in a gentlemanly fashion to help her down, and she hesitated. "Where are we?" she asked.

"The White Mountains, of course," he answered. "Now, come down off this high horse and make yourself at home here among the riffraff." He extended his hand closer to her, and she took it and dismounted. As soon as her feet hit the cold stone ground, she released his hand and wiped hers on her riding coat.

Kent's energy was nasty and full of negativity, narcissism, and envy. How could anyone so full of himself be so jealous of others at the same time? Greed. Greed makes men want what they don't have and don't deserve. And greed makes them think they deserve whatever they desire. Kent DeGrane's greed was legendary and felt like a handful of greasy iron nails.

He was sardonically bowing to her. "Welcome to our humble abode."

"Inside the mountain?" Briget asked as she looked around at the odd encampment. She could see mats laid out at one end of the cavern. Everything else was barren except for one far corner that seemed to hold a fire pit. Briget tried to commit every detail to memory immediately.

"We find the solitude soothing," he answered.

Briget thought to herself, *more like easier to hide. No wonder I couldn't sense his presence. Hiding in the mountains shielded him from my ability to detect his energy.*

The young man on the horse she had been riding slid off the other side, and from across the horse's back, she finally got a look at the face under the hood, most of it. His eyes and hair were still covered. A strong jaw and square chin with a bit of stubble jutted out into the light. His full lips and narrow nose didn't seem to match each other, and his ivory complexion made her wonder if he'd spent his whole life inside the cave.

"It's about time I got a break from her," he snarled, pulling off the blanket off the horse. She couldn't see his eyes but imagined they held the same content his tone did.

"Now, now, Wyndle," Kent chided. "Be nice to our guest. We need her to fulfill our mission."

"My name is Shade," he hissed from under his hood.

"Your name is Wyndle," Kent answered. "Until you have proven your value as a wizard, you will use your real name."

Briget wanted to mention how neither name suited the brute, but she only watched in silence as he gave the horse a smack to get it to move to the other side of the cavern. He turned from her before removing his hood and walking away. She wondered why he was hiding those eyes.

...

The dirt road back toward Krayvyn's cottage was cast in early evening shadow. Birds sang and crickets chirped cheerful tones as the rescue team rode to the place of fallen trees where Serena's mother had been kidnapped. The looming darkness had Mikal on edge, and he kept looking at Tom and Tod for assurance that they were alert and ready for an ambush. Serena was surprisingly relaxed in her saddle. The songbirds were a sign to her that evil no longer lurked in these woods. It had moved on and left them to search for clues as to where it had gone.

The carpenter was sullen and trailed behind Mikal and Serena. Having Tom behind him bringing up the tail reminded him they didn't fully trust him, and he understood why. He would never be fully trusted by anyone ever again unless he proved himself to those that mattered most.

As they came around a curve, Serena could see where trees completely blocked the road. They stacked almost neatly, like a child would stack twigs to make a home for a trapped turtle. The downed giants left huge gaps on both sides of the road. But near the ground, all that she could see were enormous balls of roots and dirt still attached to the trunks.

Serena marveled at the amount of force and the directional control that was needed to create what she understood to be a makeshift jail cell. There was no way a wizard whose magic was bound could have done this. An instance of terrible dread struck Serena, but she took a deep breath and squashed it. She knew Briget must still be alive. She could feel it.

"Wow!" Mikal marveled beside her. "It is just as Krayvyn described."

"Creepy," Tod said, as he pulled his horse on the other side of Serena.

"Amazing!" Serena corrected him. "This," she paused, looking for the best word, "structure took an enormous amount of power to create."

Tod gave her a sideways glance. "Could you do it?"

"I don't know," she answered quietly. "I would never think to try." She turned in her saddle to see Trevor and Tom catching up with them. Trevor's face showed what Serena thought to be at first shock and then mild amusement.

Mikal caught it, too. "What say you, Mr. Ash?" he asked. "What do you think of the most unnatural roadblock?"

The carpenter cleared his throat. "I'd say it could make a lot of benches." No one laughed at his attempt at humor, and Tom just glared at him in disgust.

Mikal dismounted and helped Serena down from the horse that king's guard had loaned her. It was a beautiful animal bred for bravery and battle. They insisted she take it instead of her own gentle mare. Against her better judgment, she accepted because she realized arguing was futile and they were quickly losing daylight.

Mikal looked at Tom, Tod, and Trevor. "Stay here," he ordered. "Keep watch." Then he followed Serena, already steps ahead of him, to get a closer look at the downed trees.

The stack was chest high on all four sides, with gaps between the trunks and branches. None were big enough to fit even a small child through. "How did Krayvyn get Erik out without help?" Mikal asked.

"Magic," Serena answered matter-of-factly.

Mikal looked at her with a raised eyebrow and the obvious question of how his magic might work, but he did not speak. Serena noticed the look but did not answer. She kept her focus on the task at hand. Thankful she was still wearing riding britches, she looked for a foothold and started climbing the wall of the tree jail in front of her.

Slightly surprised, Mikal followed her lead, and the two clamored up and over, landing inside with two less than graceful thuds, but they both landed on their feet.

They looked around at the cell for clues. "Here's where Erik went down," Mikal said. He pointed to a corner where drops of blood splattered the ground and the lowest nearby tree bark.

"Yes, and Mother stood here," Serena added, noting Briget's footprints in the dirt. She would have been standing over his body, hoping to shield him from more harm. The boot prints showed Briget had turned from facing Erik and the wall behind him toward the opposite side. She drew a line in the air with her fingers following the turn, "And their attackers approached there."

Mikal agreed and looked for signs of a struggle but found none. "Your mother didn't put up a fight," he said. There was no answer from Serena. He noticed something on the horizontal tree trunk at eye level in front of her had captured her focus. "Serena, what is that?" he asked and stepped closer. It looked like a small tree frog carved from black stone.

"A friend," she finally answered as she picked it up to hold it in both hands. She kept it gently in one and placed the other over it as if she expected this inanimate out-of-place figurine to escape. Before Mikal could say anything, she lifted her index finger in the universal signal for "give me a moment." So, he watched in silence as she whispered to the carving, "Show me."

Nothing happened, at least as far as Mikal could tell. Then he noticed that Serena's eyes were focused elsewhere and nowhere at the same time. Maybe something was happening.

Serena's mind went spinning back to the moment Briget froze the little frog in time with her brilliant fake sneeze. "Got you!" she had really said and caught the poor little witness on his perch so he couldn't move, but he could see her circumstances. Through his eyes, Serena watched as Kent and his thugs spoke with her mother, warned her away from Erik without even looking down at the injured bodyguard, and helped her climb over the makeshift cell wall.

"She went willingly," Serena finally said. "She wanted to see where he would take her."

"A carving of a tree frog told you that?" Mikal asked, disbelief tingeing his voice.

"No," she said quietly. "A real frog showed me that. He shared his memory with me." Mikal watched as Serena set the frog back where she had found him. Gently, she touched a finger to its head and whispered, "Thank you. Now you're free."

Immediately, the animal moved, and no longer looked like plain black stone, but shook his greenish brown little body awake. It seemed to nod to Serena before turning from her and jumping away, down off the tree trunk to the other side of the makeshift wall.

The captain was stunned into silence. He had never, ever seen anything like that before, and he wasn't exactly sure what he had just witnessed. He stared at the spot the frog had vacated, and for a moment, thought that "witch" might not be a misnomer for Serena. If she could do that, whatever that was, what else could she do?

Her voice brought him out of his wonder. "Captain?" she asked, obviously not for the first time. She was waving one hand at him, trying to get his attention.

No, he thought, now focused on the young woman in front of him. *Witches are evil, and she is pure good.* He pushed the doubt away and gave a curious smile. "What just happened?" was all he could say.

"It's hard to explain," she answered softly, almost shyly.

"That really was a frog?"

She nodded and took a deep breath. "When I was younger, I used to chase bunnies down by the riverbank. I wanted one for a pet. Of course, Mother knew I'd never actually lay a hand on one because they were far too fast and agile. So, she let me believe that if I caught one, I could keep it." She paused for a second to decide how much detail Mikal really needed, and she settled on just enough. "One day, I surprised us—her, me, and rabbit—by just sneaking up quietly and barely getting my hands on one. And I was so excited that I yelled, 'Got you!' and my joy turned to horror when this soft little creature suddenly turned to stone.

"I cried uncontrollably. You see, I had accidentally said magic words. I didn't realize I could do magic until that day. I only knew I could help people feel better. Mother picked up the bunny and made me hold it. I could feel a heartbeat inside it, and when I focused on the heartbeat, I saw how frightened I had made it. I mean literally I saw through its own eyes myself grabbing the poor thing. I apologized and cried more. Mother then told me how to undo my mistake and the rabbit reanimated and ran away when I set it down. I promised to never chase bunnies again."

"I bet not." The captain's face showed something like amusement and concern at the same time.

"So, you see," Serena continued, "when I saw the little stone frog, I knew my mother did that. I knew she remembered that day and she knew I would, too."

"So, what did the frog show you?" he asked, trying to ignore the strangeness of this whole question, and she told him. When she was done, the captain looked at her with what she thought could be disbelief.

Serena lowered her eyes and sighed. "Don't look at me that way."

He blinked. "What way?"

"Like you don't believe me."

He shook his head as if shaking off a dream. "No," he said. "I do believe you. I just..." he struggled to find the words. "I've never met anyone like you, and it seems hard to believe that you are real. I mean, I know you're real, but..." He trailed off, knowing he was digging a deeper hole.

Serena only shrugged. "I guess I'm not like other women or ladies of the court, but I'm just as real as any of them." She studied his face and added, "I'm not the only one who hides the whole story." It was an accusation she had been biting down all afternoon. His face showed confusion, so she clarified. "You knew I was the king's niece, and you said nothing."

Mikal swallowed hard. "The king made me swear not to say anything. Yes, he told me, but it wasn't my place to tell you."

"So last night, when we danced, when we kissed," she lowered her eyes again. "How do I know... how can I know if you were dancing with me or the king's niece?" She raised her eyes to his again, searching for the truth in them.

He shook his head slowly. "I guess you can't."

So, there they stood for a moment, two souls wanting to trust each other but questioning if it was even possible. Mikal knew Serena would not directly lie to him, but what other powerful talents was she hiding or even just not telling him about? Likewise, Serena wondered what other secrets the king had sworn him to keep. Were there any bigger than her heritage or did the size of the secret even matter? If he pledged his loyalty to Liam above all others, could she expect to trust him to be true to her, too? She'd never really had secrets before, but suddenly it seemed safer to hold her own emotions close. A lack of confidence in her ability to be regent if called upon; or worse, a blossoming affinity for a man in her life could be told to the king and disproportionately used against her. No, Serena realized she must keep this captain of the king's guard at arm's length, and it saddened her.

Mikal felt the change in her gaze upon him, the subtle way her features shifted. She would shut him off now, and it might hurt, but it was probably for the best. Cooling their relationship would put his focus solely on their mission. No distraction by her presence or her proximity could be allowed. He wanted to beg her to trust him, if not for his own sake, then for the sake of their security on this journey, but he knew she would trust his judgment as the king's captain. He feared her personal confidence in him as Mikal, the man she kissed less than a day before, was waning. He had to let it be and try not to wonder if he could ever regain her trust like that again.

Mikal dropped his gaze to the ground at their feet and a new thought occurred to him about Briget's captors. He pointed to the blood droplets where Erik's head hit the ground. "You said they didn't let your mother help Erik, right?"

"Correct," Serena answered, remembering what the little frog showed her. "The leader didn't even acknowledge him with eye contact. It was like he didn't exist."

"That says much about his mentality."

"That he's cruel? I gathered that," she said.

"No, more than that. Don't you see? They left him there. They left him for dead because his life had no value. His death had no value either, or they would have finished him. No, they were completely apathetic to his condition. So, they acted as though he meant nothing, like he didn't exist. These people value nothing unless it furthers their cause."

Serena thought for a moment. "I guess that's good to know. He'll keep Mother alive if he thinks he'll need her."

"Exactly," Mikal confirmed. "Your mother is more important alive, and that tells us he needs her to break the binding." He looked at her, waiting for the moment of recognition in her face, showing she was following his logic.

"So, if he needs her, he couldn't have done this!" she exclaimed, sweeping our hands in reference to the fallen trees around them.

Mikal clapped his hands together excitedly. "Someone in his company is a powerful wizard, but not the leader. Given your description and Krayvyn's, we can assume the leader is Kent DeGrane, but he is not the powerful player. Another wizard is taking orders from the old man."

...

Inside Mount Pilkin, Briget sat by the campfire and watched the smoke drifting away and up the wall of the cavern. She could make out small cracks in the stone where it made its escape. And she imagined there must be another chamber, or better, an exit, those cracks led to.

She watched Kent's men interact with each other, or in the case of the one who called himself Shade, not interact. The young man sat off to the side, away from everyone as if he should have been ringing a bell and shouting "unclean" to anyone who came close. Briget wondered if the solitude was self-inflicted or if the rest of the group was avoiding the bundle of negative energy wrapped so tightly inside himself.

She watched as the others drank fresh water and lamented the general lack of ale and women in the White Mountains. Normally, bad men wanting for objects of lust would worry her, but none of them so much as glanced in her direction. She was off limits and not to be thought of as anything but Kent's captive. A rare smirk crossed her face when she silently reminded herself that she was there mostly voluntarily and could use magic for protection if they pushed her to it.

Finally, she watched Kent DeGrane. The old wizard, the ringleader of the three who had caused so much pain and suffering a decade ago for most of the people of Myribell, their king, and, more poignantly, her own little family. She could see the scars on his hands that were made when he fought against the binding spell as Waylon and she cast it.

The two of them—she and her husband—had been a force for good in the darkness of those days. They fought as hard as Liam's troops to keep their kingdom free from the tyranny of the warlord, Ranald, and his dark magicians. The power of light over darkness was clear in their victory and in Kent's scars, but his evil had left its mark on her life. Her husband was a casualty of that final battle, and her daughter had bravely faced her teenage years without a father to guide her. Briget hoped her love and instruction had been enough of a foundation to get Serena through whatever struggles she may face in adulthood.

That last battle wasn't really so final. There Kent was again in front of her, intentionally ignoring her, and plotting to regain his former power. She knew he wasn't the one who fell those trees or sent the cyclone. In fact, she was pretty sure it was the man named Shade, or Wyndle, or whatever he deserved to be called. He had the brooding rage to create serious trouble, but he needed guidance on how to control it. That student-teacher relationship must be the reason for his presence. Kent probably promised the world for his help in vengeance and recapturing his own power. Yet would he keep those promises?

Briget imagined Kent would not want the young wizard to become more powerful than himself once he had his own powers restored. Which, of course, she could never allow. In fact, she had sworn to the order to keep all dark powers at bay, and it appeared Shade was a new threat.

She pondered the eyes that he hid from her. He must have made a deal with a powerful soul-bart, at the very least, to gain such control over nature itself. His eyes must hold the clue to which one. The entity would be able to use Shade's eyes as its own whenever needed. Briget could only think of a handful of demons who could impart the ability to create storms and turn trees into jail cells. Each had its own elements associated with it and colors associated with those elements. Shade's eyes were probably no longer the color he was born with. They could be dark violet, burned orange, yellow, green, or blood red. Any variation of those hues would be creepy enough to keep the rest of Kent's band from wanting to get close.

They all looked less like wizards and more like hired thugs, possibly even on loan from the warlord himself. They might have been men of good repute at some point, but poor choices and dire circumstances often lead weak men to do bad things. Anyone looking for an easy path could find himself in the Dark Territory quickly. All it takes is following the leader walking toward the shallows and promising a chance for more... more of anything, really. Greed always leads in one direction.

Briget's thoughts were interrupted when one of those men waved at her and shouted across the cavern. "Hey, witch lady, do you want some water?" His words had an odd inflection, as if the language were not native to him. Briget nodded, and he brought a canteen to her.

The water tasted cleaner than she expected. As she drank, she noticed details about him she hadn't really seen before. He had long but thinning hair on top of his head swept over to hide a bald spot. His long sideburns made up for that same bald spot. His rough little goatee added to the pointedness of his chin and did little to draw attention from his big dark eyes and flat nose. Everything about his features seemed just slightly off, just a little disproportionate. Even his ears looked a little low.

He watched her drink eagerly and asked, "Thirsty, eh?"

"Yes," Briget answered after nearly emptying the canteen. "I'm sorry if I drank too much. I've had nothing since lunchtime and that seems ages ago." She paused and added, "Thank you." He took the canteen and nodded.

"Someone should have offered sooner, but we weren't sure Kent would allow it."

"So, you are the brave one?" she asked.

He laughed a quick snort of laugh. "No, I'm the one who realized he never had us tie you up. You're not bound, so why treat you like a kidnapping or hostage?" He gave a weak smile, and those big eyes betrayed a hint of goodness in him.

"What's your name?" she asked.

"Elian," he replied with a half bow.

"Well, Elian, thank you for the water. It was refreshing."

"It comes from these mountains, you know. They say it has mystical properties." He laughed again. "I mean, of course you know. You're a witch, right?"

"An energy worker," she corrected him.

"Isn't that the same thing?" His tone was earnest, with no hint of sarcasm, so she explained.

"No, a witch, like a wizard, must make a pact with a demon. Her soul in exchange for specific powers. An energy worker makes no contracts and is born with her abilities."

"Oh," Elian said. "I guess that is a big difference." He looked pensive and turned to leave her.

"Thank you again for the water," Briget said behind him. She could see him nod as he walked back to the group, and she knew he was thinking hard about what she had just told him.

...

Nightfall found the rescue party at Krayvyn's cottage. He told the king they were welcome to use it for the night to rest for whatever lay before them the next day. Serena picked some rosemary and mint from his garden and made a herbal infusion. Tom and Tod unpacked a loaf of bread and venison jerky. For his part, Trevor did what Trevor did best by saying nothing and staying out of the way. Mikal sat at the table and stared at the scrolled map of the White Mountains. One by one, they all joined him at the wooden table.

"So, what's the plan, Captain?" Tom asked.

Mikal pointed to a spot on the map just a few miles from Krayvyn's cottage. "I do not doubt the trail will lead here," he said. "We've always suspected Kent was hiding in the White Mountains."

"Why?" Trevor's curiosity finally broke his silence.

Mikal glanced at him quickly and then at the others around the table. "No one ever saw him leaving the mountains or anywhere beyond them, not in the ten years since he fled. Our friends in the kingdoms beyond the range have been watching for him. They know his danger and would never allow him to live in peace in their own dominions. No one claims jurisdiction over the White Mountains. Because of their innate power, they have always been neutral territory."

"I would think someone would want to claim that power," Trevor stated.

The captain shook his head. "They would not know what to do with it. They sense it, and they know it's there, but they fear it. It's easier to call the range haunted and avoid it than to claim it and conquer it."

Tod asked, "If we've always suspected he was there, why didn't we look for him?"

Serena answered intuitively, "Because he wasn't causing trouble and his powers had been bound."

Mikal nodded. "Why waste manpower when, for all we know, he could never be a threat again?"

"I meant why do you think the trail will lead us to that spot?" Trevor clarified his earlier question.

"Because it is the only path wide enough for horses that leads from this kingdom into the mountains. There is only one way for them to get in or out."

"If that is true," Trevor said, "then why wasn't there an armed guard manning that point?"

Serena had wondered the same thing.

"There should have been," Mikal answered with the first hint of uncertainty in his voice. "Two guards were assigned to the post. I will have to assume that Kent's band somehow dispatched them."

Tod spoke this time. "You mean killed them?"

Mikal nodded gravely. "I hope I'm wrong, but what else could explain it?"

Serena didn't know the missing soldiers, so she couldn't reach out for them and confirm psychically. Instead, she sent up a quiet prayer for their souls, alive or dead.

They finished their dinner in relative silence and found empty places on the floor in the small cottage to bed down for the night. Mikal tried to give Serena the bed, but she refused his chivalry, not from spite. She knew that sleeping in Krayvyn's bed could affect her dreams and her energy. It would be unwise, so Mikal took the bed and slept as well as the head of the rescue party could, which in the end, was not very well.

Chapter 6

Day 5

SERENA KNEW SHE WAS dreaming because she heard her mother's voice. "My Daughter, do not worry," Briget soothed her. "I am unharmed and waiting for you, but so is Kent. He knows you will follow me."

The space around Serena was a gray, misty world with no light source and no darkness, either. Her mother's presence didn't surprise her. In fact, she had hoped for it and made herself sleep in order to find it. "Where are you?" she pleaded, searching the nothingness for a vision of her mother.

The echo of her voice was all that was granted. "In the mountain," Briget answered, "Follow the trail to the green that should not be. There was a portal there. We crossed through it, but I don't know if you can open it."

"The green that should not be," Serena repeated. "What do you mean 'in the mountain'? A cavern?"

"I'm sorry, but I can't show it to you. The stone limits our telepathy. One more thing, Daughter," Briget's voice was fading. "Beware of Shade." Then she was gone. The gray faded to black, and Serena opened her eyes to the first light of dawn creeping through the windows. "Beware of shade," she repeated quietly. What did that mean?

...

The warlord's eyes flashed with rage. "You are worthless to me now," he told Shay.

She was standing before him in the great hall of a small castle beyond the forests of Myribell's northern border. Despite her long ride through foreign lands, her appearance was still impeccable. She still wore her ball gown and added her favorite tiara, which she fit in the hastily packed bag she flung onto her stallion when she left her home. She had changed in the servants' quarters just before presenting herself to the warlord, Ranald.

"How can I be worth nothing?" she asked incredulously. "I am the princess of Myribell, rightful heir to my father's throne."

"You were," he corrected her. "The messengers told me what happened."

Of course, he had spies who beat her there. Why hadn't she considered that? "My father's betrayal does not remove my blood ties to the throne." She kept her head held high and looked him directly in the eyes.

"You left in a huff like an angry child. I needed you in that castle for our plan to work. You are useless here."

"Clearly," she argued without raising her voice. "Your spies have that position covered."

"And what exactly can I expect from you here, other than snobbery and complaints?" He tapped his fingers on the hilt of the sword on his side and glared at her.

Shay had never realized how much he must have despised her until that moment. There was no respect in his stare. She saw only contempt mixed with something akin to anger. It was only then that she missed the safety of her father's castle and wondered silently how big a mistake she had made, but it was too late to turn back. She was ready for his questions, but not his hatred. With a hint of insolence in her voice, she answered, "You could claim you captured me and demand a ransom."

Ranald blinked once, and for a moment seemed to consider it before scoffing. "They wouldn't pay it."

"Why not?" Shay demanded.

"Because your father doesn't trust you." He practically spat. "He'll see right through it."

"I disagree." Her words were calm but pointed. "While he may not trust me, he doesn't trust you either. He still loves me. He wouldn't want to see me hurt. And if he thinks you are threatening my life, he will err on the side of caution."

The warlord's eyes narrowed, "My plan is an invasion, not a sack of gold. I mean to take the kingdom. You do not give your father enough credit if you think he would hand over his kingdom for the life of a spoiled princess."

"And you do not give him credit for loving his daughter," Shay's words burned in her mouth. She knew the king loved her, but she had never thought about how much he might be willing to sacrifice for her safety. "His compassion for his own child could be his downfall and exactly the leverage you need."

Ranald never lifted his gaze from her, and it chilled her with its ice and ire. "We shall see," he said and stomped his right foot on the marble floor. A door to Shay's right opened and two of his mercenaries entered and stood at attention. "It seems we have a new prisoner," he told them. "Take her to the tower. She can wait there while I think."

They followed his orders, grabbing her roughly by the shoulders and moving her toward the door. *I'm so stupid*, she thought for the first time in her life, and she heard the hem of her gown tear as she stumbled under the weight of their grasps.

...

Mikal led the way to the narrow pass from Myribell's border to the White Mountains. His thoughts were focused on the dream Serena had described to him. How could they travel a mountain path and avoid shade? The mountains cast their shadows throughout the day. Maybe traveling at night was the only option. Technically, night was just one long shadow, though. He knew he must be overthinking it.

They had decided to find the portal Briget had described but were still debating whether to enter it. Kent might expect them to come that way. There had to be another route inside, or he would never have known a cavern was there to begin with.

They passed a small village and came upon the place where the border guards should have been. Tom and Tod silently dismounted and crept toward the small, somewhat camouflaged building at the edge of the forest. Tom knocked twice on the door while his twin stood aside, ready to pounce. There was no answer. Tom tried to open the door but didn't budge. Both sent questioning looks back to their captain, who mimed kicking in the door. Tom nodded, squared himself with the door, and gave a violent kick. There was a loud thud on the other side of it as the thing cracked off its hinges and tried to fall inward, but something unseen held it up.

Mikal suddenly had a horrible feeling in the pit of his stomach as Tod stepped up to help his brother shove the door aside. With the door out of the way, Tom could see into the building, and just as they had all feared, was staring at the two guardsmen in a heap at his feet. Dead.

"Sticks," Tom said and gave the signal to Mikal.

"Sticks," Mikal whispered. He slid off his horse and told Serena and Trevor to stay there. Serena nodded and watched the captain approach the guardhouse. He walked into its shadows and came back out quickly. "Serena," he called. "Your help, please."

She dismounted quickly, and although not invited, Trevor followed. What she saw upon entering the room stole her breath. Inside, the two guards who had been leaning against the door were now in a heap on the floor. Terror was in their still-open eyes. Their hair was sticking straight out, and both had markings on their skin shaped like long streaks of lightning.

Serena gasped. She'd seen similar marks before on a farmer who had been struck by lightning in his field. The scarring on his body forever marked him as the lucky survivor of a terribly improbable event. "But how?" Serena asked aloud.

"How what?" asked Tom.

She looked up to see all four men had turned their attention to her, and she realized she had spoken her question out loud. She shook her head and cleared her thoughts. Then she pointed at the victims' skin. "Those marks," she told them, "tell me that these guards were struck by lightning." She paused to let that thought sink in and saw the understanding in their eyes. "They blocked the door from the inside, and I see no opening to the outside world."

Mikal finally spoke. "Were they trying to escape or make sure they were safe inside?"

Trevor cleared his throat, and the group looked at him expectantly. He just shrugged and tapped his neck. "Sorry," he whispered.

Serena told them, "I think they were hiding from a storm that wasn't natural."

Tom and Tod nodded simultaneously, and Mikal agreed. "This was definitely not natural," he observed. "So again, we see evidence that we're dealing with someone who can manipulate the sky."

"This person is obviously dangerous, but it isn't Kent," Serena observed.

Trevor gave a subtle nod, and Mikal noticed it. "Do you know who could have done this?" the captain asked.

The former wizard shook his head thoughtfully. "No, and I'm not sure we want to meet him."

Serena explained, "Whoever could create weather and bend it to do his will is probably in league with a powerful soul-bart and also probably not in full control. Demons like that use their so-called partners as tools while fooling them, at first, into thinking they have free will. By the time the sorcerer realizes he's a puppet, it is too late. The only way to separate himself from the evil entity controlling him is death, and the demon decides when that death comes."

The captain looked back at the dead border guards and shook his head with controlled fury. "I want to meet him," he said. "I want to make sure he never does this again."

"How?" Serena asked.

"I'm not sure, but there is always a way." He motioned to the door. "We need to keep moving."

"We're just going to leave them like that?" Tod asked.

"For now," Mikal answered. "We'll have to. We need to find Briget and the one who did this."

Tod nodded in understanding, and the group returned to their horses and rode away from the struck guardsmen.

Serena would never see their bodies again, but the image was seared into her memory. Those poor men who probably never expected to have to actively guard the border of Myribell, and who died in what must have been a moment of sheer terror, would never spend time with their families again. Anger galvanized her, and she prepared herself for what surely would be required ahead.

She was still thinking about the guardsmen when the trail narrowed into the pass that led up into the mountains. The feeling of her horse tensing under her brought her focus back to her own situation. The energy of the white range seemed like a shield in front of them, and their animals sensed it first.

In front of the line, Mikal's gelding paused, then backed up a few steps, but the captain coaxed the animal forward and it went. He shouted over his shoulder to them to follow, but he knew the horses would be hesitant. Tod and Tom went next. Their horses snorted in disapproval but kept moving. Serena's horse was unsure and despite her attempt to steady him, he reared and bucked. She felt herself go airborne and braced for impact against the mountain as she sailed toward it. In a hot blue flash, it was all over.

Serena was lying on the ground, eyes open, staring up at the blue sky above her. She felt... fine. It was as if she landed on goose down, not hard granite. Mikal was beside her in a heartbeat, asking if she could move. She found her voice and answered. "Yes, I'm alright." The look on his face told her he didn't believe her, so she lifted herself on her elbows and repeated, "I'm alright." He stood and held his hands out to help her to her feet. She took them and rose with no trouble.

"But how?" asked Trevor, his horse still at the edge of the pass.

"What was that blue light?" Tod wondered.

Serena felt a warmth against her chest and touched her grandmother's necklace. The sapphire glowed slightly, and she smiled. "This," she whispered. "It worked."

"Thank heavens," Mikal said quietly.

Serena looked around. "Where's my horse?" she asked.

"It's probably halfway back to the castle by now. What spooked it?" Tod asked.

"The energy shift at this pass. He probably felt it, and then I shifted my own to match." She shrugged and looked accusingly at Mikal. "Next time I ask to use my own horse for an adventure, please let me. She never would have dumped me."

The captain nodded but said, "That was a seasoned warhorse just like ours. He shouldn't have reacted like that."

"Has he ever been exposed to magic?" she asked.

"Not to my knowledge," he answered honestly.

"Well, there you have it." She crossed her arms and looked down at the necklace. Its warmth was fading because the threat to her had passed.

The captain whistled, hoping the runaway horse had not gotten too far, but after a few moments, he lost hope. Tod was probably right. The horse wasn't coming back, and they needed to move forward.

"You'll ride on my horse," he told Serena.

"I'll walk," she said.

"No, we need you alert and not tired."

The look in his eyes was commanding, but she insisted. "I could say the same of you." She looked at Tom and Tod, who were both watching and waiting for a decision, and then she looked at Trevor, who seemed to do his best to fade into the scenery. "I'll share Trevor's horse," she announced.

Mikal put himself between her and the carpenter with his back to him. "Do you think that is wise?" he whispered to her.

"I do," she whispered back and put her hand on his arm, giving it a light squeeze the same way she had the first day they met—the day she saw his past through that touch.

After a moment, the understanding showed in the captain's eyes. "If you say so." He turned back toward Trevor and asked, "What say you?"

Trevor nodded and answered, "I would happily share if the horse doesn't mind."

Mikal nodded in response and added, "You'd better walk him through the pass, so we don't lose him, too."

"No worries," the powerless wizard answered and kicked his heels into the animal's sides. It trotted through the narrow passage and stopped on the other side, where Trevor motioned for Serena to hop on, and she did.

...

Tall wrought iron candelabras lit the round table in the corner of the throne room with flickering light. King Liam sat with Erik and the exiled fire wizard and spoke in low tones. The big guard looked much better after resting most of the day. He was describing how the earth shook and the trees fell and then his world went black.

"And how is that head of yours?" the king asked him.

"Much better. Thank you, Sire." He touched his forehead. "The young lady is a miracle worker." There was barely even a mark where once had been a deep bloody gash. "It hardly even aches now," he added.

Krayvyn studied Serena's handiwork. "Tomorrow morning, there will be no outward sign it ever happened."

"Ah, yes," Liam agreed, "But the memory and the pain of losing your charge won't fade as easily." He saw the guilt cross Erik's face. "Don't worry, my friend. I know you could have done nothing to stop it. I am not blaming you, but I know you. You blame yourself, don't you?" Erik nodded. "That is why I trust you as I do. Your sense of responsibility is admirable."

The king turned his attention to Krayvyn. "And you, sir, I have a few questions for you."

"I will do my best to answer them."

"What kind of wizard are you?"

"A fire wizard, Sire."

The king pondered the answer for a moment and continued. "And what is your oath?"

Krayvyn smiled genuinely to know that Liam understood how wizardry worked. "I may only use my power to help the truly helpless."

"Ah, yes," Liam nodded toward Erik. "He was most definitely truly helpless."

Erik agreed and asked his own question. "Why are you in exile, then?"

The smile left the blond wizard's face as he said, "That I cannot answer. All I can say is that plans to help others went dreadfully wrong, and I was told to leave or risk all that my family had."

"So you left to save them?" Liam asked.

"Yes."

"And you did not save them through fire?"

"No, Sire."

"Then, may I deduce they were not truly helpless?"

"You may."

"And you were sworn not to tell some horrible secret or risk their all?"

"Precisely."

Liam frowned. "Briget did not see you as a threat, so I will not either. In fact, you appear to be a friend and a potential asset to the kingdom, so I will not press you for any more information than you can give."

"Thank you."

...

After what seemed like hours of squinting through bright sunlight glinting off the quartz mountains, clouds began to fill the sky. Serena welcomed the relief for her eyes but worried the building clouds meant rough weather for her and her friends, and Trevor, whatever he might be. She rode behind him on his horse, her arms loose around his waist. She had tried to read his thoughts and his energy, but all she could feel was a strange base energy that she'd never encountered before. It rippled and pulsed when she tried to reach through it, reminding her of a sort of psychic jelly. The feeling it gave her was on the verge of repulsion, so she quit trying. Instead, she engaged him in casual conversation.

"I wonder if we somehow missed the green place my mother described," she said.

"How could we?" he replied. "The pass is so narrow with no trails veering off it, it must still be ahead."

"Maybe it has been hidden from us."

"Kent wants you to find it. He wouldn't hide it."

"What makes you so sure?" Serena was a little surprised at his matter-of-fact statement.

Trevor sighed and tensed at the same time. "I think it should be obvious that he took your mother to draw you to her. He needs both of you to break the bounds and give him back his power."

"Huh." Serena thought about that possibility, but Kent might be sorely disappointed if that was his goal. She neither knew how to do it, nor would she ever willingly release the man responsible for her father's death. "No chance of that happening," she said flatly.

"Never say never. Kent can be persuasive in his way."

Serena brushed away the thoughts of what types of persuasion the dark wizard might employ and took the opportunity to learn more about her riding partner.

"So, tell me, how did he persuade you to follow him?"

Trevor scoffed, "Me follow Kent? Kent and I were equals. He had much more experience, but he was not my leader. We worked for Ranald."

"The warlord? Why?"

"He promised us the life we could only dream of—power and wealth and importance in the vast kingdom he was building."

"You mean destroying lives and peace to create from other kingdoms?"

"He did what it took." The response was cold, unapologetic. With a shock, Serena got her first real insight into the personality of Trevor Ash.

"And you did whatever he asked, even if it meant hurting innocent people?"

"I served him, yes." He took a deep breath, let it out slowly, and added, "As did the others."

Serena shifted her weight in the saddle behind him, wishing she could put space between them without falling off the horse. Trevor felt the movement and tried to change the direction of the conversation. "Why do you serve King Liam?"

"I serve no one."

"What about your parents?"

Serena had to think about that one. In the last few days, she discovered her knowledge of her parents to be utterly incomplete. One thing she was sure of, though, was that they were not the types to swear allegiance for power or wealth. She gathered herself and answered intuitively, "My parents were friends and consultants to the king. They aided him as needed, but they did so out of loyalty and love. They were not servants, and they wanted no wealth or power for their help."

"Of course," he said, "That's how you ended up a farm girl."

"My parents preferred a simpler life outside the city gates, yes. They did not want me growing up in a castle, becoming spoiled by material possessions, and turning into someone like Shay." It suddenly made perfect sense. "If I lived that life, I might have become too self-centered to ever live up to my true calling, which is healing others."

"So, by making you a simple farm girl, they saved you from yourself."

"Or the potential bad me, yes."

"Would that we were all so lucky to have parents like yours?" There was a tinge of bitterness in his voice.

"In a way, my parents did the same for you," she told him, not unkindly.

"How so?"

"They bound you from injuring yourself or others by use of magic. They saved you from yourself."

Anger welled up inside the former wizard, and Serena felt an unfamiliar heat emanating from his core. His next words were meant to hide his feelings, but it was too late for that. His psychic wall of jelly was falling. "I suppose I should thank your mother when I see her."

The tamped-down rage flustered Serena. She couldn't stay on the horse so close to him any longer. She felt the amulet on her necklace warming and gave a glance behind her to Tod. When she caught his eye, she mouthed silently, "Get me away from him."

He nodded an understanding in faked a cough. "Captain!" Tod yelled from the rear. "I need a break for some water and stretching."

Mikal halted his horse and turned in his saddle. He was going to deny the request, but the dull blue glow of Serena's necklace caught his attention. Her eyes pleaded with him, and he realized Tod was trying to help her. "Alright," he said. "Dismount. We can use a quick break."

The moment Serena's feet hit the crystal ground, she felt relief, safe and grounded. The glow of her amulet faded as fast, and the carpenter never seemed to have noticed it. She nodded a thank you to Tod and went to Mikal who was holding a canteen of water.

He offered it to her and, watching to make sure Trevor stayed out of earshot, whispered, "What happened?"

"He still harbors resentment toward my mother."

"No surprise there."

Serena shook her head. "I tried to read him by touch, but he had a weird sort of wall blocking me. So, I got him talking, and I drew him out that way. Only he lost his cool and was getting angry, so I got Tod's attention."

"You'll ride with me now," Mikal told her.

"No," she answered. "I will walk. We must be close, and the earth here grounds me. I need that focus right now."

Mikal clinched his jaw and considered it. "Then I'll walk, too. You may feel grounded, but it puts you at a disadvantage if we come across any challenges."

"By that logic," she said, "you're putting yourself at a disadvantage."

"You are under my protection, and the best way for me to protect you is to be beside you, even if you are walking."

Serena sighed but secretly appreciated his valor. "Alright, then," she sipped from the canteen and smiled at him.

"You said he had a wall blocking you. What does that mean?"

Serena thought about how to best explain. "It's a sort of psychic defense mechanism."

"Magic?" Mikal looked surprised.

"Not really. Anyone can do it," she told him. "It just takes practice. It wasn't very strong, but it was enough to keep me out and it felt gross."

"So, it's something I could do?"

Serena saw his point. "I can teach you, but you won't need it against me. I promised."

"I know you did, but others have your gift for reading people, too, yes?"

"Yes."

"Then I would like to defend myself against them."

She nodded. "Alright, I'll explain while we walk."

...

The room where the guards left Shay waiting was empty and small. Broken tiles barely covered the dirt underneath. Dust gathered in the corners and cobwebs hung loosely from the ceiling. The longer she waited for them to return, the tighter the room felt.

For a little while, she paced back and forth, turning over the answers Ranald might have to her suggestion. If he caved and went along with her plan, she could return to the castle. If he stubbornly considered her worthless, he might let her leave, or worse. She didn't want to think about what he might do if he thought she could pose a threat. Of course, he wouldn't think that, right?

In that moment, she had no soldiers to command, clout, or power. At best, he could take her up on her offer and send word to her father that she was captured and in danger. At worse, he might leave her in the tiny room to waste away.

The more she paced, the more her feet hurt, and she cursed herself for not changing into riding clothes before storming out of Myribell. Standing still didn't help, but sitting on a dirt floor was out of the question. No princess would stoop to that level, and after all, she was still the daughter of a king!

Time ticked away, but without a window to show her the march of daylight, Shay had no sense of how long she had been alone when the same two guards returned for her.

The one with the thick neck and missing teeth spoke as he grabbed her upper arm and pulled her toward the doorway. "Master Ranald wants a word with you."

The other guard, a man with a rough beard and a broken nose, gave a mocking bow and stuck his foot out in front of him. "Your Highness," he said with a sneer while the first gave her arm a yank, causing her to trip over the second one's extended leg.

Shay landed in a heap of ice-blue silk and gray dust. It took her a moment to bite back her temper, knowing that they had the upper hand. She slowly raised herself to her hands and knees, looking down at her own body to make sure there was no blood. Her palms hurt, and she slowly sat back on her calves and raised them. Tiny pieces of tile were embedded in her skin, so she wiped them on her dress. Then, she slowly stood, warily eying the guards as she did.

"Oh, look at what you did!" Crooked Nose said. "That's too bad about your dress. Did you have another one in your bag?"

"Where is my bag?" Shay demanded.

"It's with your horse," Toothless answered. "I'm sure the stable boy is taking good care of them, but I wouldn't expect to see them again." He spat at her feet.

The bearded guard took her by the arm this time, while the other gave her a shove in the back as she passed.

"Why are you doing this?" Shay asked.

"Doing what?" Crooked Nose replied.

She decided not to dignify his feigned ignorance with an answer, and they walked through the dingy hallways in silence.

...

The afternoon sun reflected off the tops of the White Mountains while the ridges cast the trail through them in shadows. Briget's warning of "beware of shade" echoed in Serena's mind while she explained how to put up a psychic wall to Mikal.

He listened intently and asked good questions, but his eyes were always set on the path ahead of them. Its twists and turns could easily hide an ambush, and the growing shadows as the sun moved beyond the peaks concerned him, too.

As they went around another steep ridge, they saw it. The green meadow was out of place amidst the stark white stone and loose gray dirt they'd seen everywhere else. It looked like someone had thrown a rug made of grass down at the foot of a rise. Small yellow flowers dotted the patch of green that was at least fifty feet in diameter. The edge of the grass was as distinct as a hem with no stray blade beyond it.

Serena and Mikal stopped so suddenly that Tom, Tod, and Trevor had not gotten a glimpse yet.

"Why did we stop?" Tom whispered.

Serena answered in full voice, "Because we found the green that should not be." Then, she and Mikal took a few careful steps forward, so the others could see it.

"Whoa!" Tom said. "This was what your mother said to look for, right?"

"Yes," Serena answered, looking back at them. She noticed Trevor's face showed no surprise or amazement.

"Is it safe?" Mikal asked her.

Serena stepped toward the edge of the grass and felt Mikal's hand on her arm. "Wait," he said. "I should go first."

"I'm sure it's safe," she told him. "Mother said to look for it, not to run from it."

He nodded slowly and reluctantly let go of her, but quickly stepped up beside her. "We go together, then," he told her.

Serena nodded to him, and they each took a measured step into the grass and waited. When nothing happened, they moved a few more paces into the circle. Then Mikal motioned to the others to follow.

"So, what is this place?" Tom asked as he dismounted, and his horse immediately started to graze.

"I'm not sure," Serena said. "I mean, obviously it's a meadow, but there shouldn't be green grass anywhere in these mountains, right?" She looked at Mikal for assurance.

"It's not natural," he answered. "It can't be."

They all looked at Trevor, who remained apathetic and just shrugged before dismounting.

Tod observed, "The horses seem to think it's pretty nice, though." All four horses were enjoying the break by the mouthful.

Serena made a full turn to take it all in before walking cautiously across the field. Mikal stayed with the rest and rummaged in one of his supply bags for a snack.

The grass under her feet felt different from what she was used to. It seemed to have an energy that intensified as she got closer to the center of the circle. It almost seemed to shimmer, but there was no breeze to move it. As she bent down to touch it with her right hand, she felt a pull from her left side. At first, it was gentle, but it quickly turned into a tug that knocked her off balance. And then everything went black.

...

Briget sat against the cool wall of the cave with her eyes closed, waiting for a change in the atmosphere to signal her daughter had found a way in. Instead, she felt her heart flutter. Then it started racing, and her mind began to spin. Swirls of dark violet and black energy spun before her as she tried to catch her breath. She opened her eyes to get her bearings.

Nothing had changed in the cave.

Her heart was beating in her ears, but the spinning sensation subsided. She knew immediately that the feelings weren't hers. "Serena!" she whispered.

...

As Mikal's hand found the apple that had sunk to the bottom of his bag, he saw something dark cross the meadow from the corner of his eye and heard the other men gasp. "What?" Not waiting for an answer, he looked toward the center of the green, and Serena was gone.

The unnatural sense of panic struck him. "What? Where?" He looked all around them. "No!"

Tom's and Tod's faces were pale, and even Trevor looked surprised. "It's like the earth swallowed her where she kneeled!" Tod finally said.

"A portal," Trevor told them with a hint of amusement in his voice.

The tone angered Mikal, who drew his sword. "You did this!" he yelled at Trevor.

The carpenter stepped back with his hands up. "No, sir. I didn't," he said adamantly. "How could I?"

...

Serena hit the ground hard and caught her breath. Underneath her cheek was gravel and dirt, not the soft, shimmering grass she had just been touching. In her peripheral vision, the soft blue glow of her grandmother's pendant faded. The stone was beside her, still attached to its long chain.

Serena used one hand to push herself up, so that she was sitting on her knees. The ground wasn't the only different thing. She seemed to be on a path in a dark forest. The canopy was so thick that she couldn't tell if it was day or night. She listened intently but heard no birds or animal sounds. All was deathly quiet.

Serena sat for a moment and concentrated on taking slow, deep breaths to calm her nerves. What had just happened?

All she remembered was a tug from her side, and suddenly, she was spiraling through violet-streaked darkness. The energized grass must be a clue, but she couldn't quite piece it together.

The grass. It was the "green that should not be" that her mother told her to take the trail to. The energy she felt must have been the portal opening, but where was her mother?

Serena looked around her carefully. There was no sign of Briget, or anyone else. A dull light glowed from somewhere in the forest to her left. The trees were old and reached across the path in a way that made them look like hands grasping for each other. To her right, she felt darkness as much as she could see it. When she turned to look behind her, she thought she glimpsed a pair of eyes blink out.

She quickly stood up and spun to get a better look at the path behind her. It disappeared into inky blackness just twenty feet away. Staring into it, she searched for any feeling of life, but what she felt was an emptiness that seemed to press toward her.

Taking a few careful steps backward, she felt it follow, so she paused. The soft glow was to her right now, and it seemed to be the color of her grandmother's pendant, but duller. Serena weighed her choices: turn and run down the path from whatever stalked her and risk making it chase or head into the woods to find the source of the light.

Two fiery orange eyes appeared in the darkness again, and this time they glared at her for several seconds before blinking out. She knew then it was not her imagination. They were about eye-level to her, so whatever they were part of was not small, and she had a feeling it wasn't kind either.

She took a slow step to her right and waited. There was no sound or sign of movement from the thing in the darkness, so she took another. After several measured steps off the path and closer to the edge of the woods, she cautiously turned to face the direction she meant to walk.

Feeling like a field mouse hoping the hawk wasn't hungry, Serena took one purposeful step at a time until she broke the wood line, where she paused again to listen. When she heard nothing, she stepped a little faster in the direction that seemed to hold the source of the glow.

She decided not to question why the thing didn't follow her. Instead, she concentrated on focusing her energy outward from her body. She imagined herself walking within a bubble of light that extended a few feet away from her—just far enough to keep the darkness behind her at bay.

When it felt like she'd been walking for an hour, she stopped to rest. The dull glow still emanated from somewhere beyond the trees, but seemed no closer. Turning in a circle, she surveyed the forest. There were still no animal sounds, but she could hear something faintly carried on a light breeze. It was coming from the direction of the glow.

Serena breathed deeply and started walking again. As she did, the sound grew louder, and she finally recognized it as running water. Just a few minutes later, she came upon a brook, peacefully making its way toward the light.

She followed it and observed the lack of animal prints along its edge. Usually, water sources were places for animals of all sizes to congregate for relief, but not this one. The thought was odd, and she wondered what kind of forest lacked life.

After what felt like miles, the brook gradually widened until it opened into a lake of sparkling blue water that reminded Serena of the crystal inside the pendant she was wearing. The water here was still, except where the brook joined it. There were no waves and no sign of fish.

Serena couldn't see to the other side of the lake, but about fifteen feet from where she stood on the shore, she saw what looked like a low stone wall stretching from her right to her left. Her curiosity piqued; she walked along the shoreline to see where the wall led.

About a bowshot down, the wall met a stone archway that looked like it had once been part of a small castle gate, but there was nothing beyond it other than water. And the glow.

The light shone from beyond the arched doorway. It was coming from the water, and something was surfacing.

Serena took a few steps back from the edge of the lake and watched as a bright orb of white light broke the surface and rose into the air. It stopped above the archway and was almost too bright to look at.

She squinted at the orb and realized it was illuminating words on the inner rocks. She was too far away to make out the writing etched into the stone, and the thought of wading into the water to get closer worried her.

"I can't," she whispered to herself.

"You must," a voice said. It startled her. Like a whisper in her ear, but somehow coming from all around her, it was gentle.

"What? Why?" She turned in a quick circle to look for its source.

There was nobody there.

"It is your birthright," the voice said, and Serena watched as the orb lowered to better illuminate the writing on the arch wall.

She still couldn't make out what it said, so she studied the water. Then she looked at the pendant on her chest. It wasn't glowing, so she couldn't really be in danger, right?

Serena dipped the toe of her riding boot in to see if the ground under the water felt solid, and it did. So, she took a step in. When nothing happened, she took another step. Just as cautiously as when she left the path in the darkness, she walked toward the arch. To her relief, the water stayed about ankle-deep all the way to the gateway.

As she approached, the orb lifted as if to give her space. Its light still illuminated the words on the stone, and Serena read, "Only children of the Mystic Moon may pass."

Serena's breath caught in her throat. "The Mystic Moon?" Wasn't that the order named on the ledger she had found at home?

"What is this place?" she asked aloud.

For a moment, she heard only the water lapping against the land. Looking around her for any other clue, she saw a symbol on the opposite inner wall of the archway. It looked like a crescent moon with a flower nesting in the lower tip. When she stepped closer to the stone for a better view, the orb of light moved to ensure she could see it clearly. To her amazement, inside the center of the flower was etched the letter $\underline{S}$.

The voice whispered in her ear, "That's you."

"Me?"

"Daisy," the voice said.

Just then, the water around her ankles began to swirl counterclockwise, and she felt the ground beneath her roll. Serena struggled to keep her footing as the water sloshed around her.

The orb rose higher in the sky and brighter until she was blinded by it, and she felt herself start to fall as the ground gave way beneath her. "Not again," she thought.

...

Mikal stared at Trevor over the tip of his sword. The tanned carpenter was still standing with his hands raised in surrender. Tom and Tod stood to the side, unsure of what to do other than watch their captain's response.

Mikal slowly lowered his weapon but didn't sheath it. "What do you know of portals?" he asked.

"Kent used them for faster, stealthier movement. I never mastered them," Trevor answered in a steady voice. He lowered his arms to his sides.

"Kent?" Mikal looked back toward the center of the green where he last saw Serena. "Do you think this was his?"

"I don't know anyone else who works with portals, so it's possible."

Tod muttered, "The green that should not be."

Mikal glanced at the young soldier and winced. "I should have been more cautious." The slight nod of agreement Trevor gave only angered him more. "You knew it was here!" Mikal shouted.

"I suspected, but I knew nothing," Trevor answered calmly. "I mean look at this place. It's not natural, so it must be magical."

Tom and Tod exchanged glances as the understanding dawned on them simultaneously. "Magic," Tom whispered.

"Why didn't you say anything?" Mikal asked with anger in his voice.

"I didn't really have a chance," Trevor lied.

"Sir?" Tod asked, pointing down the path where they had entered the green.

Mikal looked around the horses toward the trail and saw Serena walking toward them. "How the..."

Serena plodded back into the meadow with a confused look in her eyes. Her clothes were dingier than they had been, and her boots looked wet. She wore exhaustion like a heavy cloak and came to a stop when she reached the edge of the grass. To everyone's surprise, she plopped down on the white stone just outside the circle and sighed.

Mikal ran toward her but hesitated just a few feet from her. With concern crossing his face, he raised his sword toward her.

"Captain!" Tod yelled as he and Tom ran toward them. "What are you doing?"

"It's not her," Mikal answered without lifting his gaze from Serena. "It can't be."

"I beg your pardon?" Serena said incredulously.

"You're a fake."

"What?" Serena stood, and Mikal followed her motion with his outstretched sword. "I am not."

"You lie. You're fae."

"Fae?" she asked. "Like a changeling or something?"

"Exactly."

"What is wrong with you, Captain?" she asked.

Trevor sauntered over to better hear the conversation and smirked.

Mikal answered, "There is no way that Serena disappeared from the center of the green and less than five minutes later arrived here looking like you do."

Serena looked down at her clothes and then it hit her. "Five minutes?" she asked and sat back down.

"Yes," Mikal answered, still aiming his sword at her.

"I walked for hours," she whispered. "How?"

"Prove yourself," Mikal said sternly. Sweat broke out on his forehead.

"How?" she asked.

"Serena would know."

She lowered her eyes to the ground in thought and sighed. Finally, she told him, "You were there when your sister died."

"Common knowledge," he stated.

"I didn't know it until I touched your arm." The pendant tucked under her tunic started to glow faintly.

Tod elbowed Tom in the arm and pointed to it. "Sir?" he said, but Mikal didn't seem to see it.

"Captain?" Tom said louder than Tod had spoken. "Her necklace."

Serena looked down and noticed the light and pulled her pendant out for all to see. "You would kill me?" she asked with tears in her eyes.

For a moment, no one so much as breathed.

Then Mikal lowered his sword. "No, I would kill an impostor." He was breathing heavy from the strain of trying to decide if this Serena was the true Serena.

The twins relaxed, and Trevor turned back to the horses.

Mikal sheathed his sword and offered his hands to help Serena stand.

She wiped tears from her eyes and told him, "No, thank you. I think I'm going to stay here for a while."

He looked back at Tom and Tod, who were still watching with curiosity. "Go," he told them. "Tend the horses and eat something."

"Yes, sir," they said in unison and left the two alone.

Mikal waited until they were out of earshot and sat down beside Serena. He took a moment to stare at the grass in front of them before saying quietly, "My apologies, my lady. It makes no sense. You disappeared in a flash and then, just moments later, you were walking up the path."

"Looking like this," Serena added.

He looked at her, "Well, yes."

"How was I only gone a few minutes? I don't understand what happened either."

"Tell me where you were."

"I don't know. One second, I was looking at how the grass shimmered and the next, I was lying on a path in dark woods." She paused. "There were swirls of color in between, but it happened so fast."

"Dark woods?"

"Yes, darker than any forest I've ever been in." She described the forest as he listened quietly. "And there was something down the path, waiting in the darkness. It felt like a predator. All I could see were eyes like fire when it opened them. When it closed them, I only saw darkness."

"What did you do?" Mikal asked with concern in his eyes.

"I moved slowly away toward the light in the woods," she answered and explained how she carefully left the trail and walked for miles before reaching the water's edge. Serena told him about the stone wall and archway and how a ball of light illuminated the carvings.

Mikal listened intently and shook his head when she finished. "When you came back through the portal, it dumped you on the trail down the mountain?"

"Yes, and I recognized it, so I came back this way. I wasn't sure you'd still be here because I'd been gone for so long."

"But you weren't."

"But I was."

Mikal put his arm around Serena's shoulder and kissed her forehead. "I'm glad you came back to us."

"I am, too."

They sat in silence for a few minutes before Mikal asked her, "How much time do you need to rest?"

Serena shook her head and stood up. "That was enough. We need to find Mother, and we're wasting daylight."

Mikal stood, too, and looked over toward the others as they lounged in the grass near the grazing horses. "Alright, then. Let's find her."

Serena hesitated to walk into the grass.

"Oh, right," Mikal said and looked down at it. "You said the grass shimmered right before you... I don't even know what to call what happened."

"It did." Serena looked around the green, and it all looked very normal apart from being in the middle of mountains where nothing should grow. She took a careful step into it and paused, waiting for something to happen.

Mikal was patient and didn't take his eyes off her. When she felt comfortable, she took another step and nodded.

"I think we're safe," he told her. "If you see a shimmer, yell this time."

"Yes, sir," she said, and they walked toward the others.

...

Inside the castle at Myribell, King Liam sat at the table in his library, chatting quietly with Erik as they waited for news about the rescue mission.

"It will take at least three days, Sire," Erik assured him. "To get to the borderlands, retrieve Briget, and return requires long rides and little rest."

"I'm not so much concerned about how long they'll take, but how long will it take us to learn of their success? I expected Mikal to send word about their progress with one of the border guards, but we've heard nothing."

Erik nodded and was about to speak when a young soldier with a prematurely receding hairline appeared at the door. He paused, waiting to be acknowledged, and shifted his weight from foot to foot. Erik addressed him after a nod from Liam. "Yes, soldier? What is it?"

"I have news, sir."

The king's eyes brightened. "Yes, son, what is it?"

"It's about your daughter, Sire. The princess is being held at the old manor house Ranald claimed for himself."

Liam slumped in his chair and bowed his head.

The soldier hesitated and looked at Erik for a sign of what to do next.

"Who told you this?" Erik asked.

"Ranald sent a messenger. He's down in the stables awaiting a reply."

"A reply?" Liam asked, lifting his eyes toward the young man.

"Sire," the soldier said quietly, "he says she's being held for ransom. He asked if you'd trade your kingdom for your only daughter." The young man knelt as if he'd asked the question himself. "I'm sorry, Sire."

The king looked at Erik with sadness in his eyes. "I was right. She ran straight to my enemy." Then, realizing the young man was still on one knee, he said. "Stand up. Return to the messenger and tell him to wait for my answer. Offer him food and water, but do not let him leave the stables. He may be a spy, and I'd rather him not see more of the castle than he needs to."

The young man stood up and left the room quickly.

"So, she thought Ranald would help her?" Erik asked.

"Likely so," Liam answered.

"Do you think he's lying?"

The king lowered his gaze to the table in front of him and paused before answering. "I'm not sure. If she went seeking help, that means they were plotting against me as we suspected, but her actions have left her without any clout, so he'd have no use for her now."

"But would he hold her for ransom, or would he pretend to hold her for ransom?"

"I wouldn't put either option past him." Liam stroked his chin in thought. "If he believed I would hand my kingdom over for a daughter who betrayed me, he might ransom her."

"Would you, Sire?"

"Would I what?"

"Trade the kingdom for her life?"

Liam lifted his eyes again to meet Erik's. "I hope I don't need to."

...

Kent's men lounged in seemingly random groups around the big cave. Most never gave Briget a second thought, but a few would glance her way with curious eyes. She imagined they wondered why Kent was keeping her alive. They wouldn't understand how bindings work. Magic needs to be undone by the same blood that made it work in the first place.

None of the men came close to Briget while they rested. Kent didn't seem worried that she'd try to escape. He was always overly sure of himself, but she remembered he wasn't the powerful one anymore. No, Shade was the new protégé, and he radiated dark energy. She still hadn't seen his eyes, but she had worked through the possible soul-barts that he could have dealt with as she rested and waited.

After her quick telepathic hit from Serena, Briget tried to reach out to her daughter to find out what caused it, but she couldn't make contact. Instead, she prayed for Serena's protection and searched the walls of the cave for signs of alternative entrances. While the entire gang easily passed through Shade's portal, someone must have entered the cave by more mundane means in the past. A hole big enough for a curious man would be big enough for her to slip through.

Occasionally, she felt a light breeze coming from somewhere, but the direction always shifted. Could there be more than one entrance?

As her gaze moved across the far wall, movement toward her attracted her attention. Kent was heading her way. Briget dropped her eyes to her lap for a moment and feigned a yawn.

"Not enough excitement for you?" Kent asked as he approached.

"I expected more," she answered dryly.

"Wait for it," he assured her. "We have big things planned." He waved his scarred hands as if to illuminate the cave.

"Do tell."

He looked her over with disdain. "No, I think I'll let you be surprised." He knelt to meet Briget at eye level. "When your daughter and her guardsmen come looking for you, you'll see we're full of surprises."

"What makes you sure she'll be the one looking for me?"

"She's your daughter, right? And Waylon's? It's in her blood to be a hound dog, whether she knows it or not."

Briget let herself smile.

"You're proud of her, and yet you've hidden the truth from her."

"How would you know that?"

"I have eyes and ears everywhere, always have." He sneered. "Even without the demon's influence, I have my ways."

"Ways?" she mocked. "You have Ranald's henchmen."

"They count, too," he said with confidence and added, "If you only knew how much they count."

"So, he has spies in Myribell? We already knew that." Briget told him. "The most obvious one left of her own accord, though."

"Eh?"

"The Princess Shaylea. The king finally had enough of her entitled attitude and stripped her of her inheritance, so she left." Briget watched as the news hit Kent hard. Shay's tantrum meant a change of plans for the king's enemies.

He quickly recovered, though. "No matter. I don't need her, anyway. I only need your dear sweet daughter to come save her mother."

"Don't underestimate her," Briget told him.

"She's nothing," he scoffed.

"You said yourself," Briget nearly growled, "she's my daughter."

"And you," Kent whispered, "Why have you not fought back?"

Briget threw glances at the men scattered throughout the spacious cave. "I'm clearly outnumbered."

Kent stood, and a dark grin crossed his scarred face. "So, you are." He looked around the cave. "It's too bad." He turned and strolled across the cave, back into the shadows.

"I could have been a powerful witch," Briget whispered to herself, "But that's not the path I chose."

...

As Mikal watched Trevor stroke his horse's neck, he considered the man's past. After a moment, he asked in a measured tone, "What do you know of portals, Mister Ash?"

Trevor allowed a smile to cross his face before meeting Mikal's gaze. "I know a little."

"Can you tell me how they work?"

"No," Trevor answered coolly.

Serena watched Mikal strain to hold his temper. "Why not?" she asked on his behalf.

Trevor turned to face her and explained, "I'm not sure anyone knows how they work."

"Ah," Serena nodded. "Magic can be complicated."

"Truly," Trevor said.

Mikal shook his head. "Let me start again," he said. "How does a wizard create a portal?"

"Now that is a better question," Trevor nodded. "It takes knowing the right incantation, having the right kind of place, and," he paused, "more power than I've ever had."

"Really?" Serena asked and thought for a moment. "You couldn't have done that?"

"No, not even at my best."

Mikal looked at the area where Serena had disappeared and scratched his head. "I thought you were one of the top three of your time," he finally said to Trevor.

"I was. It looks like Kent found someone better."

While they talked, Serena had a hit of intuition about the carpenter. "You are a natural?" she asked.

Trevor looked at her with a glint of pride in his eyes. "Yes."

She nodded and said quietly, "That explains so much."

Mikal looked confused. "What does that explain?"

Serena answered, "There are different types of wizards. Naturals can be powerful in their own right, but there are certain things they can't do, like bending the laws of nature to their will. For that, a wizard must find a soul-bart."

"Soul-bart?" Tom asked. He and Tod had been listening quietly and pretending to be focused on their horses, but now his attention was outwardly on the conversation.

"Yes," Serena answered. "Trevor could probably explain better, but it's a sort of demon that lends a wizard power in return for their soul when they eventually die."

Tom gulped hard. "You mean demons are real?"

Tod stood up and chimed in, "But Father told us they were just stories the old priest made up to keep us in line."

Trevor scoffed. "Demons are most definitely real."

"Have you seen one?" Tom asked.

Trevor stared at his feet for a moment before answering, "I have seen the shadow of one. When it learned I wasn't interested in a trade, it went back into the darkness from which it came."

"I have to admire that," Serena said.

Mikal glared at her, and she felt his disapproval.

"What did it look like?" Tod asked eagerly.

"Just a shadow, but darker than dark, and it had glowing eyes like fire."

Serena felt sick when she heard his description, and Mikal's disapproving glare shifted to concern. "Like fire," she repeated.

"Yes," Trevor said, and he gave her a sideways glance.

Tom asked the next question. "How can you tell if a wizard met a ... what do you call it? Soul-bart?"

"His eyes will have the glow of the demon's eyes. They'll be the same color as the demon's, and the demon will use his eyes to see the world around them."

Tom frowned. "So, if a wizard looks at you with the demon's glow, it's really the demon looking at you?"

"In a way, but the wizard is looking at you just the same. They share the same eyes until the wizard dies. Then the demon consumes his soul," Trevor explained. "Or hers," he added.

"Wait," Tom said, "a woman can be a wizard?"

"We would call her a witch," Trevor said.

"That's why calling an energy healer a witch is an insult," Serena told them. "We come by it naturally, and our only goal is to heal. A witch gets her power unnaturally, and her goal is to do whatever it takes to gain more power. Same as a soul-bart's wizard."

Tom and Tod nodded in unison.

"So, Trevor," Mikal said, "You were the most powerful of the wizards until they traded up."

"You could say that."

"What kept you from doing the same?" Mikal asked.

"Fear," Trevor admitted. "Or pride. Or both."

"You're smarter than I gave you credit for," Mikal told him.

Trevor laughed. "Thanks, I guess."

Serena brought the conversation back to the portal. "So, Kent must have a powerful, unnatural wizard working for him."

"It seems that way," Trevor said. "Kent would know the incantation, but with your mother's binding, he'd need someone else to do the work."

"Same as with the storm and the trees twisting into a cage?" Tod asked.

"Yes," Trevor answered.

"Any ideas who that might be?" Trevor asked.

"I'm sorry to say I've been out of that life for so long that I do not know who else might be around to do it."

Serena wondered if the apology was for not being able to answer or not being able to live his old life.

Mikal continued questioning, "Does a portal have to lead to the same place every time you use it?"

"I don't think so," Trevor answered and thought about it for a second. "No, we had one that Kent created that would take him anywhere he wanted." He looked at Mikal's astonishment, and added, "Except for the castle of Myribell." Then he looked at Serena. "Your parents made sure of that."

"So, this portal that took Serena wherever she was could also take us to her mother?"

"In theory, yes."

"How can we harness that?"

Trevor laughed again. "Your guess is as good as mine!"

...

Shay stared into the dingy mirror across the small room from the old bed where she sat and wondered if her father would step up and ransom her. This room was an improvement from the cell where Ranald first held her, but it was not fit for the Princess of Myribell. Her treatment wasn't either. The guards still acted as though she might run at any time even though she came to Ranald of her own volition and helped him devise the new plan.

They didn't knock before they opened the door to let her know Ranald had news for her. They didn't bow when they told her they were going to take her to him. The men were gruff and apathetic, but at least they weren't mishandling her the way they did when she first arrived.

She followed the two brutes down the dim corridors to the throne room where Ranald waited. He sat in a large, upholstered chair with a wrought iron frame that hadn't been cleaned in years—much like the rest of the bare-bones castle. The longer Shay was there, the more she realized this building was held together by not much more than Ranald's delusions of grandeur. He had taken it when the former owner abandoned it for a palatial estate farther from the borderlands, and he was just a squatter plotting to take something bigger and better, with her help.

A smirk crossed his bearded face when she entered the room. In his left hand, he held a parchment letter. "This is from your father," he told her as he unrolled it. "Ranald, I have received your offer," he read, "but I cannot afford the ransom you ask. You expect me to sacrifice the safety of my people in exchange for a daughter who never appreciated all I gave her? Although I love her dearly, the exchange does not seem fair. I'm sure by now, you have seen her true personality shine through. If you decide she's too much to live with, feel free to return her to Myribell. She will be welcomed back with open arms, but not open coffers."

Shay held her composure despite the blow. She had been sure her father would agree to anything to assure her safety. Her mind raced through the possibilities of what might happen to her now.

Ranald rose from his throne so that he towered over her. "Your father is smarter than you give him credit for." She said nothing. "Now, the question is what shall I do with a broken princess that nobody wants."

Shay winced. "I can still get you into the castle."

"How?" Ranald asked, raising an eyebrow.

"You heard him. Send me back. You said yourself I'm worth more inside." Ranald rolled his eyes. "I'll go back with my tail between my legs, make some lame apologies, and be on the inside to open the gates when your men are ready."

"Why would he trust you to do anything but sit in your chamber and sulk?"

"My point exactly. He wouldn't, so he wouldn't expect me to betray him after you decided you had no use for me."

"He'll be watching you."

"Not if you distract him."

Ranald sat back down and pondered his next move. After what seemed like minutes, he nodded. "My plan will have to change, but I can make this work."

"And when you're inside, we will take control and rule Myribell together."

The smirk returned. "Yes, when I'm inside, your world will change forever."

...

"Dusk nears," Serena whispered to Mikal. They were still standing in the grassy meadow, contemplating their options while the horses rested and the other three lounged nearby, awaiting orders.

"I know," he answered softly. "Without magic, we're not opening the portal. We'll have to find another way to reach your mother."

"I think she's inside the mountain," Serena nodded toward the white peak rising to the side of the green grass. They were halfway up in elevation but had yet to see a cave entrance. "There must be a way in big enough for a man to fit, or they never would have found shelter inside."

Mikal nodded absently. "We need to move on, then, and keep climbing."

Serena thought for a moment, turning to face the patch of grass where the portal had opened earlier. "What if we can open it?"

"You heard Trevor. He doesn't know how. Do you?"

"No, but I'm not above trying."

Mikal furrowed his brow. "Is there something you're not telling me?"

Serena put her hands on her hips and answered sharply, "No."

"Then, how do you plan to do something natural healers can't do without help?"

Serena glanced at Trevor and then back to Mikal. "I think if he works with me, we can do it together."

Mikal bristled. "You're forgetting something about Mister Ash."

"Oh, right. He can't do magic," Serena said. "But why do I keep feeling like he can?"

As if he'd heard the conversation from thirty feet away, Trevor stood and strode over to join them. Mikal greeted him with a suspicious look.

"Were your ears burning?" Serena asked.

Trevor shrugged. "Should they have been?"

Mikal pointed at Serena. "She gets the feeling you can still do magic," he told Trevor.

"She should know better," he replied. "Her parents bound me."

"They bound you from harming anyone with magic," Mikal said.

"Yes."

Serena's eyes lit up. "That's it! They bound you from harming anyone, but did they bind you from doing any magic?"

Defeat crossed Trevor's face and his eyes darkened. "They didn't have to."

"What do you mean?" Mikal asked.

"I mean, the king made sure I never did magic for any reason. As part of his merciful leniency, for me to make a respectable life for myself in Myribell, I had to swear never to use any magic for any reason."

"And you swore?" Mikal asked.

"I did."

"But the king couldn't possibly have known a situation would arise all these years later that would require your gifts," Serena assured them.

"I can't do it," Trevor said, grimacing. "If I want to stay in Myribell, I can't break that promise."

"Why do you want to stay in Myribell?" Mikal asked him.

Trevor paused for a long moment before answering, "My daughter is there."

Mikal nodded, and confusion hit Serena. "Your daughter?" she asked.

"Long story," Trevor said as he shot Mikal a glance.

Serena put her hands on her hips and shot them both a look of disgust. "What are you <u>both</u> not telling me now?"

Mikal dropped his gaze to the grass at her feet. Trevor shrugged again before admitting, "The king's granddaughter is my daughter."

Serena's jaw dropped. She stood still, staring at him for a moment before forming the question, "You and Shay?"

A bit of pride glinted from Trevor's eyes, and his mouth curled into a smile. "Don't look so surprised. It was a long time ago, and I was in my prime."

Serena stifled the urge to laugh. Trevor was not a bad-looking man, but to consider him having a relationship with the spoiled, beautiful princess was more than she could comprehend.

Mikal said softly, "Some women are attracted to powerful men."

Serena shook her head. "I guess," she said, "I never really got to know her, so I wouldn't know what to expect of her." She let a small laugh escape. "Yes, why not?"

The three stood in awkward silence before Serena remembered her initial question. "But you can do magic?"

Trevor sighed. "Yes, technically, but the king would expel me from the realm, and that would be the end of my chance at seeing my daughter ever again."

Mikal gave him a look of deep consideration. "You just met her for the first time, though, right?"

"Yes, the king finally decided I earned a meeting."

"You'd never met her before?" Serena said, disbelieving.

"No, she's been a well-kept secret. The king said I needed to prove myself worthy before he'd let me near her."

"She is the heir to the throne now," Mikal said in approval of the king's decision.

Serena recalled her conversation with the king. The child was the heir, but if anything should happen to Liam before she came of age, Serena would be regent. It was all too much to think about, so she reminded herself of the task at hand.

"Trevor, I need you to help me open the portal."

"No," he said flatly.

"It's alright," she urged. "I'll vouch for you with the king. I'll tell him I begged you to do it to help find my mother faster."

"I swore no magic." He looked at Mikal and then back into Serena's pleading eyes. "Besides, the captain here is the one I'd need to vouch for me."

"You will," Serena said to Mikal, "won't you?"

Mikal drew a deep breath and let it out. "I would rather find another way." He looked at Serena. "If neither of you knows what you're doing, why do you think it will work?"

"I know that magic is based on intention, and our intention is to find my mother and bring her home safely. The incantation is secondary."

Trevor laughed. "I'm not so sure about that."

"What's the worst that can happen?" she asked.

"We end up part of a cave wall."

"What?" Mikal asked, incredulously.

"How?" Serena asked.

"We don't know how to bend the rules of nature, so if we mess up, any number of unnatural, catastrophic things might happen. That seems like the worst possibility to my imagination, but there's probably worse."

"If we don't try it," Serena said, "Who knows how long it will take to find a way into the mountain?"

Mikal asked Trevor, "Do you know of any openings to the caves Kent uses inside Mount Pilkin?"

"No," he answered quickly.

"Have you ever been inside the mountain?" Mikal asked.

Trevor hesitated. "I don't know."

"What do you mean, you don't know?"

"I've been inside _a_ mountain, but it might not have been _that_ mountain."

Serena asked, "Does it matter to open the portal?"

"You're not opening a portal," Mikal told her sharply.

"I don't know," Trevor answered her.

"It will be the quickest way to Mother," Serena said, looking at Mikal.

"You heard the man; it's not safe," he replied.

"I think I can protect us," Serena urged.

"With what? A bubble?" There was condescension in Mikal's voice now.

Trevor shook his head. "All your energy will need to be focused on the portal. It's too hard to do both."

"Then _you_ protect us," she told Trevor.

"No," Mikal said.

"If he can still do magic, he can protect us." Serena could see Trevor weighing his options, so she continued. "Look, we can try to find an entrance to Mount Pilkin and hope nobody is guarding it, or we can try it this way. Finding our way in could take a long time since we don't know where to start, but if I can open a portal with Trevor's help, our mission will end much faster."

Trevor stayed quiet while Mikal aired his thoughts. "What makes you think you can suddenly go from healing and light bubbles to opening portals? Trevor just said that takes a demon's influence. You didn't make a deal with one when you disappeared and did not tell me, did you?"

Serena shook her head. "No." The memory of those blazing eyes flashed through her mind, and she added, "At least I didn't speak to it."

Trevor glared at her. "What?"

Mikal held up his hand to stop her from answering Trevor and repeated, "What makes you think you can do it?"

"I can't tell you. A feeling, maybe? An intuition?" Serena answered.

Before Mikal could reply, Trevor answered. "If you promise to back me if the king inquires, I'll do what I can to protect us."

"Now you think she can do this?" Mikal asked incredulously.

"I'm not sure, but if she wants to try, who am I to stop her?"

The captain threw his hands up in frustration.

"I can do this," Serena said with more confidence than she felt. "Magic is all about intention, right?"

"And talent and power," Trevor added.

"I have a strong intention of finding my mother and bring her home safely."

"But you don't know the incantation, and you've never done anything like this before," Mikal argued.

She looked at Trevor, "Do you recall the words Kent used?"

He thought for a moment before answering, "No."

"Doesn't matter," she told him.

"It doesn't?" Mikal asked.

"I mean, it shouldn't matter," she corrected herself. "I use no words for most of the healing work I do."

"What do you use, then?" Trevor asked, looking perplexed.

"Just energy and intention. I visualize the person being healed with the sickness leaving their body or their wound closing or whatever is necessary to make it happen."

"Interesting," he said.

Mikal looked back at Tom, Tod, and the horses. "Can you protect all of us, including the animals?"

"I can," Trevor answered, "but I need your assurance before I do anything."

"Granted," Mikal said coolly.

...

Cut off from natural light, Briget had no idea what time it was, but she guessed the sun must be setting by now. Hours in the cave had yielded plenty of time to think and observe but little else. She watched the smoke from the small campfires around the space rise toward the ceiling and slowly spread out in all directions. She noticed where it seemed trapped in alcoves and how, in one corner, there seemed to be a place for it to flow. It was the same corner she thought a light breeze occasionally flowed from.

Now the campfires were being used to warm water and simple meals of red potatoes and deer meat. She wondered where they hunted. Without natural grassy areas in the White Mountains, deer were rare here. As she pondered, the odd little man, Elian, returned to her with water and a hot potato.

"Kent allowed me to bring you some food," he said quietly.

"That was nice of you to ask him," Briget said as she took it from him.

"You must be hungry," he said, looking around nervously.

"I am, but I have another need, as well," Briget whispered.

"Aye?" He asked.

"Yes," she leaned closer to him and said softly, "I need to relieve myself."

"Oh! Oh," he blushed a little.

"Is there somewhere I can have just a little privacy for that purpose?" she asked.

"Um," he hesitated, looking back toward Kent, whose back was facing them.

"I'm sure you understand. A woman needs to feel comfortable for that."

"Ah, well..."

"Is there an alcove I can duck down, just out of sight for a moment?" She paused and looked at the walls of the cave. "Or are those all tunnels?"

"Oh, no," he replied. "There's only one tunnel out. The rest are alcoves or dead ends."

"Surely one of them would be safe to use?" she asked, trying to hide her satisfaction at receiving confirmation on the way out.

Elian looked back toward Kent again, and after a moment, he seemed convinced that the dark wizard was too involved in conversation to notice. He turned back to Briget and nodded. "Quickly, come this way."

"Thank you," Briget whispered, trying to sound desperate for relief.

...

Tom and Tod spoke in hushed tones as they prepared the horses to leave the meadow.

"Do you think they can do it?" Tom asked his twin.

"I'm not willing to put coin on it."

"Ah, come on. Just a little wager."

"Pa always told us not to bet on unknowns."

Tom shook his head, "But it's the unknowns that make it fun!"

Tod looked at Serena, sitting on the grass with her eyes closed. "Is she praying?"

"I would be," Tom laughed quietly.

"Do you think it's safe?"

"Don't know. It can't be worse than sitting here waiting for an ambush, can it?"

Tod shrugged. "If they know we're looking for her, why don't they just come fetch us? It would save us a lot of time."

"Because," Mikal said from behind him, "Kent wants to make us work for our prize. He needs Serena and Briget alive, and he needs us unprepared."

Tod winced. "Ah."

Tom asked, "And how do we prepare to go through a portal, if the young lady can create one?"

Mikal answered, "Keep your eyes open with one hand on the horses' reins, and one hand on your weapon. Be ready to feel sick or out of sorts. Serena said her trip through the portal was dizzying, but she recovered quickly."

"What if it makes the horses sick, or worse. What if they bolt?" Tom wondered.

"Kent must take his horses through when they shelter in the cave. Otherwise, we'd see them out here somewhere." Mikal patted his horse on the neck. "Ours should be able to handle it as they handled entering the mountain pass."

"Right," Tod said. "The one that couldn't handle magic already bolted."

"Just in case, though," Mikal said, "we walk the horses through. It should be safer than riding them."

The twins nodded, and Mikal motioned that they follow him to where Serena sat with Trevor kneeling beside her.

Trevor acknowledged them as they came closer. "We're nearly ready. She's focusing her energy on the same spot where the portal opened before. I'll shield us when it opens, and we'll enter as a group."

"Are we to expect a bubble of light like she used in the farmhouse?" Tod asked Mikal.

Mikal answered, "That is a question for Mister Ash."

Trevor shook his head. "I don't work like that. A healer works with white light. I work with raw energy."

Tom squinted at him as he tried to understand.

Trevor continued, "My protection is less subtle, but it works. I can't explain it to someone who's never done magic before. So, just stick close and do as we say, and you should be fine."

Mikal shrugged, and the twins gave each other sideways glances.

"I'm ready," Serena said calmly and opened her eyes.

She stood and looked at each man to assure herself they were ready, too. Mikal's face was set like stone. The twins faked smiles, and Trevor looked at her with the same look he had given her on the village green. His eyes were intense but friendly, so she took it as a good sign. "Alright, let's do this. Everyone, focus on a positive outcome for saving my mother."

They nodded agreement as she rubbed her hands together for a moment. Then she pushed her palms away from her, spread her fingers, and focused her energy on the grass in front of her. She stood like that for a minute as everyone waited for something to change.

Nothing happened.

She dropped her hands and looked at Trevor. He gave her the same look but tinged with a slight grin this time. "Shake it off," he told her. "Try again."

She looked back at the others, and they all shot her weak smiles and nods.

"Alright," she said. "I can do this." The last part was more to herself than to them.

"You can," Trevor told her.

She rubbed her hands together again, but this time, she raised them to the sky and exclaimed, "Creator of all that is, ancients who know the words, helpers who assist those who love, and Order of the Mystic Moon, lend me your will!"

There was a loud crack of thunder despite the cloudless sky. Mikal watched as Serena's hands started to glow. At first, they took on a golden aura, but it faded and pulsed to light green, then to sea blue and finally to violet before swirling into rainbows like a kaleidoscope made by a perfectly carved crystal held to the sunlight.

Keeping her arms stretched out but lowering them toward the space in front of her, she yelled, "Open the path to our success!"

The grass began to shimmer beneath them, and the air started to move. The colors that had pulsed around Serena's hands shot out from them and hit an invisible wall. It sparked and began to swirl counterclockwise in front of her, and for just an instant, she saw the image of a daisy in her mind's eye.

"Trevor, now!" she yelled, and Trevor spread his arms wide, raised his palms facing out to the sides, and said, "Follow me!"

While Serena held the portal open, Trevor led them into the swirling colors. As he hit the wall, sparks shot from his still-raised palms and found their targets in men and horses. Mikal watched as one took aim and hit him square in the chest. The impact made him shudder, and a heat like fire spread through him. He looked down to make sure there were no flames before walking toward the portal. The twins followed, and they noticed Serena was not hit by Trevor's magic.

Walking through the swirling colors disoriented them, but they kept their balance. One by one, they emerged, but to where? They were standing in total darkness. Colors still circled behind them, and Trevor whisper-yelled to Serena, "We're here! Cross through!"

They all heard another crack of thunder and saw a figure punch through the shrinking circles and stumble into Trevor.

He caught Serena by the arms and held her up as she found her footing. "I have you," he whispered.

"Thanks," she said, leaning on him and trying to catch her breath. Her balance felt a little off, and when she opened her eyes, she realized the darkness she sensed was literal.

"I think we're here," Mikal whispered.

"Where?" Tod asked quietly, following the captain's lead with hushed tones.

"In the cave," Mikal answered.

"That would explain the darkness," Tom observed. "We didn't totally think that through, did we? Could've used a lantern or torch."

Serena tried to step away from Trevor, who had moved his hands from her arms to an embrace, but she lost her footing and ended up on her knees. "Ouch!"

"I said I had you," Trevor sounded hurt.

"I'm sorry, but I need space," Serena whispered. "My head is still... off kilter." She took a few deep breaths and planted her hands on the cold stone below her. "We're definitely in a cave. I can feel the energy of Mount Pilkin's quartz."

She felt a hand on her shoulder. "There you are," Mikal said quietly.

"Yes," Serena said and patted his hand. He clasped hers and helped her stand again. She heard Trevor take two steps away from them.

Tom broke his silence. "Begging my lady's pardon, but if you can stretch the fabric of time and space, do you think you can procure us some light?

Tod quipped. "That shouldn't be hard at all."

Serena chuckled. Despite the seriousness of the situation, it was funny. "I'm sorry, you only get one magic trick per show," she answered.

"Do you smell that?" Tom asked.

Serena inhaled deeply. "Yes."

"Smells like dinner," Trevor said.

Mikal hushed them. "Campfires in a cave. Serena, you did it!" he whispered.

"But how can we tell which way to go? The smell surrounds us," she wondered.

They stood in silence for a moment. Then one of the horses stomped the ground, and she saw a spark.

"That's it," Mikal said.

"What?" Tod and Tom asked in unison.

"Find two good sized rocks," he told them. "Quietly, now. And we need some fabric and alcohol."

"Where will we find alcohol?" Serena asked.

Tod giggled.

"Oh," she said. "I have fabric." She reached down and ripped the hem of her tunic that was already frayed from her first trip through the portal. She handed it blindly to Mikal who felt her bump him with it. She heard him unsheathe his sword.

"I found two stones," Tom whispered.

"Bring them here," Mikal told him.

"Where?"

"Follow my voice. There. Thank you."

Serena hoped that meant Mikal now had the stones.

"Here's the drink," Tod said quietly. "It's not much."

"I'm not one to judge at the moment," Mikal assured him.

After almost a minute of near silence, there was a <u>clack</u>. Then another, and sparks flew. After two more, the fabric provided a tiny flame, and Serena noticed it seemed to be wrapped around the sharp end of Mikal's sword.

"Smart," said Trevor. "Don't you think they'll see us now?"

"No," said Mikal. "They're camping in a cave lit by fire. Our little flame won't even catch their eyes."

Now that Serena could see each of their faces in the dim light, she let out a sigh of relief that none of them had been fused to the cave wall, and the horses had made it through, too.

...

Inside a shallow alcove behind the cover of a stalagmite, Briget stood quietly and took stock of her situation. She had done what she told Elian she needed to but was taking her time to return to him. She could see him waiting patiently, with his back to her.

She scanned the large cave, sighting Kent eating with a few of his larger men. They looked like giants compared to him, and he was still taller than she was. Briget also noted that many of the horses seemed restless suddenly. She stilled her breath and listened intently. Was that thunder? Surely, they couldn't hear a storm this deep inside the mountain.

Her thoughts turned to Serena, and she instantly felt the answer. Her rescue party was on the way. Now she had to decide if she should stay sheltered in the alcove or be out in the open when they found their way to the grand hall of Mount Pilkin. Unsure how Kent's men would respond to their entrance or what they planned to do, she hurried back to Elian and told him she was ready to enjoy that potato he'd brought her.

"Ay, lady," he said as he walked with her to her spot by the cave wall. "We never know when our next meal will come." After a short bow, he turned and walked to join the other men.

...

Shay's arrival at the castle gates sparked whispers and pointed fingers. Despite her tattered dress and tired eyes, she sat upright and as proud as ever on her stallion.

"I hoped to never see her again," she heard one old lady whisper to another.

"Don't let her hear you," the other whispered back.

"Why not?" the first said in a bolder voice. "It's not like she can do anything about it now."

Shay kept her focus on the guard at the gate, who eyed her suspiciously. "I need to speak to my father," she told him in a casual tone.

The guard said nothing, but nodded, and knocked on the heavy wood with his long spear. The door swung open and allowed Shay to enter without dismounting. "Thank you," she said without looking at the guard again.

He furrowed his brow in disbelief and watched her enter, and the gate swung shut behind her.

Inside the walls of the castle, Shay directed her horse into the stables. Always courteous, the stable boy took the reins as she dismounted and gave her a quick bow. Then he quickly guided the horse to a stall and out of her sight.

"I think His Majesty will be relieved to see you," the graying guard said as he stepped out from a shadow.

Shay recognized him as Erik, one of her father's favorites. "I'm sure you're right," she replied without thinking. Then, remembering that she was supposed to be humiliated, she added, "I hope."

Erik stepped toward the side door that led into the winding hallways of the lower floor of the castle and told her, "Follow me."

Shay obeyed and followed the man through the halls and up the stairs until they reached the small dining room off the kitchen, where Liam sat with Eleanor, finishing a quiet dinner of quail and green beans.

Shay's throat caught at the sight of her daughter, whom she hadn't laid eyes on in years. The child was beautiful with the sun-kissed skin and dark eyes and hair of her father, but her delicate cheeks and lips favored Shay's own features.

"Excuse me, Sire, but you requested when your daughter arrives, that I bring her directly to you."

"Thank you, Erik," Liam said with a nod. He turned to Shay with assessing eyes. "My daughter, I am thankful you are alive. Ranald could have done worse than to let you return."

Erik stepped out into the hallway to leave them alone.

"I am grateful to be alive, too," Shay said as humbly as she could. She glanced at their nearly empty plates but did not look again at the child. "I could use a meal, if you don't mind."

"Ah, yes!" Liam said with enthusiasm. "Eleanor, my dear, be a sweetheart and let your mom know we need another plate for the princess."

Without a word, the little girl scooted her chair from the table, curtsied to the king, and ran through the servant's door to alert Jeryl of their need.

"She's such a bright child," Liam said fondly as he watched her go. "Quite sweet, too." He looked back at Shay and motioned for her to take the chair next to him. "Please, sit."

She took her place beside him and tried to keep her expression neutral. "I appreciate the hospitality," she told him quietly. "I am not sure I would do the same."

"I'm sure you wouldn't," the king said with a laugh. "If I left the safety of the castle, you would change the locks and wish me dead." There was no malice in his voice, despite the truth of what he said.

Shay didn't know how to reply, so she said nothing and only looked down at her hands, dirty for the grime of Ranald's old castle and the reins of her horse.

Liam continued, "My daughter, I have given you all I could since you came into this world, and yet, you've returned nothing but resentment and betrayal. Yet, I am still grateful you are here, and that Ranald did not harm more than your ego. You can live safely in this castle until your last breath, if you choose, but if you leave again, I may remember the old wounds and lose my ability to forgive one last time."

Shay understood the threat in Liam's declaration, but not the love. How could the old man forgive her behavior and expect her to believe he could act like she had never left? It didn't matter. In just a day, Ranald's plan would be in motion and her father would meet his fate. She only had to pretend she'd learned some stupid lesson long enough to let the enemy inside. "I thank you, Sire," she said softly and waited in silence for her dinner.

...

The bit of fabric wrapped around Mikal's sword burned faster than they hoped it would as the small rescue party led the horses as quietly as possible through the narrow passage toward the much larger part of the cave system. With each step, Serena heard the voices of Kent's men grow louder and prayed they were making enough noise to keep them from noticing the horses' hooves against the stone floor.

They arrived at the opening to the great hall of Mount Pilkin from the side opposite the wall Briget was leaning against, and their motion immediately caught her attention. "Mother!" Serena whispered.

Briget gave her a slight nod to let her know she saw them and touched her hair to signal she was unhurt.

Mikal put his hand on Serena's shoulder to keep her from moving further as he assessed the men in the cave. She did the same and noticed that a man in wizard's robes was chatting with two large goons wearing long swords. Beside them sat men of more normal sizes who seemed to be finishing a meal. Others were scattered around small campfires throughout the vast space in various stages of dining and relaxing. A few even looked as though they were sleeping with rolls of cloth under their heads. None of them seemed to expect company.

"Kent?" she whispered with her finger pointing toward the robed man.

Mikal nodded.

"Where's the soul-traded one?" she asked.

From behind her, Trevor tapped her right shoulder and drew her attention to a man in a hooded cloak leaning against the cave wall, alone and about thirty feet from Kent. Serena shuddered. Her intuition told her the man felt like ice but had eyes of fire. And then she saw them.

As if on cue, the young man raised his chin just enough to allow the hood to fall backward and show his face. He opened his eyes to stare directly at Serena. She involuntarily took a step back into Trevor, who put his hands on her sides to steady her. "Do you see his eyes?" she asked.

In unison, Mikal and Trevor answered, "Yes."

The demon looked out from the young man's face with flaming orange eyes.

"I've seen those before," Serena whispered. "When I first went through the portal and landed in the dark forest."

"He was waiting for you," Trevor said knowingly.

She turned her head to face him. "How do you know that?"

"He was waiting for me when I met him."

"That was him?" Tod whispered. "The one who wanted you?"

"Sh!" Mikal hushed them. "He sees us, but let's not draw any more attention."

Everything in Serena's gut warned her to run, but Trevor held her steady. Or was he holding her still? She suddenly didn't trust his touch. He had said a demon tried bartering for his soul, and he turned it down. But did he really? Did it matter?

Her mother sat against one wall, the soul-bartered wizard sat against another, and they still weren't sure where the way out was.

The demon blinked slowly at Serena and her blood ran cold. She closed her eyes and shook her head to clear her mind. Her mother's voice in her ear said, "We stand together now." It was so close and so real that Serena opened her eyes and looked beside her. There was nothing but cold quartz, so she looked back toward where her mother still sat.

Briget nodded again.

"Alright," Serena whispered, and forcibly broke Trevor's hold on her waist. "What's the plan, Captain?"

Mikal was watching the young wizard stand. "We move to protect your mother. You stay behind all of us, including the horses. We're your shield."

Kent noticed the young man's change in position and followed the direction his demonic eyes stared.

"Now!" Mikal didn't bother whispering anymore, and the group pulled the horses across the distance to Briget quickly. Briget stood and grabbed Serena's hand as they neared and pulled her against the wall, behind the horses as Mikal hoped she would.

Serena gave Briget an unsure glance, but Briget's smile was real, and her touch was reassuring. "It will be alright." Briget said. "We can..."

Kent's voice echoing through the cavern cut her words off. "Well, what do we have here? A rescue party?"

Mikal, Tod, and Tom stood in front of their horses with their swords raised, ready for battle. Serena noticed Trevor stood a few feet to the side. "He's unarmed," she whispered to Briget. "He should be back here."

"He's always armed," Briget said.

Kent held one hand out toward the young wizard, who had started walking toward the group. His eyes still burned with the demon's power, but he obeyed the older man. "Good, Shade," Kent said to him. "Thank you."

The young man blinked in response, and the flames in his eyes seemed to shrink. He seemed surprised by Kent's words.

"Shade?" Serena asked.

"Yes," Briget said.

Suddenly "Beware of shade" took on a whole new meaning Serena never would have expected.

"He's powerful, demon-possessed, and just barely in control."

"He is," Kent agreed as he closed the distance between himself and the rescue party. "I suspect that he's happier to see you than I am."

Trevor snorted, and the whole group looked at him. "What?" he asked. "Demons aren't as patient as you'd think."

Shade stared at Trevor in recognition and said, "I know you."

"Yes, yes, we all know Trevor Ash," Kent said dismissively. "The wizard who went good." There was sarcasm in his tone.

Trevor stiffened. "I had my reasons."

"Of course you did. We all have our reasons," Kent told him. "Briget had her reasons for binding us, the captain has his reasons for fighting us, and young Miss Serena back there will soon have her own reasons for hating us."

"I hate no one," Serena said reflexively.

"Oh? How nice," he said with the insincerity of a lion apologizing to its dinner.

Mikal finally spoke. "We're here now. What is your plan, Kent? We know you needed Serena and Briget together."

Kent gestured widely to the gathering men. "It was so nice for you to deliver her directly to us." The men laughed. "What's my plan?" Kent repeated. "My plan is to undo the binding that's kept me from gaining what's mine all these years."

"What's yours?" Tod asked.

"My power. My wealth. My freedom." Kent answered casually. "My revenge," he added. "Now, young miss, I suggest you keep holding your mother's hand through this next part. You'll need her strength... at least until it's gone."

He pointed toward the little group and his men descended on them quickly. Mikal engaged and found the mercenaries had weapons, but little skill in combat. Tod and Tom instinctively took their stand back-to-back, swords facing out. They began to rotate, wielding their swords with all the agility of a trained team. Serena realized the fun and antics she witnessed at the celebration dinner were training for real combat.

Trevor stepped farther to the side and started mumbling to himself. The horses scattered, and Shade took a few steps closer and raised his hands toward the cave ceiling.

A wind began to blow through the cavern, twisting the campfires and stirring ash into the air.

"Watch the ash," Briget whispered.

Serena looked at Trevor, whose eyes were closed, and lips were moving.

"Not him, the fire ash," Briget said with a squeeze of Serena's hand.

Serena focused on the campfires and tried to ignore her outnumbered friends battling for their lives just steps away. The gray smoke and ash swirled upward at first and then trailed toward one corner of the cave, not fifty feet from where they stood. "The way out?" she asked quietly.

Briget nodded. "We need to get there quickly."

"I can't leave them," Serena said, refocusing on her friends.

"Then don't," Briget said with a sly grin.

Serena instinctively reached for her grandmother's pendant for assurance and realized it was no longer on her neck. "Oh, no!" she gasped.

"What?" Briget asked.

"My necklace is gone."

Serena looked around and realized it was dangling from one of Trevor's closed fists. "He stole it," she said, pointing at him.

"Never trust a wizard," her mother told her.

The wind whipped around them and caught their hair and skirts. She could see the energy transforming from straight lines to twisting whirls, reminding her of the tornado that hit their home just a few days before.

"Make a bubble?" Serena asked.

"No time," Briget yelled, and she raised her hands to mirror Shade's. "Love and light, quench this storm!"

Serena wasn't sure what to expect, but nothing happened at first. Then Shade's focus faltered.

"Say it with me," her mother told her.

Serena raised her hands like her mother's and together they yelled, "Love and light, quench this storm!"

As if the sun's rays had burst through the mountain, the cave filled with bright white light. In a flash, it surrounded them and showed them a path toward the exit.

Shade lowered his hands to rub his eyes. When he opened them, they were... hazel.

"Where'd the orange flames go?" Serena asked.

"Not far. Come now," Briget pulled her in a frantic run toward the way out.

Serena ran for a moment, but then resisted. She turned back toward Trevor and her friends. "Come with us!" she shouted.

Mikal yelled, "Just go!"

Trevor saw his opportunity and ran toward Shade, but Kent stepped between them and yelled, "Stop!"

Trevor halted, and Shade blinked. The demon's eyes returned.

"Jealous, are we?" Kent said over the din of the fight. "You're foolish if you think you'll wrestle with a demon and win."

"You're foolish to think the demon will let you live," Trevor replied, but Serena wasn't sure who he was talking to, Shade, Kent, or both.

Before Kent could say anything else, Shade grabbed him by the shoulders and threw him against the wall. The old wizard landed in a heap and didn't move. Then Shade moved toward Trevor, who held out the pendant in a show of force. He said some words Serena didn't recognize, and Shade stopped in his tracks.

Serena yelled, "That's mine, you thief!"

Trevor didn't even glance her way. "I need it more," he said dryly.

Shade tilted his head to one side like a dog sizing up a weak owner. Before he could make his next move, Serena ran toward Trevor in a blind rage.

"No!" Mikal pushed the mercenary he was fighting aside and punched him in the throat. The man hit the ground, and Mikal ran toward Serena to stop her. She brushed past him just as he grabbed for her arm, and he stood helplessly and watched.

With an outstretched hand, Serena touched the crystal pendant and blue light shot out of it in a blinding flash that made the white light leading toward the exit shimmer.

Trevor held on, and the two struggled over the necklace. When she couldn't wrestle it away from him, she finally did the only thing she could think of and touched his arm. "Got you!" she yelled.

Trevor went rigid, releasing the pendant.

Mikal watched as the demon-controlled wizard grabbed at Serena and barely missed her. The pendant glowed brightly as she put it on while running back to Briget.

The men who had been fighting Tom and Tod realized their master wasn't moving and lost their motivation, only half-heartedly sparring with the twins as they became more distracted by everything around them.

Mikal signaled to them to move toward the exit and yelled, "Grab the horses!" As they made their way toward the opening that would lead outside, Serena looked back and watched as Shade focused his energy on the petrified Trevor Ash and hit him square in the nose with an open fist. The carpenter exploded into a million shards like a dark crystal goblet dropped on a brick floor.

Shade didn't pause longer than a second before he turned to watch the group flee.

"Keep running!" Briget's voice brought her attention back to their situation. The passageway out of Mount Pilkin was tall enough for riders on horseback in single file, but not wide enough for the group to run out of easily. The horses whinnied as they instinctively ran toward the exit, practically dragging the twins along with them. Mikal was behind Serena and Briget helping each woman as they stumbled on the uneven quartz floor toward the waning light outside the cave.

Serena could see sunlight, and the white light that lit their escape faded as they neared the open air. Following the others through the cave opening, she quickly realized that she didn't recognize where they were. Green grass and tall pines didn't fit at all with the White Mountains they'd started in.

The group stopped to catch their breath as Mikal listened for anyone who might have followed them out. After a moment, he shook his head and exhaled. "We're good. Although we shouldn't stay here long."

Serena nodded and looked at the others for the first time since the fighting started. Tom had a black eye and several cuts on his arms that were bleeding through his shirt sleeves, but his eyes were bright, and he was smiling as he leaned over with his hands on his thighs, catching his breath.

Tod looked worse for wear; a cut above his left ear was bleeding down his neck, and he was holding his side and wincing in pain. Serena wasted no time and ran to help him. "Mother!" she called, and Briget was immediately by her side, laying him down on the grass.

"I'm okay," Tod said, but it came out more of a wheeze than a confident declaration.

"Let me see it," Briget told him as she lifted his blood-soaked shirt away from the wound. The cut was long but not deep enough to have destroyed organs. "You'll live," she told him, "But we need to clean it, and I don't have my healer's bag." She looked at Serena, who shrugged.

"Mine was on the horse I was riding here. It bolted when we crossed into the mountain pass."

Both women turned to Mikal, who was already rummaging through the bags strapped to his horse. "I have water and a clean shirt, but that's about it." He handed them to Serena.

"It will do for now," Briget told him. "Do you have a knife to cut this bloody shirt off him?"

Tom handed her the knife from his belt before Mikal could react. "Here," he said, looking at his brother with concern. "What can I do?"

Briget took the knife and answered, "Just give us space and pray."

Tom and Mikal both took a few steps back and watched, remembering how Serena had almost immediately healed Erik. Only, this time, she didn't have her crystals to help with the process.

Serena whispered to her mother, hoping the other men wouldn't hear her as she gently maneuvered to rest Tod's head on her lap and start cleaning the cut above his ear. "How do we do this without our tools?"

Briget looked at her naïve daughter and regretted not teaching her more than she had until now. "My child, you don't need crystals to heal."

"What?" Serena's disbelieving eyes met her mother's.

"It's true."

"How?"

Briget took the canteen from Serena's hands and placed it on her own lap. "Give me your hands," Briget said.

Serena held her hands out to Briget, palms down, and Briget gently took them and turned them over. She traced a circle in the center of each palm and told Serena, "These hands hold the same power your crystals do. We use the crystals to help us focus that power more easily, but you don't need them. They are crutches. You only need your hands."

Serena looked at her palms, still not sure she understood. "But the crystals..."

"Are unnecessary. When we make an energy bubble, we use our hands, yes?"

"Yes."

"When we illuminated the pathway out, we used our hands, too."

Serena remembered opening the portal despite not knowing exactly what she was doing. "And I opened the portal into Mount Pilkin," she started.

"Yes!" Briget interrupted. "Without crystals. We only use tools to help work more efficiently, but we can do as much without them. Watch."

Tod's eyes were closed, but Serena was sure he was listening because a small smile crossed his face as they spoke. "You're in better hands than mine," she told him.

Briget used the knife to open the shirt all the way so she could work on the wound more easily. Taking the water from Serena's lap, she poured just enough to cover the wound and dabbed at it with Mikal's clean shirt. When she was satisfied that the still bleeding wound was free from debris, she put the canteen and the shirt down beside them and put her hands together as if she were going to pray.

"You don't need to say anything, but words help you focus your intent," she told Serena. Then she said, "Help me heal this young soldier," and placed her hands, palms down, just an inch over Tod's wound.

Serena heard a hissing sound as the water droplets left on the wound seemed to bubble and burst. "They're carrying away disease," Briget told her. Then Serena watched as the skin around the wound pulsed, glowed, and then closed. The entire process took just a minute, and there was nothing left but a light scar.

"Wow!" Tom was astonished. "Can you do that for me, too?"

Mikal stepped in. "Later, if you can wait. We need to get moving. We're losing daylight and are too close to the cave entrance for comfort. Let's find a safe place to camp and get our bearings."

"Oh, right then." Tom nodded.

"Can you get up?" Serena asked Tod.

"Yes, I think I can." As she helped him rise to a sitting position, he looked down at his side and shrugged off what was left of his tunic. "Thank you, ladies. I'm in your debt."

"No, you aren't," Briget insisted. "This is what we do."

"You've done much more than that today," Mikal told her as he reached out his hands to help her stand.

...

The elder wizard's robes rippled with motion as the mercenaries looked on. First, he came to his hands and knees with the wariness of a person with a head wound. They couldn't see his face because his hood covered it, but they heard his moans as he reached one hand up to gently touch his head.

"Sir?" Elian spoke softly as he cautiously approached Kent.

Kent raised his head to look at the little man. Under the cover of his hood, they could see a forced smile. And then he laughed. The uncanny sound echoed through the cavern and made hair stand on end.

Elian took a few steps back and reflexively raised his hands in surrender, although he had done nothing wrong. Then he glanced at the young wizard they now called Shade. He stood motionless, with blazing eyes, staring at their uncrumpling leader.

Kent slowly raised himself to his feet and straightened his back. He reached his scarred hands up to his hood and slowly lowered it to reveal his face, wearing a grin that inspired fear. To their astonishment, he looked unharmed.

"How?" Shade's voice betrayed a nervousness he'd never shown before, even with the demon almost completely in control.

Kent laughed again, and all in the cave stood motionless. "Magic, of course," he said without pause.

The demon's voice took over—a guttural sound coming from Shade's lips that made the words hard to understand. "You were bound!"

"I was," Kent agreed, "from doing harm to others. I was never bound from protecting myself." He made a show of straightening his robes and dusting them off. "I assure you," he continued after a moment, "your power cannot reach me. I suggest you bide your time some other way than aim your energy at me."

Shade's voice returned to normal when he replied, "It wasn't me."

Kent took a few steps toward him and waved him off. "I know, son, but you're a vessel and you're breaking."

"I can do better," the young wizard said with a hint of desperation in his voice.

"I expect you to." Then Kent turned to the men, who were still looking on. Seeing several with bleeding wounds and a few others lying where the rescue party left them, he motioned in their direction. "Check your brethren. Help them or bury them. Then, prepare to move. We're meeting the warlord soon."

"What about the healers?" Elian asked.

"That was a test of their abilities," Kent answered. "I let them escape."

"A test?" Shade asked.

"Yes, and it was also a test of yours. You failed."

Shade hung his head and blinked a few times. The fire gave way to hazel again, and he pulled his hood back over his face to hide embarrassment.

Kent added, "See to your horse and meditate on your mission. The next test won't be so easy."

...

Amongst the tall pines in a small meadow far enough from the road to be safe, the healers and the soldiers made quick camp. The hobbled horses grazed to one side while the humans laid out cloaks and anything soft that they could spare to sleep on.

Tod sat beside a tree and chewed a piece of deer jerky thoughtfully before asking quietly, "Captain, why can't Serena just open a portal to Myribell?"

Mikal looked up from cleaning his sword and nodded toward Serena and Briget, "Ask her."

Tod nodded but hesitated and looked at his brother. Tom gestured his encouragement and whispered, "Yes, ask her."

Tod cleared his throat to get the ladies' attention. "Ahem, my lady, Serena," he started, "Would it be possible to speed our way home through a portal... or something?"

Briget gave him an endearing smile before looking at her daughter and saying, "Ah, yes! I meant to ask about how you managed to get into a closed-off portion of the cave."

Sitting on her cloak with her arms wrapped around her knees, Serena beamed with uncharacteristic pride. "I did it, Mother! I opened a portal from the grassy meadow on the mountain!"

"By yourself?" Briget asked, not unkindly.

"Yes, I opened the portal, and Trevor used his magic to protect everyone as they entered."

Briget glanced at Mikal who nodded in agreement. "It turns out the carpenter had some ability left to him."

Briget shrugged, "Well, we couldn't leave them defenseless," she told them matter-of-factly. "That would have made us as bad as they were."

"Them?" Tod asked.

"Yes, the wizards," Briget answered. "We bound them from ever harming others again, but we didn't bind them from magic that would allow self-defense or positive actions."

Serena lowered her head and shook it sadly. "I killed him."

Briget moved closer to her daughter and put her arm around her. "Trevor Ash?"

"Yes," she answered as sorrow filled her eyes. "I didn't mean for him to die. I just wanted my pendant back."

"You didn't kill him," Mikal corrected her as he set his sword down and leaned toward her. "He did himself in."

"The way I saw it," Tom spoke up, "that wizard with the blazing eyes killed him. Hit him square in the nose."

Serena shook her head again. "No, he wouldn't have shattered like that if I hadn't frozen him. It's my fault he didn't make it out with us."

Briget gave Serena's shoulders a gentle squeeze. "No, daughter, the captain is right. He made a poor choice, and he paid for it."

Serena turned her head to Briget with disbelief in her eyes. "He didn't deserve to die for stealing my necklace."

"No, but that was just one in a very long line of poor choices that caught up with him," Mikal assured her.

Briget nodded, "He wasn't a good man. He pretended to be changed because he wanted more than what we left him with. Whether playing Shay's pride or your generosity, the king and I were sure he was just waiting for a chance to make a move."

Tod raised his hand. "I have a question."

"Yes?" Briget asked.

"What did he think that little necklace was going to do for him against that Shade person?"

Mikal answered, "I think he thought it would protect whoever held it."

"Wrong," Tom smirked.

"He was out for himself, or he would have left it on Serena," Briget told them and turned to face her daughter again. "If that doesn't prove he wasn't acting for the good of all, I don't know what would."

Serena nodded weakly. "I guess, but I still feel so guilty."

"Don't," Mikal said sharply. "He never felt an ounce of guilt for those he killed in his youth."

"Never?" Serena asked.

"No," Mikal answered.

"Then why was he allowed to stay in Myribell?" she asked.

"Because our king is..." Tom stopped himself.

Mikal finished his sentence with more sense than Tom, "a generous man who hopes for the best."

"That's what I was going to say," Tom told them.

"Sure," Tod said with a grin. "Not to be uncaring, but back to my original question—why don't we just portal our way home?"

Everyone looked at Serena with expectant eyes, except for Briget. She studied Serena's face and answered for her, "Because my dear daughter is tired and needs rest. Opening a portal isn't easy. It's impressive for someone who's never been trained to do it without assistance." There was a hint of pride in her voice.

"But I had help," Serena insisted.

"From whom?" Briget asked.

"The Order," she told her mom.

Briget sat back, astonished. "How do you know about the Order?"

"Oh, there's so much to tell you," Serena said. "The captain and I found a ledger, and then I fell through a portal..."

Mikal interrupted, "Not all at the same time."

"Yes, no, not all at once," Serena agreed.

Briget smiled. "Much has happened in a short time, I see. But I also see you're weary. You can tell me after you rest."

Serena didn't argue as she yawned and stretched her arms. "Yes, Mother, you're right. My soul needs sleep."

"Alright, then," Mikal told them, "No fire tonight, so we don't attract attention. I'll take the first watch. Tod, you'll be up in a few hours, so sleep now."

"Yes, sir," Tod replied, and they all stretched out and tried to rest.

But Serena couldn't sleep. Every time she started to drift off, her mind flashed between the soul-bart's glowing eyes and the image of Trevor shattering into a million pieces. Exhausted and traumatized, she gave up after an hour.

She rolled over on her side and opened her eyes. The horses were still. Her mother slept soundly, and the twins snored on the other side of her. Serena could see Mikal standing at the edge of the clearing, staring into the woods. Or was he just staring into nothingness?

Quietly, she got up and walked over to stand beside him. He sensed her approach and turned to watch her come nearer. A smile warmed his eyes. "You should be sleeping," he whispered.

"I can't," Serena said.

He gave her a careful look and sighed. "I understand. I couldn't sleep either after my first battle."

"When was that?" she asked, keeping her voice low.

"Years ago. I was fifteen and had just started squiring for the king."

"That young?"

"Yes; I had little choice. The king made my family an offer they couldn't refuse."

Serena raised an eyebrow. "What sort of offer?"

"The king said he saw potential in me, and he'd take me on, let me live in the castle, and see to my education. We didn't have much, my sister had just passed, and my brother was needed to help with the farm. So, my parents sent me on my way."

"Wow!" Serena looked at the captain with fresh admiration. "You didn't squire for a knight first? Straight to the king's guard?"

"Something like that."

"And your first battle was when?"

"Just a few months later," Mikal said. "Ironically, it involved some of the same men, including Kent and Trevor."

Serena gasped, and the captain nodded. She thought for a moment, piecing the timeline together. "Was my father there?" she finally asked.

"Yes, and your mother."

"Both?"

Mikal looked past Serena to ensure Briget was still sleeping. "Yes, and this might not be my story to tell."

Serena frowned. "You were there, so it is your story."

Mikal inhaled deeply and let it out slowly. "My first battle was your father's last, and we hoped it would have also been the last one your mother had to see." He paused and studied Serena's face for a sign of understanding. "Do you take my meaning?" he asked.

A tear rolled from her eye, and he knew she understood. She lowered her eyes to the ground, and he put his arms around her and pulled her close to comfort her. She melted into him and let her head rest on his chest as she fought back more tears. "It's so strange," she whispered. "I barely remember him, yet I was old enough that I should."

"Yes, strange indeed," Mikal agreed. "Maybe it's better this way."

Serena pushed away from him and was about to argue, but his attention shifted. His eyes were drawn back toward the woods, toward the road. He raised his forefinger to his lips to tell her to stay quiet. She listened intently and could just hear the murmurs of someone passing.

As the voices came closer, she could make out some of their words:

"Why couldn't this wait until dawn?"

"DeGrane said we need to move quickly. Ranald doesn't like to be kept waiting."

"I, for one, am glad we're finally doing something. That cave life was dull."

"Dull? Did you not just watch the demon boy shatter that other man?"

Serena's eyes grew wide, and she instinctively sat on the ground and bowed her head low. Mikal knelt beside her. "They can't see us. We're too far back." His voice was barely audible. She nodded, afraid to speak.

It seemed like ages passed before the voices became a murmur again and eventually faded away. Once he was sure they were far out of earshot, Mikal said, "I know where we are now. We're on the border road to the east of the White Mountains. It runs between the northern edge of Myribell's lands and the land Ranald stole."

"Ranald?" Serena asked. The name sounded vaguely familiar, but she couldn't place it.

"He's a warlord. He thinks everything should be his because his family was once royalty."

"In Myribell?"

"No, but that hasn't stopped him from trying to invade. It seems he's pulling the wizard's strings again."

Serena remembered what she was going to say earlier, but it suddenly didn't seem as urgent. There was much she didn't recall about the time before her father passed, including the details of how it happened. Tonight, she was learning more than she expected, and she wasn't sure how she felt about any of it. Looking at her mother sleeping peacefully made her wish she could slip into dreamland, but she'd already seen the nightmares that threatened her if she closed her eyes again.

Mikal watched her with concern. "You need rest. We have a long trek tomorrow, unless you want to try opening another portal, and for that, your mother said you need rest, anyway."

"I just keep seeing them when I try to sleep," she told him. "Trevor and Shade."

Mikal nodded in understanding. "Let me rouse Tom for his watch. If you're willing to let me, maybe I can keep the nightmares at bay."

The young soldier woke with just a gentle tap from the captain's boot. "Your turn," Mikal whispered. As Tod rubbed his eyes and found his canteen, Mikal filled him in on what they'd overheard when the mercenaries passed.

"Right," Tod said quietly. "You got the toughest part. All I have to do is wait until sunrise."

"If you get too sleepy, wake your brother and give him a turn. We don't know if they have anyone looking for us. Otherwise, wake us at dawn. We have a long day ahead."

Tod nodded at each of them and walked toward the opposite side of the meadow to start his watch.

When Mikal was satisfied that they could relax, he spread an old wool blanket out on the grass and lay down on his side. Then he motioned for Serena to join him. She hesitated and looked at her mother as if expecting her to awaken and protest. "It's alright," Mikal told her. "I won't do anything to hurt your reputation. I just want to protect you."

Serena nodded and made her way closer to him. She lay down facing him, staring into his eyes, and wondering what to do next. Mikal could tell she was overthinking it. Stretching an arm toward her, he said, "Whatever makes you most comfortable. I'll hold you until morning so you can relax and rest."

Serena scooted closer to him and rolled to face her mother and Tom. Somehow focusing on them helped her remember she wasn't doing anything wrong. Mikal's arms were powerful around her, and his embrace was warm, but she still fought closing her eyes... until she couldn't anymore, and at last, she slept.

Chapter 7
The Final Battle

Day 6

WHEN THE SUN'S RAYS broke through the branches of the trees, Tom was standing watch. Serena felt Mikal stir behind her and realized she had slept without dreaming. She opened her eyes and moved her hand to rub her face, and the movement let Mikal know she was awake. With his arms still around her, he gave her a gentle hug before letting her go.

"Good morning," she said quietly as she put her hands on his forearms and squeezed back. She could feel the roughness of his new beard on the back of her neck.

"Good morning, my lady," he replied.

"Did you sleep?"

"Just enough," he assured her.

Serena saw her mother's eyes open and immediately rest on the two of them lying on the old wool blanket. Serena gave a little gasp, and Mikal released his arms. She scampered to her feet and brushed little bits of grass from her clothes.

"Good morning," Briget said, trying to hide a smile.

"Mother, I was..."

"Resting," her mother finished for her. Briget sat upright and looked around the camp. "I'm glad you were able to."

"Yes," Serena said, her eyes downcast.

Mikal stood and rolled up the blanket. "Tom, any news?"

"No, Captain," the young man replied. "Tod woke me a while ago and fell right to sleep. It's been a quiet early morning."

"Good," Mikal nodded. "Wake your brother. We have a long trek back to Myribell."

"No portal, then?" Tom asked.

Mikal looked at Serena, who was sipping water from a canteen. "What say you, Serena?"

Briget didn't give her a chance to answer, telling them, "It won't work."

Serena looked at her mother, wide-eyed. "Why not?"

"We placed wards around the castle and outside the gates. The closest we can get is our cottage, and there may still be wards there, even after the storm hit it."

"Wards?" Tom asked as he walked over to Tod and gave him a gentle nudge.

"Yes, wards—protection spells to keep people like Kent from taking us by surprise."

"Ah," Tom nodded.

Tod rolled over and covered his eyes.

"Wakey, wakey," Tom told him. "The captain's ready to go."

With the realization that it was an order, Tod quickly scrambled to his feet, eyes barely open, and nearly tripped trying to roll up his blanket before he had fully stepped off it.

Mikal grinned at the sight. "Don't hurt yourself. We'll need you later."

"Aye, sir." Tod nodded, sheepishly.

Turning his attention back to Briget and Serena, Mikal said, "I'm sure we can make it back by late afternoon on horseback, if we get started now. I know a short cut."

"Where are we?" Briget asked.

"Near the northern border. We saw Kent's men heading to Ranald's run-down castle last night."

Briget scowled. "Let's not waste time then. We need to warn Liam."

"Right," Mikal agreed. "Tom, do you know the game path back to the castle from here?"

"Yes, sir."

"That's what we're taking. Ride ahead and tell the king what we saw. He needs to know as soon as possible."

"Yes, sir." Tom quickly mounted his horse and headed towards the woods opposite the road.

"Be safe," Briget told him as he rode past her.

"I will," he replied, and they watched as he disappeared into the thick trees.

...

Outside the nearly crumbling tower of Ranald's confiscated castle, Kent's men slept in quickly pitched tents. The night's march had tired them, and Kent promised them a few hours' rest before letting Ranald take command.

Inside the crumbling walls, Kent and Ranald sat in a small room at an old wooden table. Ranald leaned back in his chair, looking more relaxed than a man about to make an offensive move should. Kent rested his elbows on the table and leaned closer to Ranald, speaking in low tones. "How do you know the princess will make way for us?"

Ranald smirked. "She wants her father off the throne as badly as we do. She'll be ready."

Kent shook his head. "She knows nothing about wards and portals."

"She knows enough."

"This will be a very brief battle if you're wrong."

"If I'm wrong," Ranald said, sitting up straight, "The battle will happen the old-fashioned way. Either way, I'm taking Myribell, and you will share in its treasures."

"And after that? What will you do with the princess?" Kent's eyes narrowed. "You have concern for her?"

"No, merely curious."

"I'll do whatever I want with her. She offered herself to me." Ranald's tone was prideful, not lustful.

Kent nodded and stood. "I must rest. I told my men they could have until midday."

"No rush. The princess won't be ready until dusk."

...

Serena and Briget shared Trevor's horse as the small group traveled the old game trail through the forest toward Myribell with Briget riding in front and Serena holding her mother's waist. They could see Tom's horse's tracks ahead of them and knew he would be near the castle gates within the hour.

Although she had many questions for her mother, Serena didn't know where to start. Who was the Order of the Mystic Moon? Who was it who showed her the daisy symbol on the gate in the lake? Why didn't she have more memories of her father? And most importantly, why had her mother kept so much from her?

Concerns over trust and fear of misguidance bounced in her head as the horse dashed through the woods. She watched Mikal riding ahead of them and thought of how he knew of her relation to the king before she did and wondered how she did not know he was her uncle until recently. What else was being kept from her?

She turned to look back at Tod, and he gave her a warm smile. At least, he seemed to be as naïve as she felt. He was just a soldier following orders. She returned his smile and turned to face forward again.

"Serena," Briget's voice broke her string of questions, "when we arrive at the castle, I want you to head straight for the library. I'll meet you there shortly."

"Where will you go?" Serena asked, with a little more anxiety in her voice than she liked.

"I will head to our rooms and bring what I think we'll need for the evening."

"Like what, Mother?"

"I'm not sure yet. I'll know when I need to know."

Serena was glad her mother couldn't see her frown. After a moment, she asked, "If there are wards protecting the castle, why are we concerned about Kent's men coming? Won't that stop them?"

"The wards will stop them from using a portal to enter the town and the tower, but that magic cannot protect against brute force. We need to act fast when we get there to reinforce the wards and to help the king. Whatever he asks of us, he will have."

"Yes, Mother," Serena agreed, recalling the king had asked her to be regent in the case of his death. Did Briget know about that conversation? Before she could ask, Mikal stopped his horse and put his hand up to halt them.

"What is it?" Briget whispered.

Mikal put his finger to his lips to hush her and quickly pointed up to the treetops above them. Looking down on them were easily three dozen crows. Not one made a sound, but one looked very different from the others. A larger bird on a lower branch had thin rings of white around each red eye.

Serena's breath caught in her throat when she saw it. There was something unnerving and unnatural about the way it studied the group on horseback. "Mother," she whispered, but Briget gave her the same signal to keep quiet.

Slowly, Mikal took a rock and slingshot from his saddlebag, but before he could use them, the enormous bird dropped from the tree with claws outstretched toward the captain. It cawed loudly, and the others came swooping down upon them. Serena threw her arms up to cover her head and face as she felt a crow rake her hair. Claws stung her scalp, and she was afraid to lower her arms to steady herself as the horse reared in fright.

The cawing, clawing, neighing, and yelling only lasted a minute before there was a crack of thunder that shook the ground. Then silence.

Serena slowly lowered her arms, relieved to see that her mother was still on the horse in front of her. Mikal had a fresh cut on his forehead that was bleeding down the side of his face. She turned back to look at Tod and found him crouching on the ground with his face in the leaf litter and his arms over his head and neck.

Since the birds were nowhere to be seen, she started to dismount, but her mother caught her by the arm.

"Wait!" Briget told her.

"Tod," Mikal shouted at the young man. "Are you alright?"

Tod slowly lifted himself to a kneeling position and looked around. Dirt clung to his unshaven cheeks, and fear filled his eyes. "Yes, sir. What was that about?"

Mikal shook his head. "The wizard's spies."

"I haven't seen them since our last battle," Briget told him.

"No," Mikal nodded, "and I haven't thought of them since. How is it possible?" Mikal sounded exasperated.

Thunder rolled in a heavy wave over them again.

"The soul-bart!" Briget exclaimed. "We have to hurry."

Mikal turned his attention back to Tod and ordered, "Mount up and ride quickly."

Tod stood quickly and grabbed his horse's reins. "Aye!"

Mikal asked Briget and Serena, "Are you alright to move faster through these trees?"

Serena nodded, and Briget gave a confident "yes." So, as Mikal faced his horse forward down the trail, Serena tightened her grip on her mother's waist, and they were quickly racing through the forest.

There was no time for questions anymore. All Serena could do was hold on and dodge branches as they tried to beat the demon's storm to Myribell.

...

In the shadows of the small side gate of the castle wall, the princess, dressed in dark gray riding breeches and a black tunic, used the heel of her boot to kick a stone loose from the ground. It was just plain gray stone about the size of a breadbasket, but underneath it, she found what she was looking for. A small, fabric pouch was half-buried in the dirt. She bent down, picked it up, and brushed it off. Not bothering to look inside, she put it inside her waistband and replaced the gray stone.

Looking around to ensure no prying eyes were following her, she followed the wall around toward the back of the tower and crept inside, heading back toward her chambers.

...

In a field beside Ranald's crumbling castle, crows guarded a tent. Shade sat inside, cross-legged on the ground with his hood lowered over his flaming eyes. His deep focus made him as rigid as a statue, and the demon's magic made the tent feel like an oven. Kent sat across from him, watching as the young wizard silently sent a storm after the mother and daughter that he needed alive.

Kent could hear the distant thunder crack and roll over the forest. The goal was to keep them off-balance and make them think they had less time than they did. As his men began to rise, eat, and break camp, he would have the soul-bart stir fear in their hearts. The horses would arrive in Myribell exhausted, and the women would need to regroup. But, he assured himself, they wouldn't have time to prepare.

Cawing from outside the tent alerted Kent to an approaching visitor. A tall man in dingy armor poked his head through the opening and announced, "Ranald gives you one hour to have your men ready."

Kent gave the man a sideways glance before nodding and waving him out. He must not disturb Shade until the last moment. The soul-bart didn't move, and satisfied that he was still in a trance, Kent rose and exited the tent.

A large crow with white rings around its red eyes bowed to him as he stepped out into dappled sunlight. Kent returned the bow and said, "Hello, old friend. Thank you for your help. Stay and keep watch."

The bird bobbed its head in response and turned toward the tent opening obediently.

Kent walked to the next tent down and told his leaders to spread the word that the warlord wanted to leave within the hour. Then each started walking the rows of the camp, announcing it was time to pack up and prepare for battle.

...

As what was left of the rescue group approached Myribell's town gates, Mikal yelled a greeting to the guards. "Hail Myribell, prepare!"

"Hail!" The two soldiers yelled back and opened the tall gate doors just wide enough to let the group through.

When they were close enough to talk in a normal voice, Mikal asked them, "Did Tom make it back?"

"Yes, sir," the shorter one answered. "He arrived about thirty minutes ago. Said he was chased by bird, sir."

Mikal nodded. "I'm not surprised. Once we pass, close the gates and let no one else through. A battle is coming. This is not a drill."

Both men nodded with determination in their eyes.

When they approached the stables, three boys ran to greet them, and quickly took the reins of each horse. Serena noticed how sweaty hers was as she and Briget dismounted. The poor things had run for nearly an hour through trees and brush to bring them safely home. She wished she could pause to give them healing energy, but water and food would have to be enough.

"Serena," Briget gave her a stern look. "Remember what I told you; go straight to the library. I'll be there shortly."

Mikal ordered Tod to report to the armory and make sure the guardsmen knew all he could tell them. Then, he came to Serena's side. "I'll walk with you, my lady. If Tom has done his work, the king will be there waiting."

"Yes, of course," Serena said absently as she watched her mother hastily walking away.

"Serena," Mikal said quietly, sensing her anxiety, "it will be alright. We've been preparing for this event for years."

They started toward the doors to the tower's interior hallway. "For years?" Serena repeated.

"Yes, we knew Ranald was biding his time, and we suspected Kent would still partner with him if he could prove his value. We just didn't know when it would happen."

A realization suddenly hit Serena. "That's why the king requested we move into the castle when the blacksmith died? Because magic was used, and he knew the time was coming?"

"Yes."

"But do you think Shade killed the blacksmith? From what I heard, his death looked more normal than a lightning strike."

"I'm still not sure whose magic it was, but it provided the telltale sign we'd been waiting for."

Serena stopped walking, and Mikal looked down to face her. "What?" he asked.

"You were waiting for someone to kill the blacksmith?" she said with a gasp.

"What? No," Mikal assured her. "No, that's not what I meant." They started walking again. "No, I meant we knew their first move would be magic-born. We did not know when or who would be targeted."

"So, why the blacksmith?" Serena asked, willing her tired legs to keep up with Mikal's fast strides through the stone halls.

"My guess is because he was in charge of sword making. His talent is crucial for defense, but they didn't target his apprentice or assistants, so they either didn't know of them, or they just wanted to send a message."

"They were younger?" Serena asked.

"Yes, closer to your age."

"They didn't know of them."

"We can't be sure," Mikal said as they started climbing a narrow stairway to the second floor. "We suspected Trevor Ash had some hand in it, too, and he would have known them."

"But how?"

"As your mother said, he was bound from doing harm and barred from doing magic, but he could use it as long as it was not against anyone."

Serena's steps slowed as she thought about the carpenter's last moments.

"Don't," Mikal seemed to read her mind. "Don't dwell on him. He was not worth your concern."

Serena shook her head to banish her guilt over his death. As they turned the corner and entered the library, the sight of the king and the fire wizard interrupted her thoughts.

Liam stood in full, shining armor with a sword at his side. A young soldier was behind him, tying a piece of fabric with the family's coat of arms to his shoulders. It wasn't quite a cloak, but it was thicker than a flag. Serena had seen nothing quite like it before.

As the young man stepped back, Liam turned his back to them so they could get a better look at the fabric. Serena's eyes widened as she recognized some symbols on the crest: a golden crescent moon was embroidered at the top with two dark stallions facing opposite directions, away from a castle tower at the center.

"Very nice, Sire," Mikal said. "So, you are ready?"

"As ready as ever," he said with a touch of sadness in his voice. "Tom told of crows and distant thunder. He said Kent marched his men to the warlord's old castle overnight."

"If you could call it marching," Mikal confirmed. "They're not very organized and obviously inexperienced mercenaries. We'll be able to tell Ranald's men from Kent's fairly easily."

"Good," the king nodded. "And how about you, dear Serena?"

"Sire?" Serena wasn't sure what the question was.

"Are you prepared for battle?"

Before she could answer, Eleanor came running into the library without a care in the world, but she stopped short when she saw Liam. Jeryl trotted in behind her, apologizing. "I'm sorry, Your Highness, but she heard you in the hallway and was excited to see you."

The king bent over to kiss the young girl. "Hello, my dear. I'm afraid we don't have time for a visit."

Eleanor just stared wide-eyed, and Jeryl arrived at her side and took her hand. She looked at Mikal and said, "I noticed the carpenter did not return with you?"

"You noticed?" Mikal asked.

"We saw your approach through the window of her room. I'm glad the ladies are safe, but what of him?"

Mikal looked down at Eleanor and back to Jeryl and shook his head in the negative. "He was lost."

Liam cleared his throat. "Ah, no surprise. You can fill me in later. Jeryl, please take Eleanor to the secret room."

"A secret?" Eleanor gasped.

"Oh, yes!" Jeryl said with false pleasure in her voice. "There's no place I'd rather be right now!"

Eleanor's face lit up with delight as she followed Jeryl out of the room.

Liam turned his attention back to Mikal and Serena. "I'm not sure how much of this she should remember..." He paused as he remembered whom he was speaking to.

"Sire," Mikal changed the subject, "I need to suit up. Can I leave the lady with you? Her mother should join you soon."

"Ah, yes." Liam nodded. "On your way, Captain. God speed."

Mikal gave a slight bow to the king and then to Serena. "You will be in skilled hands with your mother. I must inspect my men." And without waiting for a response, he quickly left the library.

Liam gave Serena an assessing look. "This will be your first battle, am I right?"

"Yes, Sire," Serena said with reluctance in her voice.

"I am afraid we have not prepared you the way we should have, and I'm tempted to send you with the cook and my granddaughter."

"Sire?"

"You are as important as she is," Liam said, looking toward the doorway as if he could still see them walking away.

Serena could not think of a suitable response, so she kept quiet and glanced at Krayvyn, who stood quietly observing.

"My dear, battle is no place for a healer. We will need you when it's over, for certain, but without the proper training, you can only do so much against what's coming."

"I can make a protective bubble!" Serena said confidently. "And I've learned to open portals."

Krayvyn gasped, and Liam raised an eyebrow. "Portals?"

"Yes, that's how we found Mother."

"Impressive," the king said as he walked over to the table and leaned on a chair. "How did you learn such a thing?"

Serena looked at her feet. "I don't... I don't know." She finally admitted. "It took a couple of tries, but I did it."

The king studied her as if he were deciding whether to believe her. From the doorway, her mother's voice broke the silence between them.

"She's a natural, Liam." Briget said as she entered. Serena noticed she'd changed into a clean tunic and skirt and was carrying the ledger and her healer's bag. She had pulled her hair back into a loose bun, and there was a fierceness in her eyes. "All the power we poured into her—why shouldn't she be?"

The king nodded. "I see that now. And you, Briget? You look no worse for wear."

Briget curtsied quickly and assured him, "I'm fine. Kent was testing us."

"Testing?" Serena asked.

"Yes," Briget answered. "He wanted to see what you were capable of before deciding on his next move."

"But his next move seems to be to attack Myribell," Serena said.

"Yes," Liam agreed. "But your mother knows how Kent thinks. The castle is one part of his plan. The binding is another."

"I don't even know how a binding works," Serena shrugged.

"I'll explain later," Briget told her, and turned her attention fully to Liam. "First, we must check the wards, unless you have already?"

"No, no, I haven't. Please, check them, although very few know of them or where the points are."

"Come, Serena," Briget said, taking her daughter by the hand. "I'll explain what I can. We must hurry."

...

Ranald and Kent stood side by side in the field beside the small castle, the warlord's soldiers and the wizard's mercenaries formed loose lines of ten side-by-side. It was easy to tell the soldiers wearing proper armor from the wizard's men, who only had thick leather vests and wooden shields.

Kent inspected the lines and wondered how many of his men thought they were being promised enough to risk their lives. The spoils of Myribell were tempting, but split between those that survived the battle, would it be enough?

Shade stood off to the right side of the lines, leaning against a tree. His hood covered his eyes, but Kent could tell the demon was on edge. As long as the boy stuck to the plan, the demon would have its fun. After all, wreaking havoc was its favorite pastime. But if the demon made him question Kent's power again... he didn't want to consider what might happen.

Ranald strode up to Kent's side, wearing a broad grin. His armor was black, and he wore a dark gray cloak with blood red embroidery showing two swords crossing over the waves of a river. For a man who lived in a stolen castle, the symbols were impressive—a reminder that the warlord's family was truly powerful generations ago.

"Are you ready?" Ranald asked Kent.

"As ready as ever," the old wizard said quietly. "Are you?"

"Of course!" He turned his attention to the gathered army. "And you?" Ranald shouted, "Are you ready to take a kingdom?"

The men shouted a cacophony of answers—all in the affirmative.

"Soul-bart, are you ready?" Ranald yelled in Shade's direction. The men all turned their attention to the young wizard, who stood tall and lowered his hood so they could see his face.

"Yes," he hissed. His eyes glowed with the demon's fire, and his grin chilled their bones.

For a moment, there was silence, but Ranald lost no time. "Then, we march now! Through the ether to the town; we'll take Myribell or burn it down!"

The army yelled their agreement as Kent gave Shade the sign to open the portal to Myribell. Within moments, a swirl of dark colors—violet, midnight blue, and wine reds—appeared in front of them and grew as wide as the ten lines of men. On Ranald's signal, led by Shade, the men started marching forward, except for Kent. He stood still, hands raised toward the sky, as he drew energy from the portal to protect their passage.

...

Under the waning sun, Serena followed her mother's brisk footsteps from the front gates to the next checkpoint for the wards. So far, they had found all the pouches intact. Each held a point of white quartz, a garnet the size of a garden pea, and a wooden carving of a crescent moon about the width of a man's thumb. Serena didn't know what to expect when she peeked into the first pouch, but those items didn't seem powerful enough to keep out an army.

"I assure you," her mother said, "they hold enough power to hold hell at bay, but they all must be in place to work. We have four more to check."

Before they made it to the point near the guard's tower above the river, they heard a crack of thunder. "No!" Briget yelled.

"That came from the other side of town," Serena said, looking in that direction, although she couldn't see through the buildings.

"It's too soon."

"Do you mean..."

"Yes, there's a breech. Don't you feel it?" Briget turned her head wildly, looking for soldiers moving toward the side gate.

Serena held her hands out and focused on her palms. "Yes, there's a tingling."

"They've opened a portal. Someone broke that ward."

"But who?"

"I don't know," Briget said, grabbing Serena's left hand and running back toward the main gates.

"Where are we going?" Serena yelled, trying to keep up.

"To get a better view!"

They ran at breakneck speed along the town wall until they found a guard's tower with an open door. Inside, they raced up a narrow spiral staircase until they reached the top. As they made it to the doorway, they quickly froze because a guard stood with a sword drawn toward them.

"Please!" Briget threw her hands up to shield her chest.

"My lady!" The guard lowered his sword. "What's happening?"

The sky above them darkened with thick black clouds, and thunder rolled over the town. The wind whipped around them, blowing her skirt and pulling at their hair. "It's dark magic!" Briget yelled over the thunder. "The side gate is breeched. The battle is here!"

The guard rushed to the side of the tower facing the side gate and watched in horror as lines of men started pouring through a rip in the wall. "It's not the gate; it's the whole wall!"

"It's a portal," Briget said. "We need to go!" and she led the way down the staircase to the stables, which were the closest entry to the king's tower.

The ladies dodged soldiers mounting horses and stable boys searching for any tool that could become a weapon. Over the din, Briget yelled instructions for Serena. "Head to the kitchen. Jeryl will hide Eleanor there, and you need to protect them."

"The king told them to go to the secret room."

"That is the secret room!" Briget flung open the door to the castle's interior hallway. "Can you find it from here?"

"Yes," Serena said with little confidence.

"Trust your instinct. Protect the child."

"Where are you going?"

"To protect the king." Briget pointed down a side corridor as they approached. "Down the hall. Take the staircase on the right. You'll recognize where you come out."

Serena nodded and turned down the hall, but her mother grabbed her arm and pulled her close for a quick hug. "I wish I had more time to teach you, but you'll know what to do. Trust your instinct," she said again, and she pointed to Serena's pendant. "Trust this, too. It glows when danger is close."

"Yes, Mother," Serena nodded. And with a little push from her mother, she ran down the darkened corridor until she found the stairs.

...

Captain Mikal steadied his horse as he and his men watched throngs of armored soldiers and rag-tag mercenaries pour through the dark, swirling hole in the town's protective wall. Few of his guardsmen had ever seen anything like it, and the ones who had remembered too well the darkness that came with it.

"We will not let the darkness win!" Mikal yelled with his sword raised over his head.

"Aye!" the guardsmen responded as one.

On the balconies of the tower above them, archers stood ready to fire on his command. When the third row of ten came through, Mikal dropped his sword quickly and dozens of arrows flew over their heads toward the incoming army.

The wizard's men fell, but the armored soldiers were unharmed.

"Steer clear of the portal," Mikal shouted. "Stay on this side." He saw the men nearest him nod as arrows continued to fly overhead. "Ready?" More nods. "For Myribell!" He yelled and led the charge toward the invading army.

...

While the young girl peered out from a small cupboard, Jeryl made Eleanor promise to stay quiet no matter what she heard in the kitchen. "I'll be nearby," the cook promised her adopted daughter. "No one will harm you. Just stay put."

"I will," Eleanor whispered bravely. Jeryl kissed her on the forehead and shut the cabinet door. Then she grabbed a sharp knife and ducked into a pantry.

After a few quiet minutes filled with silent prayer and pounding heartbeats, Jeryl heard hard-soled shoes on the kitchen's stone floor. The steps were slow and deliberate, and they stopped near the food preparation table. Then a female voice called softly, "Eleanor! Where are you?"

Jeryl recognized the voice without question. The princess was looking for her daughter, and her motivations were never good. Jeryl sent her thoughts as strongly as she could for the child to stay quiet.

At first, Shay's calls were sickly sweet. "I have something for you, dear child," she said as she took steps here and there to look for her in corners and under tables and counters. Then her voice took on its familiar, irritated edge. "Come out at once! I'm not playing games, child!"

Jeryl prepared to pounce from the closet if she heard her daughter yell for help. The knife in her hand faced the door handle as she strained to hear any hint that Eleanor was found. Instead, she heard a second woman's voice.

"Hello, Princess. What are you doing here?"

There had been no footsteps from anyone but Shay, and from the closet, Jeryl could hear the surprise in Shay's voice as she answered, "I could ask the same of you!"

"I thought you were banished," the second voice said.

"My father is a forgiving man." Shay's footsteps moved briskly from one side of the room to the other. "And you; I'd hoped the wizard had finished you."

"How would you know about that?" Either the second woman was standing still, or she moved as silently as a cat.

"Eleanor!" Shay's voice sounded a little more desperate now. "Come out, child. I just want to talk."

"When have you ever wanted to talk to her?" the second voice asked.

"What do you know?" the princess snapped.

"I know enough."

Pans crashed to the floor suddenly, and Jeryl imagined one woman must have knocked them off the counter. The hard-soled shoes ran several steps before stopping with a thud.

"You're out of your league," the princess yelled.

"Hardly," the other kept her cool.

Jeryl could hear wood knocking on wood and smiled to think the princess might battle another using broomsticks. Then there was a sickening crack, and someone hit the floor.

The other woman's voice called to her, "Jeryl, if you're in here, I need help."

Keeping her knife at the ready, Jeryl slowly opened the pantry door and peered out to find the young healer standing over Shay's prone body.

"Oh, my!" Jeryl exclaimed as she approached.

"I couldn't help it. I had to." Serena had a bruise on her left cheek and sorrow in her eyes.

"I know, dear," the cook told her and bent down to check Shay for a pulse. "What should we do with her?"

"Do you have any way to tie her up and put her in that pantry?

Jeryl thought briefly and smiled. "I do!" She walked to a drawer and pulled out a ball of twine that she used to tie meat for fancier dishes.

"That'll do," Serena said. The two women tied the princess's arms behind her back and carried her to the pantry. They put her inside facing the back wall and stacked the flour up around her. "Hopefully, this confuses her enough to keep her still," Serena told Jeryl as they shut the door.

Looking around the room, Serena said, "Where's Ellie?" but before Jeryl could answer, she said, "No, don't tell me. She's safe wherever she is."

"Right," Jeryl said, "and she'll hear me now and know to stay put."

Serena nodded. "The danger isn't past, but I'm afraid we ruined your hiding spot."

Jeryl laughed. "My lady, I have more than one."

"Right, I'll be in the hallway, keeping watch. My charge is protecting you two."

"I think you've done enough!" Jeryl told her, but Serena shook her head.

"You haven't seen what's coming. The warlord's army has marched through a portal, and the king's guard is doing their best."

Fear crossed Jeryl's face. "We must protect Ellie."

"That's why I'm here. Now, hide," Serena told her.

...

Briget rushed into the library, but neither the king nor the fire wizard was there. "Of course not!" she said aloud. *Liam doesn't hide from battle. He embraces it.*

Realizing that he was probably on his way to the side gate with Krayvyn at his side, Briget took a minute to gather her thoughts. If the fire wizard's only calling was protection of the defenseless, he would be valuable to any of the town's citizens who weren't prepared, but could he protect Liam? The king was battle-scarred and far from defenseless.

Briget walked to the table, took the ledger from her bag, and opened it. She flipped to a page with ancient script scribbled over a drawing of the castle tower. Putting both hands on the page, she began to whisper the incantation.

"Mystic Moon, draw your power from our ancient ways, illuminate the darkness, and bring forth brighter days."

Thunder cracked overhead, and the books shook on their shelves—a distraction from her focus, but she took a deep breath and started again.

"Mystic Moon, draw your power from our ancient ways, illuminate the darkness, and bring forth brighter days." She repeated the verse five times, each time with more energy and fierceness in her voice.

From outside, she heard men scream and a single, panicked voice yell that the portal was closing. She shut the book and shoved it back into her bag, leaving the library to join the battle below.

...

As hundreds of intruders marched through the swirling darkness, the men in front were shot down or quickly engaged by the king's guard. Experienced warriors, like Mikal, used their horses and swords to keep the battle as close to the wall as possible so the town's residents had time to seek shelter in the towers and tunnels of the castle.

Mikal yelled orders to keep pushing the strangers back and hold the line of defense. He couldn't tell how many more could come through the portal, but he could tell they were slowing because they literally could not move forward into the town. His men were doing their jobs.

Then, as quickly as it opened, the portal started shrinking. It quickly went from the height of the castle wall to the size of a mirror. Over the heads of the men in front of him, he could make out the men who were being cut off and left on the other side as the portal closed.

One of Kent's men shouted with despair, "The portal is closing! Move forward!" But no more mercenaries made it through.

Mikal searched the faces of the men on this side as the castle wall was in full view once again, but he could not find Kent. He must have been left behind. Ah, but there was Ranald in his black armor and dark gray cloak, standing near the soul-bart with glowing eyes, raging at that loss of the portal.

He watched as the two moved along the edge of the battle toward the king's tower's main doors. *They must not find their way inside!*

...

The raging sky added to the sounds of war—soldier's shouts, swords clashing, horses' screams, and doors slamming. As Briget ran from the stables to the area near the side gate, the noise was deafening. She had forgotten how overwhelming the chaos of battle could be, but she didn't have time to consider it now. She needed to find Shade before he found the king.

Searching the scene for any clue to his whereabouts, she saw Mikal on his horse. He wasn't engaging with the surrounding men; instead, he was facing the main tower door. Following his gaze, she saw the young wizard and old warlord. Ranald was fighting with the guardsmen at the doors as Shade stood with his arms outstretched, commanding the storm.

Ranald was fast with his sword and quickly dispatched the guards, but before Ranald could push open the heavy oak doors, they opened from within, and King Liam stood with ten more guards, ready for battle. Briget watched in horror. She knew Liam could handle the warlord, but was he prepared for the soul-bart?

She looked for a clear path to the tower and spotted one to her right. Slapping her hands together, she created a bubble of light and stepped into it before dashing madly toward the king.

...

Mikal was watching the clash at the tower play out when, out of the corner of his right eye, he saw a bright light racing toward that fight. He turned his head to see Briget running faster than a woman of her age should be able. Without another thought, he reared his horse and took off in the same direction, leaving the defense lines to the other troops.

Fighting men jumped out of the way as his gelding barreled toward the tower. Mikal steered past as many of his own men as he could while monitoring Liam, who was settling into a battle-ready stance.

Meanwhile, the demon-ridden wizard stepped aside to let the warriors have their fight. Against the tower wall, Shade raised his hands to the sky and laughed maniacally. Orange light gathered near his palms, and lightning flashed directly above him. Mikal realized what would happen next and spurred his horse the last fifty feet.

Briget arrived at the same time and threw her energy at the young wizard. The bubble of light that surrounded her broke free and crashed into Shade, pushing him back into the wall with a thud. She hoped it would slow him, but he shook off the hit and threw his hands back up toward the sky.

Mikal dismounted and ran to her side, sword ready.

"Don't worry about me. Protect Liam!" she yelled at him.

He watched as the energy gathered around Shade's hands and the demon's eyes settled on Briget. Realizing he was no match, he yelled, "Right! God speed," and ran to the fight just yards away in the tower's doorway.

From behind, he surprised two of Ranald's men with slashes of his sword to the weak points in the necks of their armor. Both slumped to the ground, and Ranald turned his attention from the king to the captain. "Retreat!" Mikal yelled at Liam.

"Not on my life!" Liam yelled back, still swapping blows with the others.

"Your life is what I'm worried about."

"The men need to see their king."

"Not dead!"

Ranald interrupted the argument with, "Yes, dead!" and hit Mikal's shoulder hard with the tip of his sword. The vibration stung, but the armor held, and Mikal only needed a step back and a breath to recover.

...

Shade's eyes were wild with fire as the demon screamed his threats at Briget. "Your time is over, healer! Your light will fade today!"

Briget focused her energy in front of her and started whispering an incantation in the language of her ancestors.

"I hear you, witch!" The demon yelled through Shade's mouth. "They are lost to you."

Briget kept whispering. It didn't matter if the demon heard the words; it only mattered that the Order heard them.

Lightning started striking the ground around her as Shade lowered his hands from skyward to attack Briget. She remained calm and kept up her incantation, bracing herself for whatever came next.

...

Standing in the relative quiet of the hall outside the kitchen doors, Serena focused on her breath, counting to four with each inhale and exhale. She felt the tingling in her palms that told her magic was all around her, and it made her anxious to be outside with the others. But her mother told her to protect Eleanor, and she was an obedient daughter.

Suddenly, voices filled the hallway with a language she didn't recognize. It sounded familiar but strange, and as they grew louder, she realized that the loudest was her mother's. She looked around wildly, expecting to see people coming from either direction in the hall, but there was no one and no footsteps. Only voices.

Then another familiar voice spoke inside her head. "Your mother needs you."

"What?" Serena asked. "She said to stay here."

"The child is safe. Go to your mother." The voice from the Order's arch insisted.

Serena ran back inside the kitchen and yelled, "I must go. Stay hidden!"

Jeryl and Eleanor both answered, "I will."

As Serena turned down the hallway to go back to the stables, the voice said, "Not that way," and Serena stopped short.

"It's the only way I know," she told her invisible guide.

"Follow me!" With that, a small blue sphere of light about the size of a dinner roll appeared in front of her and floated down the hall in the opposite direction.

"Alright," Serena said with a reluctant nod. "This isn't strange at all."

The orb led Serena down twisting corridors and stairways to the tower's main doors. Inside the entryway, she saw Mikal, Liam, and several guardsmen battling a tall man in dark armor and a few others, looking worse for wear. In the far corner, she saw the fire wizard, watching and waiting for his chance to step in.

The ball of light flew through the doors, outside toward the side gate. She kept close to the wall, away from the fighting, and followed it.

Just outside the doors and to her left, she saw Briget on the ground. Bolts of lightning danced around her unconscious body as if celebrating her defeat. She followed the energy from her mother toward the tower wall, where Shade stood with his hands outstretched toward Briget.

Serena's palms tingled as she assessed the situation. The demon didn't seem to see her, yet, and the voice in her head yelled, "Strike while you can!"

Without a thought, Serena raised her hands and threw her own energy at the demon-ridden man. White light shot from her palms in bursts and hit him hard in the chest, throwing him back into the wall with more force than her mother had mustered. He collapsed to his hands and knees, and his hood flew down over his face.

Serena watched as he tried to catch his breath, unsure what to do next. A blue glow near her chest caught her attention, and she remembered she had protection.

The soul-bart stood, removed his hood, and blinked, and for a moment, she saw hazel eyes, but they didn't stay. The flames returned quickly, and Shade turned his full attention to Serena.

He raised his hands to gather the lightning to him, and she looked up to see bolts reaching down from the dark clouds above.

Her hands tingled again, and she understood the meaning this time. She struck first, but not fast enough. Shade lowered his palms to her and her energy met his lightning. In a bright flash, the air between them burst into a heatwave that blew both of them backward.

Her pendant popped and hissed as blue light sparked from it. To her horror, she watched as the stone cracked and its light faded.

As Shade's eyes glowed with the demon's laughter, her confidence fled. She looked at her mother, lying in the green grass, and then around her to the fighting inside and outside of the tower. She had never felt so helpless, and all she could think to do was hide.

Before Shade could gather more energy, she rushed back inside the tower and toward the stairs.

As she ran past Mikal, she heard him call her name. When she hit the doorway, she turned just in time to see Ranald land a direct blow to the king's neck.

Tears filled her eyes as a cloud of smoke filled the room, but the fire wizard was too late. Flames drove Ranald and his men back outside, but the king was on the floor. "No," she heard her voice yell as she ran toward his prone body. It felt like everything was happening in slow motion.

Mikal pointed to Liam and yelled, "Save him," as he and his guardsmen closed the heavy oak doors.

Blood was pooling on the floor and staining the broken chain mail around Liam's neck. Serena knelt beside him, afraid she'd do more damage to him if she tried to move him by herself. "Help me!" She yelled, and Mikal, still barking orders to hold the doors, ran to help her flip the king over. She held his head in her lap and saw his eyes staring up into hers, glistening with tears.

"I wish you hadn't seen that," he said weakly.

Serena's own tears ran down her nose as she looked down at him. "I can help you."

"No, child," he said. "My time has come."

Serena ignored his words and drew a circle with her index finger into her right palm and then did the same with her left. "I can do this," she told him as she felt her healing energy surge.

She placed her hands over his wound, but nothing happened. She watched as his blood spread around him and soaked her britches. "It's alright," he whispered. "You will be a great regent."

"What? No," Serena cried. "I can't. I won't."

"You will," he said and closed his eyes.

Serena had never lost a patient before. She had never felt their life force leave their body, or at least, she didn't remember it ever happening. But at that moment, she watched as Liam's energy left its worldly vessel and had a flash of déjà vu. In an instant, she saw her father's face instead of the king's, and a wave of absolute sorrow hit her in the chest. The air left her lungs, and she slumped over Liam, trying to catch her breath and quell the tears.

"Serena," Mikal's voice was soft, but it had a hint of urgency in it. "Serena, he's gone, and we have to stop Ranald and Shade."

A burst of energy slammed into the tower doors with a force that knocked the guardsmen back several feet. They quickly got up and scrambled back to hold the doors again.

Serena couldn't get control of her breathing as her lungs heaved, and she fought for a deep breath of air. "I can't," she sobbed.

Mikal put his arms around her and held her tight as the doors took another hit. "You can. Just count to four," he told her.

Serena focused on the armored arms holding her. Despite the cold metal, his warmth surrounded her, and she finally took a slower breath. She counted to four and released it. After she took another and released it, he loosened his hold. "I'm alright," she told him, wiping the tears from her eyes. "I'm good now."

"I know," Mikal told her as he moved to give her some space. He looked up at Krayvyn, who was standing just a few feet away now. "What happened?"

Krayvyn shrugged with sadness in his light blue eyes. "He wasn't truly help-less," he said. "By the time I could help him, it was too late."

Mikal nodded and pointed to Liam, still in Serena's lap. "Tom, help Krayvyn move him someplace more secure."

Shocked, Serena realized she knew the guardsman closest to them. Tom, fully suited, including a helmet with a visor, bent down, raised his visor, and gave her a weak grin. "You've got this," he whispered, as he and Krayvyn gently lifted Liam's body and headed toward the eastern corridor.

Serena sat for a moment and looked at her blood-soaked riding pants, not a single thought crossing her mind. She just stared blankly.

Mikal stood and tapped her on the shoulder. "Serena," he said, "where's your mother?"

The question snapped her back to the present, and she jumped to her feet. "Outside on the ground! Shade hit her."

"Alright," Mikal said as he pointed to the guards at the doors. "Then that's where we need to be."

A wave of terror rolled over her at the thought of facing Shade once more. "No, I can't beat him."

"You have to," Mikal told her.

"But how? He destroyed my pendant."

The guards hesitated as they watched the two work through Serena's fear.

"It was a crutch," Mikal said sternly.

"What? No, it was my grandmother's magic."

"Yes, but you don't need it."

"Of course I do!"

Mikal pointed a gloved hand toward Serena's heart. "You don't need the pendant because her magic is within you." Serena stared at him, wide-eyed, so he continued. "After you went through the portal, you told me the Order had a name for you, right?"

"Daisy," she answered.

"That was your grandmother's name for you when you were tiny."

"What?"

"She was part of the Order. She... they poured their magic into you, knowing they may never have the chance to watch you bloom."

"How do you know this?" Serena asked.

"I've been around longer than you, and I remember."

That last word stung, but Serena heard the truth in his voice. Then the voice in her head returned, "Bloom, Daisy," it said. "Our power is yours."

Serena felt the power return to her hands, stronger than ever. It burned her palms and made her fingers vibrate. She closed her hands together as if to tamp it down, but the sensations grew. "Bloom!" The voice said again, and then a chorus of voices returned, "Bloom! Bloom! And boom!"

"Boom?" she asked out loud.

Mikal gave her a curious look. "Boom?" he repeated.

A smile crossed her face as she realized their meaning, and she nodded. "Open the doors."

...

Outside, most of Kent's mercenaries were down—either injured or held at sword point. Ranald had gathered what was left of his at the stairs to the tower, and Shade stood on the grass near Briget, calling the power of the storm to him as if he were about to knock on the doors again.

"Your king is dead," Ranald said with confidence. "Surrender."

Mikal looked at Kent's men at the mercy of his own. "You have a lot of confidence for a man with less than half of the soldiers you arrived with."

"I could not care less about the mercenaries. My men are enough to take the tower."

"Or I could destroy it," Shade hissed.

Serena looked at the demon's eyes and then at her mother on the ground beside the wizard. She saw a brief movement in Briget's right hand and lifted her eyes quickly. Wondering how long Briget had been conscious, she took a step forward, crossing the threshold of the tower doors.

Mikal pretended to be concerned for her with a look but let her move a few more steps forward. "You cannot destroy this tower," Serena said confidently to Shade. Then she turned her focus toward Ranald, "and you cannot take it."

"Why not?" Ranald said, with a hint of laughter in his voice.

"The Order of the Mystic Moon protects it," Serena said confidently and as loudly as she could. "The Order of the Mystic Moon protects Myribell, and you shall not win."

Shade started laughing again, and Serena could see that the boy was no longer available to reason with. The demon was in full control. He aimed his palms at her, and said with a hiss, "Back down, healer, or die."

"I will not," Serena said, hands burning with energy that was just waiting to be unleashed. She glanced at Mikal and caught his eye, and then he followed her glance to Briget's slow movement below the wizard's leg.

Lightning gathered around Shade's hands and the demon's laughter echoed off the town's walls. "You will!" he shouted, and lightning danced around his arms.

In one quick motion, Briget grabbed Shade's calf and whispered, "Got you!"

The young man froze, but the demon's energy still headed toward Serena. She threw up her hands, palms facing him in a defensive motion, and the energy of the

Order shot from them and deflected the lightning. With another burst of energy, she hit Shade's frozen body, and it exploded into tiny shards of crystal.

Briget dove face-down in the grass and covered her head with her sleeves. Ranald tried to shield himself from the explosion, but pieces of crystal embedded themselves in his armor and hissed. Serena saw that the demon's fire imbued them, and the heat made Ranald scream in pain. He sank to his knees and tried to rip the armor plating off his arms, but he wasn't fast enough. Smoke rose from his armor, and he rose and ran toward the side gate, which was open to allow his men to retreat.

A few of the king's guardsmen ran after him. They could hear his screams and then a splash as he threw himself into the river to stop the burning.

At the same time, the storm overhead rotated, thunder rolled, and the black clouds began to take on the appearance of a twisted face. The demon's voice echoed with the thunder as it threatened, "This isn't over!"

Serena turned her palms up to the rotating darkness, but her mother shouted over the din, "Don't waste your energy!" Serena looked at Briget, who was smiling at her and pointing toward the sky. The black clouds faded to gray and then slowly disappeared, burned through by the late-day sun.

Those of Ranald's men who had not fled after him dropped their swords and knelt toward Serena and Mikal, and the king's guard cheered.

Chapter 8

A New Day

IN THE DAYS THAT passed after the battle for Myribell, they buried King Liam next to his parents in the crypt under the chapel. Ranald's body was missing, and Princess Shay was locked in her rooms, awaiting trial for treason.

There had been no word from Kent, although Briget warned Serena that the old wizard was patient and scheming, and they would face him again someday. Captain Mikal sent soldiers to secure Ranald's castle and claim the land for Myribell—an act the king had once threatened but had never followed through on. The guardsmen found no sign of the warlord or the wizard there and lifted a flag with the Myribell coat of arms over its dilapidated tower.

Serena stood in the library with Jeryl and Eleanor sitting at the big table. The little girl's dark hair flowed over her shoulders as she studied a map of the kingdom and its surrounding area. "This one looks different now," she said, pointing to the border region near the ramshackled castle.

"No, that's the same map you've been studying for months," Jeryl told her. The cook was dressed in a simple tunic and skirt and missing her favorite apron.

Serena smiled. "That's very astute of you, Ellie. That map is the same, but we're having a new one drawn, and that border will be very different."

Eleanor looked up at her and grinned proudly.

"How did you know it will be different?" Jeryl asked.

"The same way I knew we had a friend in the White Mountains."

"Oh?" Serena asked, sitting in the chair next to the child. "How is that?"

"The friendly voice told me."

Shock crossed Jeryl's face, but Serena understood. "Is the voice always talking to you?"

"No," Eleanor said, hesitating. "Only when I'm thinking about the kingdom."

Jeryl exhaled slowly, and Serena put an arm around Eleanor. "That's good, my dear. If the voice ever sounds different, you let me know, alright?"

"Yes, I will," she said and turned in her chair to face Jeryl. "Is it lunchtime, yet?"

Jeryl looked at Serena quizzically, and Serena nodded. "It is, if you're hungry."

Eleanor bounded from her chair and ran to the hallway, "Come on, Mother! I have an idea for a delicious stew!"

"Oh, you do?" asked the cook as she rose from the table.

"Yes!" Eleanor said, as she motioned for Jeryl to follow. "Yes, I think the new princess will love it!"

Serena shivered at the title. "I'm sure I will," she said as they turned the corner.

Serena looked back at the map and imagined the new boundary where Ranald's stolen lands were. The original owners were long gone, and there was no one to keep them safe from another warlord staking a claim. No one, except the rulers of Myribell.

She had never wanted to rule anything, and was still unsure of her worthiness, but the paperwork was in order, and Liam had named her regent until the little princess, who still thought she was the daughter of a cook, came of age. "Ten years," Serena said quietly to herself with a sigh. "Can I do this for ten years?"

A familiar voice from the doorway answered her, "Yes."

She turned to see the captain of the king's guard, *her* captain... hesitating in the doorway.

"May I come in?" he asked.

"Of course!" Serena told him as she rose to her feet.

"Your mother is on her way up to help plan Ellie's presentation and the installation ceremony," he told her as he crossed the room. When he was just a step away, he took her hand, put it to his lips, and planted a gentle kiss on it. "My lady," he said.

Serena blushed a little. After all they'd been through in a short time, she wasn't sure how to respond.

Before she could say anything, Mikal straightened himself and took on a more formal air. "I am here to assist you with anything you need—planning, orders, security—anything!"

"I see," Serena said with a sigh. "I appreciate your help."

Mikal gave a slight bow and touched his hand to his waistband. When he brought it forward, he had a small silk pouch in it. "I mean anything," he told her, as he gently placed it inside her hand.

Serena looked at the emerald-green fabric, and she could feel something round inside.

"Open it," Mikal urged her.

She untied the string that held it closed and turned it upside down in the palm of her right hand. A silver ring with a stone the same color blue as her grandmother's pendant shimmered in the candlelight. Serena gasped.

Mikal knelt on one knee and said, "My lady, I offer you my talents and my life."

Serena was speechless. Tears formed in her eyes, and she closed her palm around the ring and bent over to hug Mikal. He stood and hugged her back, planting a gentle kiss on her cheek.

The idea of the one person who could calm her fears and bolster her confidence in a time of uncertainty pledging himself to her was more than she could imagine. And yet, here he was in front of her, doing that very thing.

They stood in an embrace, heart-to-heart and cheek-to-cheek for what felt like an eternity... until Briget's voice broke the silence.

"Apologies for interrupting."

Serena and Mikal stepped apart, and Serena blushed. Holding the ring up for her mother to see, she said, "Mikal just presented me with this."

Briget walked over and took the ring from Serena to examine it. "Is this the same stone that was in the pendant?" she asked.

The captain nodded. "Yes, my lady. We found it in the grass near the tower. It's smaller now, but it works well in a ring. Although, I'm not sure there's any power left in it. I thought Serena should still be able to wear it."

Serena took the ring back from her mother and held it to her heart. "I don't feel any magic in it, but I feel the love."

Briget eyed Mikal carefully. "I feel like I've interrupted something more."

"Yes," Mikal said. "I've just offered your daughter my life and love."

Briget looked at Serena, who was blushing and beaming from ear to ear. "I see, and you, Daughter, did you accept?"

"I haven't had the chance to say..."

Briget put her hand up to stop her words. "Please," Briget said, "take a moment first."

Serena's smile faded and Mikal's face showed concern.

Briget continued, "I have enjoyed watching the two of you fall in love, but we are in a different world now. Circumstances have changed. Serena, you're being installed as regent in three days. Mikal, you are being promoted to commander. The two of you should work together for the good of Myribell, but not together in that way."

"What?" Serena asked. "What do you mean?"

"It will not look good for the two people who were there when the king passed to become a married couple, ruling in his place. People will talk. The word 'coup' will be used, and they will question your motives."

The weight of the idea made Serena sit down. "They wouldn't think..."

"Some would," Briget told her. "It will not look good, and they may wonder if you will turn power over to Eleanor when she reaches her age of majority."

"Of course I would!" Serena insisted. "I never wanted to rule."

"I know, dear, but not everyone will understand."

Mikal stared at the floor for a moment before finally speaking. "I am sure you are right, Briget. I had not thought that far ahead."

Briget put her hand on his shoulder. "I love that you love my daughter, but I have to warn against this union now."

The tears in Serena's eyes were sorrowful now. "What do we do, then?"

Briget stepped up to her daughter and hugged her. "My dear, you will both do your duty to the kingdom, and in ten years, you can hand rule over to Eleanor, and the two of you can decide your futures going forward."

"Ten years is so long," Serena said with thoughts of becoming an old maid making their way into her mind.

"It is," Mikal said, "But it's worth the wait."

Serena gazed at him—her handsome captain—and couldn't believe a man like him would wait a year for her, much less ten. She said nothing and only nodded.

Briget assured her, "You will be surprised how quickly ten years will pass. You grew up in the blink of an eye."

"What now?" Serena asked, trying to hold back her emotions.

"For now," Briget said, "you and the captain and the rest of the guardsmen will secure the kingdom's borders, bring the princess to trial for her treachery, and decide what's best for Eleanor and Myribell."

"As I said," Mikal told them, "I am at your service, always."

And with that, the trio moved on to the business of planning the joyful ceremonies coming in the next few days.

The End of the First Book in The Mystic Moon Chronicles

Acknowledgements

To Phil, my family, my encouragers, and these Kickstarter backers:
A heartfelt thank you.

Paul Peeler, Linda Aley, Robyn Riley, Carolyn Wilborn, Phil Spence, Valerie Anne, J.L. Hendricks, Rachael Barcellano, Maria Sawyer, Rebecca Belles. Laura Jean, Brionninn, Ryan Freytag and Marcele Reola, The Crawfords--Monsterfrest 2 Crew! Lenore Ashwood, Ricardo Noriega, Reader Nation, Florentina, José María Villada, Wendy Petrohoy, Paul, Auntie Meow Meow, Richard S. Thomas, N. Gustafson, Alexandra Corrsin, Farrah R., Allison Miller, Taylor Hussey, Mishia and Todd Edwards, Triple C and D Paranormal, TJ Muir, 'Will It Work' Dansicker, Rosa Thill, John George, Kim Toxey, and Ejoberkirsch

About the author

Nicolle Morock lives in the Triangle area of North Carolina and is an SEO content specialist for a national digital agency by day and an author, podcaster, Reiki Master, and Certified Emotion Code Practitioner on evenings and weekends. She has a B.S. in meteorology and a B.A. in communication. Her hobbies include paranormal investigation and research, reading, nature walking, and trying not to kill the plants in her garden.

With over a decade of experience investigating the paranormal, a lifetime's worth of personal stories, and years of energy work, she is uniquely qualified to write fiction and non-fiction about those subjects.

Learn more about her and find her other creative works at nicollemorock.com.

Also by

Check Out More of Nicolle's Stories
Visit **nicollemorock.com/books** for more information.

Nonfiction:

Please, don't call me psychic: Stories from my paranormal life

Fiction:

The Rayna Smith Series

The Tritium Hypothesis
The Dark Season
Grumpy's Gift (A Rayna Smith Short Story) □Free eBook!

Krayvyn: a short story of The Mystic Moon Chronicles □ Free eBook!
House of Horrors: A Paranormal Choose Your Own Adventure Story □ Free eBook!
The Companion: a short story based on a dream □ Free eBook!

Sign up for Nicolle's monthly newsletter at **nicollemorock.com** to keep up with her latest creative endeavors, get energy healing tips, and to find out when and where she'll be making public appearances.